Anonymous

Transactions of the British Homoeopathic Congress, Held at Manchester

Anatiposi

Anonymous

Transactions of the British Homoeopathic Congress, Held at Manchester

Reprint of the original, first published in 1875.

1st Edition 2024 | ISBN: 978-3-38283-104-2

Anatiposi Verlag is an imprint of Outlook Verlagsgesellschaft mbH.

Verlag (Publisher): Outlook Verlag GmbH, Zeilweg 44, 60439 Frankfurt, Deutschland
Vertretungsberechtigt (Authorized to represent): E. Roepke, Zeilweg 44, 60439 Frankfurt, Deutschland
Druck (Print): Books on Demand GmbH, In de Tarpen 42, 22848 Norderstedt, Deutschland

TRANSACTIONS

OF THE

BRITISH HOMŒOPATHIC

CONGRESS,

HELD AT MANCHESTER,

On THURSDAY, SEPTEMBER 9TH, 1875.

Published by Authority.

HENRY TURNER AND CO., OF LONDON,

77, FLEET STREET, E.C.

BOERICKE AND TAFEL, NEW YORK.

1875.

Price One Shilling.

PREFACE.

THE Annual Congress of medical men acknowledging that they practise homœopathy was held at Manchester on the 9th September, 1875. The date, 23rd September, decided on at the London Congress, was changed in order to meet a deputation from the American Institute of Homœopathy. The members of this deputation, Professors LUDLAM and TALBOT, were commissioned to invite the Members of the Congress to the International Convention in Philadelphia, in June, 1876. The suggestion that this Congress should meet in Philadelphia was negatived, and Bristol was selected by a large majority.

Dr. CLAUDE, of Paris, also attended and represented the Homœopathic Society of Paris.

In addition to the admirable address by Dr. BAYES three papers were read,—one by Dr. SHARP, on "*A Scientific Principle for Toxicology;*" one on "*Uterine Therapeutics,*" by Dr. LUDLAM, Professor of Gynæcology in Chicago; and one by Dr. MEYHOFFER, of Nice, "*On the differential diagnosis of Cancer and Ulcer of the Stomach.*"

The discussions in these papers will be found in the *Monthly Homœopathic Review* for October, 1875.

"*A few notes on the treatment of Diphtheria,*" by Dr. BRYCE of Edinburgh, were submitted, but as Dr. BRYCE was unable to attend, and the discussions on the preceding papers had occupied much time, the paper was ordered to be published in the Transactions.

On the following page is given a list of the officers elected to direct the next Meeting at Bristol, on Thursday, September 21st, 1876.

If any one does not receive an invitation in due course, application should be made to the General Secretary.

J. GIBBS BLAKE, ⎱ *Honorary*
D. MOIR,   ⎰ *Secretaries.*

1876—BRISTOL. *President*—T. HAYLE, M.D.

Vice-President—Dr. KER. *Treasurer*—E. FRASER, Esq.

General Secretary—Dr. GIBBS BLAKE, 24, Bennett's Hill, Birmingham.

Local Secretary—Dr. NICHOLSON, 3, Berkeley Crescent, Bristol.

Auditors—Dr. SHEPHERD and Dr. E. WILLIAMS.

1870—BIRMINGHAM. *President*—J. J. DRYSDALE, M.D.

1871—OXFORD. *President*—H. R. MADDEN, M.D.

1872—YORK. *President*—F. BLACK, M.D.

1873—LEAMINGTON. *President*—W. SHARP, M.D., F.R.S.

1874—LONDON. *President*—R. E. DUDGEON, M.D.

1875—MANCHESTER. *President*—W. BAYES, M.D.

Members.

Dr. BAYES, London.
Dr. C. H. BLACKLEY, Manchester.
Dr. J. G. BLACKLEY, London.
Dr. GIBBS BLAKE, Birmingham.
Mr. J. N. BLAKE, Sheffield.
Dr. BRYCE, Edinburgh.
Dr. BURNETT, Birkenhead.
Dr. CROUCHER, Hastings.
Dr. COLLINS, Leamington.
Dr. COGHLAN, Manchester.
Mr. A. C. CLIFTON, Northampton.
Dr. G. CLIFTON, Leicester.
Dr. DUDGEON, London.
Dr. DRYSDALE, Liverpool.
Dr. HAYWARD, Liverpool.
Dr. HUGHES, Brighton.
Dr. HOWDEN, Bowden.
Dr. HALL.
Dr. HAYLE, Rochdale.
Dr. HAWKES, Liverpool.
Dr. HARVEY, Southport.
Dr. KENNEDY, Newcastle-on-Tyne.

Dr. MAFFEY, Nottingham.
Dr. MOORHOUSE, Bowden.
Mr. MABERLY, Leamington.
Dr. MOIR, Manchester.
Dr. E. MADDEN, Birmingham.
Dr. MOORE, Liverpool.
Dr. MEYHOFFER, Nice.
Dr. H. NANKIVELL, Bournemouth.
Dr. PERKINS, Manchester.
Mr. PROCTOR, Liverpool.
Dr. POPE, London.
Dr. POWELL, London.
Dr. RAMSBOTHAM, Leeds.
Dr. RAYNER, Manchester.
Dr. SKINNER, Liverpool.
Dr. SCOTT, Huddersfield.
Dr. STOKES, Southport.
Dr. SHARP, F.R.S., Rugby.
Dr. J. SIMPSON, Liverpool.
Dr. C. WOLSTON, Croydon.
Dr. WALTER WOLSTON, Edinburgh.
Dr. WILDE, Weston-Super-Mare.

THE POSITION OF HOMŒOPATHY IN THE RATIONAL PRACTICE OF MEDICINE.

By W. Bayes, M.D.

Gentlemen,—The aspect under which I propose to discuss the science and art of homœopathy on the present occasion, is that of an examination into its position in relation to the rational practice of medicine.

We cannot too decidedly or too often impress upon the profession, that we follow no irrational dogma when we adopt the practice of homœopathy. We are bound not only to show a reason for our practice, but to define how far and in what directions the rule of "similars" and the art of prescribing minute or infinitesimal doses of medicinal drugs accord with the discoveries of modern science, and are correlated to other physiological, pathological and physical facts.

It is in the hope of contributing my small quota to the elucidation of a rational explanation of the rule of similars and of the curative action of infinitesimals, that I venture to read the following pages before you this morning.

Twenty-two years have passed since the homœopathic practitioners of Great Britain met in Congress in the city of Manchester. This was in the early days of British homœopathy, and was the fourth of the Annual Congresses held by the practitioners of the new system. Dr. Drysdale occupied the chair. Dr. Sharp read the opening address. About 35 gentlemen were present. Many have passed away from among us—Drs. Walker, Edward Phillips, McLeod, Atkin, Fearon, John Epps, Cameron (of Huddersfield), Laurie, Ramsbotham, Russell and Blake (of Taunton). Many others remain—men of note, men who have won their spurs in the battle, men who have upheld the banner of truth so chivalrously as to have wrung a tribute of respect even from their adversaries. None among these more worthy than our learned and much-loved colleagues Drs. Black, Drysdale and Sharp.

The first Annual Congress of British Homœopathic practitioners, was inaugurated at Cheltenham in the year 1850. It occupied two days. On the first day the late

Dr. Sherlock Willis presided; on the second day our genial friend Dr. (then Mr.) Hering occupied the chair. Drs. Black and Ker were the secretaries. Dr. Black read the opening address, and Dr. Madden read a paper on the second day " On the homœopathic treatment of inflammation and ulceration of the neck of the uterus," giving the results of 180 cases. A dinner followed, under the presidency of the late Dr. Chapman, and we are told that this first British Homœopathic Congress was successful beyond expectation.

In 1851, the second Congress was held in London, Dr. Black being president. About 60 practitioners were present.

In 1852, Edinburgh was the seat of the Congress, the late Professor Henderson being president.

Then came the fourth Congress, in 1853, in this city (Manchester), Dr. Drysdale presiding.

In 1854, Leamington was selected, Dr. Quin being president.

In 1855, London was again the seat of the Congress, Dr. Madden presiding.

The last of this series of Congresses was again held in London in 1856, under the presidency of the late Dr. Atkin.

Then came a hiatus, and no Congress was held till 1870, in which year Birmingham was selected as its seat; Dr. Drysdale being president, Dr. Gibbs Blake and Mr. Evan Frazer acting as secretaries.

The Congress in Oxford followed in 1871, Dr. Madden having been elected president, and although his sudden and lamentable illness precluded his own attendance, we had from his pen one of the most remarkable and admirable addresses ever read before a homœopathic assembly.

In 1872, the ancient city of York received the Congress under Dr. Black's presidency. In 1873, it met in Leamington, when Dr. Sharp was its president; and last year (1874) the Congress met in London, under the able presidency of Dr. Dudgeon.

In thus briefly reviewing the history of our Congresses (of the former seven, and of the five of our present series), some may be tempted to ask, in this eminently utilitarian age, "*cui bono?*" Our answer lies in a very small space. As our genial and learned friend Dr. Black said, in his opening address in 1850, " Man is eminently social, and

it is strongly inherent in his nature to form associations
as tending to his defence, happiness and knowledge. In
meeting here we follow this natural impulse; we desire
to cultivate kindly intercourse, and to discuss various
points bearing on the improvement of therapeutics; and
we feel that such labours cannot be carried on so well
singly and independently, as by hearty co-operation."

The result of these Congresses has fully justified these
words of exordium, and has shown the foresight of those
men who inaugurated these assemblies. Socially and professionally they have given a tone and an earnestness to
our body tending much to improve our position and to
increase our usefulness.

Long ago, Channing observed, " The age of individual
action is gone. Truth can hardly be heard unless shouted
by a crowd."

Congresses and meetings of associations testify, from
their universal adoption (as a means of expressing opinions)
by almost all classes of men, to the truth of Channing's
observation. Annual Congresses meet and discuss, and,
after a fashion, "shout" their truths aloud into the world's
ear; and we are only following the demands of a very
practical age in holding these congresses.

The essays which have been read before us by Drysdale,
Madden, Black, Sharp and Dudgeon, have reached the
eyes and the ears of many men who, but for our Congresses, would never have opened eye or have unstopped
ear, to see or to hear any individual exposition of the
cogent and scientific arguments brought to bear on the
varied aspects under which homœopathy may be viewed
in its relations to modern science.

The full influence which these essays may have exerted
in spreading a knowledge of homœopathy may not be immediately apparent. But the seed which they have sown
cannot fail to bear its fruit. This may not be evidenced
by immediate productiveness; but one thing is certain,
these addresses will have shown the profession that we
possess in our ranks, men of profound judgment, of acute
reasoning powers, of careful research, and of classic attainments. Indirectly, a consideration of these things gives
an antecedent probability as to the value of the theories
and practice which such writers and thinkers believe in,
and are able to vindicate so powerfully.

At the very least, our Congresses and the essays read

before them, will tend to remove much of the misunderstanding as to our principles, practice and motives, which the present policy of the ruling majority among the profession has imposed upon its members.

Perhaps one of the heaviest burdens we have to bear in the active battle of life, is the feeling that our actions are misunderstood. To have our best motives misconstrued; our endeavours to act as honest, good citizens disbelieved; our efforts, actuated by philanthropy, represented as having none but self-ending, self-aggrandizing aims; our philosophy characterized as folly; our leaders designated as knaves, our followers as fools. Yet this is the position of the misunderstood, and must be borne patiently and unrepiningly. Time alone can change this state of things. "All things come to him who waits," once said a certain French sage, and, believing in this, we shall do wisely to adopt as our motto, "we bide our time."

Strong in the consciousness of the stability of our facts, and of our power to prove the truthfulness of our deductions from them (whenever we can get our opponents to listen), what matter a few years, more or less, during which we must continue to write ourselves down as "misunderstood." Ready, at all times, to defend the scientific basis of our philosophy, we can afford to wait till it pleases the profession to unstop their ears and to listen to our reasoning, and to open their eyes to look upon our facts. Upholding, with firm hand and brave heart, a high standard of philanthropic endeavour to relieve human suffering, we can afford to smile on the taunts of those who ignorantly charge us with unworthy motives. That we are misunderstood by many who, nevertheless, are acting in honest misconception of our principles, of our practice and of our motives, should never tempt us to forsake our posture of dignified awaiting.

The desire to place ourselves right with our professional brethren of the other school, is a very natural and proper object of ambition. The removal of the misunderstandings which unfortunately exist, will tend much to bridge over the chasm which yawns between the two schools of medicine. Much has been said, of late, upon this subject, both in discussion before our Societies and in our journals. But while we acknowledge that a restoration of friendly intercourse is most desirable, both at the Scientific Societies, at the Hospitals, and in consultations, we must avoid all compromise; we must yield nothing of our distinctive principles. To do so would be to become traitors to the cause of truth. Fraught with advantage as would be the restoration of brotherly feeling between the two schools of medicine, it were wiser and more noble to accept a perpetual ostracism, rather than that we should ratify a hollow truce founded on an abandonment of any of the safeguards with which we surround the interests of the public.

In what can we yield to the demands of our opponents? Can we abandon our name? In that case, how are the public to distinguish the physician who has studied and adopted homœopathy from him who has no knowledge of this branch of therapeutics?

Can we cease the open practice of the homœopathic rule of similars? Can we agree to abjure the administration of drugs in accordance with the rule of similars? Can we agree to abandon the use of minute or infinitesimal doses of drugs where we believe in their superior efficacy?

No. Those who believe in the rule of practice handed down to us by Hahnemann, those who believe in the homœopathic action of drugs, and those who have adopted the small or infinitesimal dose, believing it to be the best mode of curing their patients, cannot, without grave dereliction of duty towards the public, abandon their name, their open avowal of belief, or their practice.

That which we believe in, we must uphold. Timid counsels are as unwise as they are pusillanimous. As our late poor friend, Dr. Cochran, used to say with regard to pains and penalties borne for the cause of truth, " We must just put on a stiff upper lip and go through with them."

What we can do conscientiously, towards more friendly relations with the majority of the profession, we ought to do. First of all, we ought to define, as accurately as possible, that which we profess to teach in the practice of medicine and in the domain of therapeutics. Let this be done modestly, temperately and scientifically, and the wall of separation which has been raised by unfortunate misunderstandings must, sooner or later, break down. In thus attempting to correct misunderstandings and misrepresentations, we must proceed with the most perfect courtesy. If we must needs enter into the field of controversy, we must keep the most perfect temper, giving our adversaries credit for the same honesty of purpose, the same high sense of duty, the same integrity in scientific research which we claim for ourselves.

When we bring forward statements of facts, new to medical science, opposed to all the former experience of physicians of the older school, we must expect the opposition of its adherents. We must be prepared to receive their outbursts of incredulity and of active opposition, with a degree of even temper which we have no right to expect them to extend to us in return. We are attacking them in their tenderest point of self-esteem. We are announcing to men who are desiring to do right, that they have unintentionally been doing wrong. To men who have been as full, as we are, of a warm philanthropy, we say, that the means by which they believed they were prolonging life were, in reality, shortening life. That while they believed themselves to be ministering angels, bringing life and health to the suffering, our facts prove that they were unconsciously assisting the destroying angel on his errand of death.

Is it to be supposed that men of ordinary passions could look with even temper and "wreathed smiles" upon a system which teaches and demonstrates such a truth as this? It is asking too much of human nature to expect it.

As soon should we have expected the priests of Egypt to have accepted the teachings of Moses, or the priests of Greece and Rome to have accepted the truths proclaimed by St. Paul and the Apostles.

Therefore, we ought to accept calmly from our opponents such treatment in word and deed as we should carefully abstain from returning in kind. Our own self-respect, based on our knowledge of the truth of the doctrines we follow, should save us from returning evil for evil. We have but to wait God's own time, and that truth, of which we are the exponents, will as surely attain its place, and those errors which it has been and still is our province to oppose will as surely perish, as have all other truths triumphed, and all other errors ultimately sunk into a merited oblivion. It may not be in our day, for the human mind is very complex in its workings, and time-honoured errors are hydra-headed and difficult to slay; but that which has been will be, and light is stronger than darkness.

The propounders of a new theory are bound to prove.

the reasonableness of their belief. The series of brilliant essays which have been read at the five preceding meetings of our Congress have each shown a facet in the diamond of truth; but truth, like a well-cut stone, is many-sided, and I venture to place homœopathy before you in yet another aspect.

HAHNEMANN founded his system on the theory that disease is a derangement of vital force, and that it is best cured—*i.e.*, most readily, most certainly, and most permanently cured—by the administration of such drugs to the sick as are capable of producing a derangement in the healthy, similar to that of the natural disease.

I am well aware that it is a matter of dispute among some of our foremost physiologists of the present day as to whether there be any vital force at all. I will not here stop to consider this point, as the settlement of that question will in no way affect my argument. Vital force is a convenient term by which to signify the activity of life, even if it lack scientific accuracy, which I, for one, doubt. Hahnemann certainly did not look upon a patient as "a complex congeries of a number of subordinate quasi-independent living units, whose life is complete in themselves." Though, had he done so, his method of symptom-treatment would have equally suited the ailments of the "quasi-independent units" as of the individual man or woman they collectively go to compose.

In Hahnemann's day physiologists were more fanciful and pathologists were more materialistic than we are at the present day. Hahnemann's propositions in the earlier part of the *Organon*, that disease is simply a want of balance of vital force, shocked the materialistic pathologists of the day, who looked on diseases as peccant matters to be cast out of the body; to be poured out in a stream of blood from the arm, or to be drawn out of the skin by a blister; to be purged out of the bowels by cathartics; to be vomited out of the stomach by emetics; to be washed out through the kidneys by diuretics; to be sweated out of the skin by sudorifics, or to be tortured out of the tissues by setons. His idea that disease is simply a derangement of vital force, was an immense step toward that "conservation of life" which is now admitted, on all sides, to be the true principle of treatment, however we may differ as to the details of the therapeutic means by which this indication is to be effected.

In the temple of Æsculapius Hahnemann was a great iconoclast, and he shared the fate of all iconoclasts. He was abused and execrated by the priests and worshippers of the false gods whom he overthrew and ground to pieces beneath the heel of his intellect. Yet the pathology he rejected is now rejected by the old school as well as by our own; and the system of treatment in his day, which was barbarous and empirical for the most part, and always complex, has been abandoned by all scientific physicians for a method founded on more exact indications.

Putting aside all the fanciful explanations of disease which found favour in his day, he reverted to first principles, and became in physic what the pre-Raphaelite is in art. He drew a severe line, which forbad the physician to indulge in speculations, telling him to form no hypothetical opinions as to this or that organ or function being in fault, but advising him to take his indications for treatment from the symptoms, subjective and objective, before him, such as are patent to the senses of the physician, or such as are revealed by the sensations of the patient.

We see, then, that Hahnemann believed in a self-regulating vital force, ruling the whole healthy body, balancing each function, repairing each organ, tissue or fluid.

Disease, in his view, is the derangement of this vital force. " It is the morbidly affected vital force alone," he says, "that produces diseases."* The only exceptions which he allows to this rule, are those diseases which come under the province of manual surgery. Hahnemann further says that there is no disease "which does not make itself known to the accurately observing physician by means of morbid signs and symptoms."†

To cure a patient, according to Hahnemann's scheme, the physician has therefore only to "remove the whole of the symptoms" collectively the evidence of the disease, and these can only be removed by restoring the healthy balance to the vital force. The "annihilation of disease is the restoration to health."

When the body is free from pain and from discomfort; when a man is not conscious of the possession of any part of his body until he calls it into action, provided it be an organ of voluntary function, such as the hand, the foot, or the brain; when he is not conscious of the possession

* *Organon*, Proposition XII.   † *Ibid.*, Proposition XIV.

of the heart, lungs, or other organ of the involuntary functions, then he is well. To be conscious of these organs, by any sensation, shows them to be either distressed or diseased.

Hence, Hahnemann considers that the symptoms observed by the physician, or related to him by the patient, are the true indications of the disease : " The sum of all the symptoms, in each individual case of disease, must be the *sole indication*, the sole guide to direct us in the choice of a curative remedy." *

These propositions of Hahnemann cannot be accepted by us in their entirety, since there are many diseases whose importance and even danger are great, yet whose symptoms are by no means prominent, or sufficient to guide us in the selection of a drug analogue. And there are other large classes of disease whose causes must afford us the indications for their treatment. We cannot therefore claim for symptom-treatment that it is the " sole indication." Such claim is too absolute and dogmatic. Pathology and etiology afford us the true indications for our treatment in a very considerable number of cases; yet even where we choose our indications from our knowledge of the pathological state or etiological conditions of a given case, we shall find that our homœopathic therapeutics enables us, not unseldom, to meet these indications with precision, as to choice of remedy, where, without Hahnemann's discovery, we should remain in doubt and difficulty.

Thus, while we reject them as too absolute and dogmatic to be our *sole guide*, we nevertheless may accept Hahnemann's propositions, as defining the true sphere of the system he advocates within the domain of medicine, and may claim for homœopathic therapeutics that they best guide us in the cure of *all such diseases as arise from a want of balance between the functional actions of the various parts and organs of the body, and are characterised by pains and sensations.*

The ruling pathology in Hahnemann's day would have restricted this field for treatment to very narrow limits. But the researches of modern physiology and pathology prove that a very large area of disease is covered by that, which owes its cause to a loss of balance between the functional activities of the nerves of motion, of sensation,

* *Organon,* Proposition XVIII.

and of organic life; and that the majority of the diseases of the secretory and excretory organs are produced by the functional exaltation or depression of one or other of these sets of nerves.

The views of disease, in its dynamic, adynamic, and non-materialistic aspects, which have been so extensively promulgated by physicians of the highest eminence, and which have been adopted by the majority of the profession during the last fifteen or twenty years, show how prophetically Hahnemann foreshadowed in his day the coming theories of our own.

I need but name Dr. Bence Jones and Dr. T. K. Chambers. Dr. Bence Jones thus wrote (in his *Lectures on Pathology and Therapeutics*, p. 276):—" You must entirely banish from your minds the notion that diseases are catastrophes or separate entities, to be destroyed within, or to be ejected, like devils, without, by which a perfect cure can only be obtained ; and you must more and more be fully possessed by the fact that *all diseases* are the increase or diminution or qualitative modification of the never-resting correlated forces which constitute life."

It is not safe, in our present state of " never-resting " scientific thought and imagination, to attempt to lay down such unconditional explanation of *all diseases*.

Dr. T. K. Chambers falls into equal error when he says " Disease, *in all cases*, is not a positive existence, but a negative ; not a new excess of action, but a deficiency; not a modification of life, but a partial death."

These physicians have less excuse for their inaccuracy than had Hahnemann ; for the microscope has given us, in this later age, revelations which were but in the womb of the future when he dogmatised in his *Organon*.

Recognising at its full worth, and within its proper limitations, the value and import of the adynamic theory of disease, and claiming its recognition as the first step toward laying a basis for a rational explanation of the homœopathic rule of therapeutics, I must stay on the very threshold of the subject, to say a few words on the necessity for an equally clear admission of the principle, that large classes of disease also exist, whose whole phenomena are not satisfactorily explained on the dynamic or adynamic theory alone.

I allude to the infectious, contagious, malarious, mal-aqueous diseases; to those of parasitic origin, and to morbid growths.

The view that infectious and contagious diseases own as their cause a "contagium vivum," and are spread by organisms of extreme minuteness, which float in the air, or which exist in our drinking water or in our food, and which, entering through the mouth, nose, or skin, are propagated within the bodies or upon the bodies of infected patients, has met with able advocates, both in this country and abroad.

Budd, Tyndall, Beale and others have demonstrated this theory by many apparently incontrovertible facts. But it is nowhere set forth with the same precision and effect as in that admirable work, Ziemssen's *Cyclopædia of the Practice of Medicine.* The most recent researches of German observers seemingly place it beyond controversy that infectious and contagious diseases depend on a "contagium vivum," or "living organisms," which, entering into the body, there multiply to an enormous extent, reproducing themselves with immense rapidity, each after its own kind, whether it be small-pox or typhus, relapsing fever or measles, and never propagating any but their kind. These organisms are extremely minute: a drop of putrid solution, according to Ehrenburg, may contain as many as 500 millions of organisms, each the 40,000th of an inch or less in length.*

Vaccine lymph has been found by Dr. Burdon Sanderson and others to contain numerous particles, the 20,000th part of an inch in diameter, floating in serous fluid. A child may be vaccinated with the fluid without effect; but if one of these little germs enter the wound, all the phenomena of vaccination follow. The researches of Professors Liebermeister, Lebert and others have shown the presence of equally minute organisms in the secretions of typhoid, relapsing fever, and other infectious or contagious diseases, and that these diseases are due to the multiplication of living organisms within the patient. If few organisms develope, the disease is slight; if their development be extensive, the illness is proportionately severe.

Now, if it be proved that these diseases own, as their cause, the rapid development of living and self-multiplying organisms within the blood and tissues of the body, their

* *See Lectures on Zymotic Poison,* by Dr. MacDougal. Reported in *Chemist and Druggist,* January 1875.

treatment must be conducted on different indications from those whose causes are wholly dynamic or adynamic; and I allude to them here, simply to point out that there exist classes of disease which, from their exceptional character, are likely to demand specific and exceptional treatment, since a purely symptomatic treatment of them would be likely to prove only very partially successful.

At the same time, it is quite possible that further investigations may greatly modify the value of these microscopical discoveries, and that some explanation may be found which may show that the rapid development of these organisms may be due to partial disintegrations of the body, owing to a temporary suspension of, or to irregular action of the functions of assimilation, secretion, and formation, and may be due to partial paralyses of peripheral and minute nerves (not yet demonstrable by the instrumental means at our command), by which the bonds which bind the " complex congeries" of " subordinate quasi-independent units" together is loosened, and by which, for a time, the component parts of the body suffer a vital disintegration. But while admitting this as a possibility, I confess that it appears to me that the weight of argument is in favour of the " contagium vivum" theory. We must remember, in discussing this subject, the powerful bearing which the facts shown by Lister's antiseptic treatment of wounds has on this theory; so also has the discovery that trichinosis and some other hitherto obscure diseases are due to parasitic developments within the body.

Bearing these exceptions in mind, we may therefore now revert to a consideration of those diseases which depend on derangements of function and of the applicability of Hahnemann's method to their cure.

The experiments conducted by Claude Bernard and other physiologists have shown that perfect health of function (of circulation, of assimilation, of secretion and of excretion, &c.) depends on the reciprocal and regular actions of the three forms of nerve fibres supplying the organs, the motor, the sensory, the sympathetic—on this tripod health sits enthroned.

Destroy all the branches of these three sets of nerves which supply any organ, and its special life ceases in that organ—it ceases to perform its function.

Destroy any one of the three branches and the balance *of health is overset*—disease ensues.

A very short quotation from Dr. Meryon's *Rational Therapeutics*,[*] in which he tersely relates Claude Bernard's experiments on certain functions of the sympathetic nerves, will enable me to illustrate my arguments as to the exact sphere of homœopathic therapeutics.

Claude Bernard has shown " that section of the sympathetic proper induces increased vascularity and elevation of temperature in the parts to which the sympathetic are supplied."

In experiments upon rabbits he found that after section of the sympathetic on one side of the neck, the temperature rose 7° Fahrenheit on that side as compared with the temperature of the uninjured side. This elevation of temperature was not merely temporary but remained till the animal was killed, although the whole body ultimately increased in temperature 3°, leaving the injured side permanently 4° hotter than the other. Dr. Wm. Ogle related a case (at the Medico-Chirurgical Society) where, owing to a tumour in the neck, the cervical sympathetic on one side was injured, and the ear on the injured side became 2° hotter than the other ear. " Another curious and instructive phenomenon occurs when (owing to the division of the sympathetic) the blood is thus transmitted in a preternatural quantity through the capillaries—the venous blood immediately becomes brighter in colour. Claude Bernard observed this fact in the coronary veins on the left side of the lip of a horse after he had divided the left cervical sympathetic."

Commenting on these facts (page 41), Dr. Meryon says: " In some forms of inflammation—and inflammation in some form or other lies at the root of most diseases—we have the pathological counterpart of the result induced by the section of the sympathetic; a state in which, owing to the loss of the inhibitory influence of the nerve fibres of Remak, blood corpuscles penetrate into those minute arterioles through which blood plasma only should be propelled.

The effect of the division of the sympathetic fibres distributed to a secretory gland shows the same effect on the circulation in that gland; firstly, it induces hyperæmia, and, secondly, it induces increased secretion. These two

---

[*] *On the Functions of the Sympathetic System of Nerves, as a Physiological Basis for a Rational System of Therapeutics.* By EDWARD MERYON, M.D. Churchill & Co.

B

results invariably follow the weakening or destruction of the nerve current of the sympathetic proper, and appear to be due to a corresponding increase in the action of the motor nerve of the same part or organ, which immediately occurs so soon as the controlling or inhibitory influence of the sympathetic proper is withdrawn or lowered.

" Now the application of a *weak* electric current to the peripheric end of the divided sympathetic reverses all this. The calibre of the distended capillaries is quickly ·reduced; the temperature is lowered, and may be depressed below the existing degree in other parts; and secretion is diminished. If the power of the current be increased the circulation may be entirely arrested; so that, if examined under a microscope, the capillary vessels will be seen to be entirely empty. Such is the invariable result of stimulation of the nerves of Remak on the capillaries; and MM. Valentin Henle and Budge have observed that the large blood vessels contract when acted on by galvanism through the medium of the grey nerve fibres which are supplied to them.

" It appears, therefore, that all the conditions of healthy circulation and secretion are fulfilled in the reciprocal action of the three forms of nerve fibres.

" Make a section of them all, or cut away, say, the renal. plexus, and all secretion of urine is arrested.

" Increase the relative power of the motor nerve fibres by section of the nerves of Remak, and you establish a hyperæmia round about the Malpighian ducts and diuresis.

" Increase the relative power of the nerves of Remak by section of the motor fibres, and you diminish circulation and secretion.

" Increase the relative balance of power of either motor or inhibitory nerve fibres either by gently exciting the sensory nerves, or by painfully irritating them, and you have in the first place increased circulation and secretion, or in the second case the very reverse." *

It appears, therefore, to be proved by the experiments of physiologists, that circulation and secretion are balanced during health between the functional actions of the motor, the sympathetic, and the sensory nerves; and that disturbance in the functions of any of the three sets of nerves will result in disturbance of the vessels or parts to which they are distributed. Over-stimulation of the one set of

* *Rational Therapeutics*, Meryon, p. 29.

nerves, or debility of the other set, will induce similar symptoms. If you over-stimulate the sympathetic branch you check circulation, and you check secretion, more or less completely according to the degree of stimulus applied. In the same way, if you destroy the relative balance between the motor nerve and the sympathetic by depressing the motor branch, circulation and secretion are proportionately diminished. If you stimulate the motor nerve then, you increase circulation and secretion; and if you depress the sympathetic nerve, thus destroying the balance between it and the motor, you also find the circulation and secretion proportionately increased.

When, therefore, we see a case of disease before us in which there is a deficiency in the circulation and in the secretion of any part or organ, we know that the fault lies either in the over-stimulation of the sympathetic nerves, or in the debility and partial paralysis of the motor nerves supplying the part or organ.

On the other hand, whenever we see a case of disease in which there is a hyperæmic or inflammatory condition, or an excessive secretion, we know that the fault lies either in depression or partial paralysis of the sympathetic nerves, or in over-stimulation of the motor nerves distributed to the part or organ affected.

Two courses are evidently open to us in the selection of the indication for treatment in such cases; either we may depress the nerves which are over-stimulated, or we may stimulate the depressed nerves; we may extend help to the weakened nerve, or weaken that which is strong.

The true art of healing tends always in the direction of the conservation of energy and of strength; and acts always on the indications of strengthening the weaker nerve and of stimulating the depressed: hence, when there is inflammation of any tract or organ, knowing this to arise from a paralysis more or less complete of certain branches of the sympathetic nerves, and the consequent uncontrolled action of the corresponding motor branches, we enjoin rest, either local or general, in order to tranquillize the excited motor nerves, and we administer such means as will tend to restore the weakened sympathetic to its proper tension or tone.

We have seen that section of the sympathetic branches of the renal plexus induces hyperæmia round about the Malpighian ducts and diuresis, but if a gentle galvanic current be passed into the divided nerve at its peripheral end, the diuresis is arrested and the hyperæmia disappears. Therefore, what we have to do in a case of diuresis, occurring from natural disease, is to find a means of gently stimulating the sympathetic branch of the renal plexus. Such a means we have at command through our knowledge of the homœopathic action of drugs. We have but to seek a remedy in such drugs as in their pathogenetic dose paralyse the sympathetic branches of the renal plexus, which will induce primarily hyperæmia with greatly increased secretion, such as *cantharides* or *terebinth*, &c., and we find ourselves in a position to cure the condition of paralysis.

But it will be said by those who have not acquainted themselves with our method and our art, this is a paradox. If there be already paralysis of the nerve more or less complete, common sense will lead us to give a stimulant and not a paralyzer.

To answer this objection we must appeal to another series of facts belonging to the range of pure therapeutics, which show that each medicinal drug has at least two apparently opposite actions, according to the dose given. That in a certain dose each medicinal drug tends to paralyze a given tract of nerve, while in a certain other dose it acts as a stimulant. If the large and pathogenetic dose of *cantharides* or *terebinth* paralyse the sympathetic branch of the renal plexus, we know, from carefully recorded experiments, that the minute or infinitesimal dose will stimulate the same nervous tract. And by Hahnemann's method we are able to adjust the degree of stimulant applied with an exactitude hitherto unattainable. The degree of paralysis is shown by the intensity or prominence of the symptoms. The frequency and the size of the dose should be regulated by the frequency and the urgency of the functional distresses.

But, it will be asked, what right have we to assume that medicinal drugs possess these opposite powers? What right have we to assert that the same drug which paralyzes in the large dose will stimulate in the minute or infinitesimal dose? Or, to reverse the proposition, that the same drug which is a stimulant in a small dose will be a narcotic or a paralyzer in a large dose?

No better example can be given, in illustration of these *points,* than that of alcohol. Its stimulating action is so well known by the fatigued in mind or body, that its power to paralyse is apt to be overlooked or forgotten. Let us devote a short time to a consideration of these two actions of alcohol.

Dr. Anstie, in his article on *Alcoholism* in Russell Reynold's *System of Medicine,* says (p. 65): "If the dose" of alcohol "be moderate, and the administration well timed, the effect upon the nervous system is simply that of a restorative stimulant. Sensations of fatigue are dispelled, the mind works more freely, a healthy sense of warmth is diffused through the body, and the arterial system acquires an increased tonicity if it were hitherto deficient in that quality. The latter fact, which is due to the influence of the remedy upon the sympathetic nerves, is capable of being demonstrated in a very interesting and convincing manner.

" The sphygmograph of M. Marey has the power of accurately representing, by its registration of the pulse-wave, the degree of arterial tonicity present; and by this unfailing test it appears that the small vessels, when relaxed in a condition of fatigue, are brought by a moderate dose of alcohol to a proper tension, from which they suffer no recoil.

" If, on the contrary, the dose has been immoderate, or administered at a time when it was not required, the pulse-waves give a precisely opposite indication, that, namely, which proves that arterial relaxation has occurred, and simultaneously with this the pulse becomes abnormally quick. At the same time other symptoms of a paralytic nature are observed, confined in the first instance to the spinal nerves of the fifth cranial nerve. The former show their weakness by the occurrence of slight feelings of numbness, and an impairment of muscular sense in the extremities. The latter indicates its affection by slight numbness of the lips. The vaso-motor fibres of the fifth nerve discover their partially-paralysed condition by flushing of the face, congestion of the conjunctivæ and lachrymation.

" The cerebral hemispheres next give notice of the alcoholic influence by the occurrence of intellectual confusion; and the hypo-glossi becoming simultaneously affected, the muscular movements of the tongue become difficult, and articulation is impeded.

" The further stages of drunkenness consist of more or

less noisy or sentimental delirium, passing gradually into coma; palsy, more and more complete, of voluntary motion and sensation; the medulla oblongata is palsied, and breathing ceases; and, last of all, the organic nerves of the heart become incapable of performing their functions, and cardiac life ceases."

Here, then, we have clear demonstration of the fact, shown not only by the symptoms but recorded by the sphygmograph, that the small dose of alcohol has power to restore arterial tonicity when it is administered to a patient in whom there is a want of this tonicity, caused by fatigue (in fact where there is a partial paralysis of the sympathetic), by which the blood-vessels have become relaxed.

But if alcohol be given in an immoderate dose, precisely the opposite effect results, and the paralysis is increased.

Still more important is the fact that, when even a moderate dose is given to a patient in health, where the pulse-wave shows no want of tonicity, then arterial relaxation, with a quick pulse, is induced, and other symptoms of a paralytic character ensue.

Alcohol, then, causes paralysis of the sympathetic nerves more or less complete according to the dose administered, when it is given to a man in perfect health. On the other hand it cures temporary paralysis of the sympathetic nerves when this condition of debility pre-exists. It increases the paralysis if the dose given be immoderate (What is this but the " medicinal aggravation " of Hahnemann). It causes death by paralysis if the dose be carried to its extreme of poisonous power.

It is difficult to conceive how any truly scientific physician, having these facts before him, can logically infer from them any other conclusion than that of the general truth of the homœopathic rule of " Similia." And once admitting this, it is impossible not also to concede the necessity for the administration of small doses, such as shall effect a cure by bringing the relaxed nerves, which are causing functional disease and disorder, to such a state of tension as shall exactly restore the balance of health, and from which they shall suffer no " recoil." For such a recoil means a relapse and, over-dosing inducing relapse, a continued round of wrong must ensue from its practice.

It would take us far beyond the limits of the time

afforded to this address were we to proceed, as could easily be done, to show that the same phenomena of stimulation and paralyzing certain tracts follow the administration of all other substances which are capable of pathogenetic action.

Opium, ipecacuanha, nux vomica, cantharides, colocynth, in fact every drug in the Materia Medica, follows the same law in its medicinal effects. Every medicinal drug has power, in its large or pathogenetic dose, to paralyse or to narcotize a certain nervous tract or tracts, each according to its affinities; and it has the power to stimulate the same tract or tracts when given in a small dose to a patient suffering from depressed vitality or partial paralysis of this nerve tract or tracts. Even a moderate dose of the drug, such as might prove curative in disease, will derange the health of a sensitive patient if given " when it is not required." A moderate dose of *opium* will narcotize a healthy man, but given to a man preternaturally drowsy from threatened apoplexy, a small dose will bring the hyperæmic vessels of the brain back to a proper state of tension by its gently-stimulating effect on the sympathetic (inhibitory) nerves supplying and controlling those vessels.

An immoderate dose, on the other hand, will increase the disease, just as an immoderate dose of alcohol will tend to induce further paralysis of the threatened sympathetic generally. The question of the dose is one, therefore, of the utmost importance, it cannot be lightly passed over, or guessed at hap hazard. As with alcohol and opium, so it will be found with ipecacuanha and with every other drug. The large dose of ipecacuanha vomits; the small dose cures vomiting when caused by weakened action of the same set of nerves which the action of ipecacuanha affects. Ipecacuanha would not cure vomiting arising from concussion of the brain—nor from tubercular meningitis. Hence, accurate diagnosis is as needful to the physician practising homœopathy as to him who practises as an allopath.

It will be seen from the foregoing remarks that a study of the paralyzing power of each drug, as affecting certain parts, tracts, or organs (whose general pathogenetic power was first insisted upon by Hahnemann, and latterly further precisionized by many of his followers, and particularly insisted upon by our learned and excellent colleague, Dr.

Sharp, in the series of papers from his pen, many of which
have been read before these Congresses) enables us to predicate the power of these same drugs to cure certain
definite conditions of disease in the same tracts, parts, or
organs, by the use of minute or infinitesimal doses of these
same drugs.

Can anything be more accurate, or more scientific, or
more in accord with the present advanced state of pathological and physiological science than a system of therapeutics founded on this basis? And it is on this basis
that the science of homœopathic therapeutics is destined
to rest, for none other explanation fits all these facts
together. There is one objection which I anticipate will
arise in certain minds. It is this. If stimulation be the
key to the whole treatment of functional diseases, why not
give alcohol as their cure? Ought it not to be an universal
panacea? Some such idea has from time to time come
before the public and even the professional mind. Witness
the treatment so strongly insisted upon by the late Dr.
Todd. Witness also the brandy and salt treatment that at
one time spread like an epidemic over the country.

The objections to this apparently simple method are
two-fold. Firstly, it wants fineness of aim; secondly, a
large number of diseases arise from disorders of the
motor or sensory nerves, as well as from disorders of the
sympathetic.

Alcohol is a stimulant or paralyser to the whole sympathetic system, but a very large number of diseases are
caused by derangements of only a very small portion of
the sympathetic system of nerves; and another large
number of diseases arise from debility or partial paralysis
of the motor and of the sensory tracts. To give alcohol
in either case would be worse than useless. We want to
stimulate the depressed nerves and these alone. The
healthy branches of the nerves require no interference.
To give a general stimulant where local debility alone
exists would be to derange one portion of the body in
attempting to restore its balance to the other.

Hence we have to seek other agents, such as will
enable us to stimulate the motor and the sensory tract,
and such as will enable us to carry force to any weakened
branch of either of the three sets of nerves which may
require aid, leaving the tract which is already healthy
and in proper tone untouched. Here our homœopathic

therapeutics find their appropriate sphere; they shew us that certain drugs can be employed to carry force to this or the other depressed nerve, or branch of a nerve, and that the rest of the body will be left untouched, and Hahnemann's method of the administration of drugs enables us to adjust the dose exactly to the requirements of the case, so that we can stimulate the weakened nerve back to its healthy standard of tonicity, so gradually and so gently that there shall be no fear of subsequent recoil.

I have said in the earlier part of my address that the promulgators of a new system are bound to prove its scientific basis, in order to overcome the opposition of candid objectors. If the views I have indicated possess the truth and the stability which I venture to claim for them, we shall have placed the Homœopathic system in a position to shew its accord with the developments of modern science. If the system we advocate does shew its correlation to every real advance in pathology and physiology, then the antecedent probability of its truth must become apparent, and much of the opposition we have hitherto met with will melt away.

It will be said that the task still remains of reconciling the practice of the administration of infinitesimal doses of medicinal drugs with the rational art of medicine. This practice, we are told by our opponents, and even by some of our friends, is contrary to common sense. I allow that it is contrary to *common sense founded on past allopathic experience,* just as the locomotive power of steam was theoretically opposed to the common sense of the old stage coachman, or as the electric telegraph was contrary to the common sense of the workers of the old semaphore, but in no other way is it more contrary to common sense than is any other new discovery. Still I accept the proposition that before we can overcome the opposition of physicians of the old school to this new practice we must be prepared to shew, firstly, that an antecedent probability exists as to the reasonableness of our belief that they will act; and secondly, we must be able, by proofs of a practical kind, to shew that they do act.

As to antecedent probability, are we acquainted with any facts which prove to us that infinitesimally small agents possess the power to attack a healthy or apparently healthy man and prostrate him with disease?

The microscope, which introduces a difficulty in the

way of the universal acceptance of our rule of " similars," as the sole indication for the cure of disease, clears away much of our difficulty as to the acceptance of the probabilities of the active powers of agents themselves of infinitesimal minuteness. Organisms of extreme minuteness, far exceeding in littleness the particles of our third dilution, are proved to be capable of inducing disease, and even of destroying the lives of thousands of human beings. We have seen, but as it were yesterday, whole communities swept off by measles in the Fiji islands. In like manner former epidemics of small-pox, scarlatina, cholera, &c., have, both in Europe and other countries, swept off thousands and even hundreds of thousands of lives. Yet the organisms which induce these diseases are invisible to the naked eye, and, in no way, can be recognized by the unaided senses, till they have entered into and have overcome the body by their malign and powerful influence.

In vacine lymph, we have seen it asserted that the organisms what reproduce it are but the 20,000th of an inch in diameter. Other of these living and prolific organisms are said to be smaller still. But, whatever their absolute size may be, the organisims which produce infectious diseases probably are relatively infinitely more minute than the blood globules of the creatures they invade. Possibly this is the law of infection. It is not yet proved to be so, but the facts at present recorded point in this direction, and the attention of many competent observers being directed to this subject, we may expect, ere long, new enlightenment upon it.

This is one of the series of examples of the power of infinitesimal organisms to induce disease. A second series, and one that comes still nearer in kind to the class of action we desire to illustrate, is to be found in the toxic power of infinitesimal agents, upon certain individuals whose idiosyncracy renders them, more than usually, sensitive to the special influence of the particular drug. The pathogenetic effects of *ipecacuanha*, in the minutest atoms, on the mucous surfaces of certain persons, is well known. So is the influence of arsenical wall-papering, which has exerted toxical effects on a large number of patients. Other individuals are so sensitive to *mercury*, that I have known an instance where even the 12th dilution (*i.e.* the quadrillionth part of a grain) could not be given without inducing mild salivation and great discomfort. So also, the sensitiveness of some patients to the action of *arnica* is most instructive. I have mentioned some instances of this susceptibility in my article on *arnica* in my work on Applied Homœopathy;* but two still more extraordinary cases have also occurred in my experience. In one, the patient (a banker advanced in years), was threatened with cerebral congestion, for which I prescribed *arnica*. He warned me that *arnica* always caused erysipelas with him. "In that case," I said, "I will give you such a dose as cannot possibly produce such an accident;" and I ordered him the 18th dilution. Next day he had decided swelling and erysipelatoid rash round the mouth and affecting specially the upper lip. I have also another patient, a lady of high rank, whose sensitiveness goes even beyond this. Her husband and children, fond of field sports, and, of course, consequently liable to troubles both from fatigue and from accidents, use, by my advice, a small quantity of *arnica* in their bath after an unusually tiring day; or an *arnica* lotion or compress for bruises or strains. But, under those circumstances, if they go into the same room where Lady —————— is, either after their bath or after using the lotion, she invariably has slight erysipelas of the face, with puffiness of both eyelids and great irritation of the skin. Her last attack of the kind was induced by her having, thoughtlessly, mixed a dose of a dilution of *arnica* for her husband, one drop of which fell on her finger, and although she immediately washed it off, she had erysipelas in the face next day.†

A consideration of these two classes of facts—firstly, the pathogenetic power of the infinitesimal organisms of

* *Applied Homœopathy; or, Specific Restorative Medicine.* By WILLIAM BAYES, M.D. London: H. Turner & Co., 77, Fleet-street.

† Although I have named but two drugs as examples, yet we have ample evidence that a similar sensitiveness to the action of all other powerful drugs exists in certain individuals; each such drug acting with special power over those who possess certain constitutional idiosyncracies. Hence we may easily understand the terrible catastrophes which are common in the practices of those men who indiscriminately, or even habitually, prescribe gross or large doses of drugs. These catastrophes (or accidents, as they are called) are certainly less common among the patients of those men who use small and infinitesimal doses. Sudden exacerbations of symptoms, or the occurrence of new siezures during an illness, appear to be relatively the more frequent, the larger the doses which are given in the treatment of the case. In my own practice catastrophes have been markedly less frequent since I have adopted the homœopathic therapeutics.

infectious and contagious diseases; secondly, the patho-genetic power of toxic infinitesimal influences—shows, at the least, a strong antecedent probability that minute and infinitesimally small doses of medicinal drugs ought also to possess beneficent powers.

Those agents which induce disease in a previously strong man, which have power to break down the usual functional habits of the healthy organization, are acting against the self-conservative powers of life. Those agents, on the other hand, by which we endeavour to restore the healthy balance and to give back regularity to the func-tional habits, have the self-conservative powers of the living body all on their side. Therefore, we do not require to use, as remedial agents, means possessing so great material force as we should need to use in order to induce toxic or pathogenetic results. To believe otherwise, would be to set aside altogether a consideration of that tendency toward healthy action and self-repair which we know to exist in the living body.

Therefore, a curative power should always be found in such a dose of the medicinal drug as is materially smaller than the agent which induced the disease.

If, then, the cause of a disease has been imponderable, invisible, infinitely minute, there exists not only an ante-cedent probability, but a scientific certainty, that the true cure—such a cure as shall leave no recoil—will be found in a dose of the correlated medicinal drug, which shall be also imponderable, invisible, and infinitesimal.

And once more, in those diseases whose cause is due to living organisms, how are these to be so readily destroyed as by employing medicinal drugs in such a state of atomic division that their particles shall be smaller than the creatures they are destined to slay? Who would not laugh at a man who fired a Krupp's cannon at a monad? Yet, in point of fact, he would be no more a just object of ridicule than the man who gives ounces or grains of crude drugs either to destroy infinitesimal organisms, or to restore the balance of nerve-force which had been upset by quadrillionths of a grain of disturbing force.

The facts relating to infection and to the special sus-ceptibility to certain drug influences induced by idiosyn-crasy, correspond in the most perfect manner to the facts we witness in our daily practice of drug-giving, in com-paratively small or in infinitesimal doses.

Every one who is exposed to infectious influences does not contract the disease.

Every one exposed to arnica, to ipecacuanha dust, or to arsenical wall-paperings, does not yield to their toxic influences.

There must be some peculiar state of health which predisposes the patient to receive their noxious influence.

It is not every one, even, who is bitten by a mad dog, who becomes hydrophobic, probably not one patient in four is so influenced.

Receptivity is an important condition in the production of these phenomena. In the same way we have no expectation that an infinitesimal or minute dose of a drug will affect a patient unless some special receptivity to its action exists. But we hold that the presence of disease, in a patient, renders him specially sensitive to the curative action of that drug which has a special affinity for the part, tract, or organ. In other words, that the depressed nerve will readily appropriate and shew, by its restoration to healthy balance of function, the action of that medicinal stimulus which is needed, although the quantity needed is so small that were it added to the healthy body, no sensation of stimulation or the reverse would be felt.

As to the actual size of the dose to be given, it would appear to be most in accordance with antecedent probabilities that it should be correlated to the pathogenetic force which has induced the disease. If the cause have been material, then the curative dose may also be required to be material. It is not, for example, pretended that the disease caused by a material dose of *arsenic* or other poison is to be met by an infinitesimal dose of an antidote. But a disease caused by an infinitesimal dose of *arsenic*, such as from wall-papering, should be met by correspondingly small or infinitesimal doses of the appropriate antidote.

We should carry our " similia," not only to kind, but also to degree—our medicinal drug must be similar to the causes in their material size, in their force, and in the sequence of their incidence. We cannot balance a pound by a grain, nor can we balance the millionth of a grain by grains.

But when we come to treat diseases which have been caused by derangements of force, diseases of an adynamic character, materialism seems to be specially out of place.

Let us revert once more to the example of the hyperæmia and subsequent diuresis which follow the division of the sympathetic branch of the renal plexus. Both hyperæmia and diuresis are arrested, and the healthy balance of function and of circulation are restored to the kidney by the gentle stimulation of the peripheral end of the nerve, by means of a mild galvanic current. But when the galvanic current is increased, an opposite condition of disease is induced, and a total arrest of both circulation and secretion ensue. It is evident, therefore, that an accurate adjustment of the amount of stimulus to a depressed nerve, is essential to true and permanent cure. Although t is needful to stimulate the depressed nerve up to the standard of health, we must be careful to induce only that amount of nerve tension which is sufficient to restore the balance of function and circulation, and no more. More than this, so far from doing more good and giving more tone to the general system, does actual harm. In that class of disease which arises from an adynamic state of certain nerves, it is a dynamic and not a material influence from which we can expect really curative results. In carrying force to the nerves we must carefully avoid over-supplying the demand.

Hahnemann's method of subdivision of medicinal substances enables us to administer the medicinal doses with a degree of nicety which has not been attempted even by the other school. Those physicians, opposed to our method, and who yet have acknowledged the necessity for giving medicines in a more finely divided state than ordinary pharmacy attempts, have fallen into the most ludicrous and often cumbrous and uncertain methods, in the hope of accomplishing this purpose, without compromising themselves by Hahnemannism. To use the simple centesimal scale of division recommended by Hahnemann, or the decimal division now so largely adopted by his followers, would bring them within the range of possible ostracism. These hyper-scientific but timid allopaths therefore hit upon the notable expedient of dosing cows and goats with drugs and giving their patients the medicated milk. The expense of the method as well as its uncertainty proved its doom. Who could afford to keep a cow or even a she-goat for each drug needed? We possess about 400 medicines; can we afford 400 medicated cows, each labelled according to her supposed medicinal properties—the mercurius cow, the arsenical cow, the phosphorus cow? &c.

Next came the pulverized medicinal sprays by which the drugs were to be given by inhalation; and in other cases powerful medicines were to be given chemically combined or pharmaceutically mixed with some drug or drugs calculated to neutralize all but an infinitesimal or minute part of their active principle.*

Can the profession long continue to ostracize us for scientifically, and with precision, preparing drugs in such form as to make their administration safe and exact, while they not only retain among their body, but even honour men who resort to such uncertain, inexact and indefinite methods for the accomplishment of the same purpose? If they acknowledge the necessity for the administration of small and even minute doses of drugs when given on the above rational indications, why should they shrink from adopting a scale of decimal or centesimal subdivision?

There have been signs, notably in the recent discussions in Birmingham, that nobler counsels than have hitherto actuated the majority of the medical profession in their conduct towards us begin to prevail in the allopathic body at large. Whether this awakening of the medical conscience will immediately result in their re-admitting us to the position we claim in the medical polity it is impossible to predicate. But, whether it does or no, our duty towards ourselves and the profession is clear, and was well expressed by our worthy colleague, Dr. Black, from this chair in 1872, when he said: "It is our duty, boldly and perseveringly, to claim the liberty of free opinion and the. right of choice, which are the heritage of all members of a scientific profession. We claim admission to all the rights and honours of our profession; and as the condition of such rights we invite the strictest scrutiny—we demand a fair field and no favour."

But our real difficulty lies in this, there is no "fair field" in the whole realm of modern British medicine in the which we may enter the lists and do battle with our adversaries. There is no tournament ground open to us

---

* I am not here alluding, in condemnation, to the use of medicated sprays where topical action of medicinal substances directly to the surface diseased is desired, but simply to the using pulverized sprays as a means of giving minute doses of medicines, which is an uncertain and a bungling way of accomplishing the indication of "minute dose."

where we can measure our strength face to face with the allopath. The age of chivalry is past, especially in the British allopathic heart, and in its place reigns the narrow policy of excluding from the lists all who are too strong for them in the field of argument. Where shall we find, in the whole realm of medicine, " a fair field," or even a noble arbiter to judge between us and our adversaries? Is there a single hospital whose staff dares try conclusions with us? None. Or whose governing body dare allow us to show our prowess against disease side by side with, or in contrast to, the other system? Is there an university which dares to follow the good example of former ages and allow us to propound and defend our theses within its academic walls? None. Is there a single college to whose senate and council we can apply with a chance of our being heard, and who dare, in the interests of science, permit a thorough investigation of the facts we are prepared to lay before them? Nay, is there a single medical Society (save our own Homœopathic Societies) where those acquainted with the system are allowed to discuss its merits?

How, then, are we to attain that which we desire, " a fair field and no favour?" The last is easy enough, the " no favour" is granted readily enough; but where is the "fair field?" It is only by continued knocking at the gates, and demanding our rights, that we can expect to attain them. This is the legitimate means of attaining our ends in religion and in politics, and it is not otherwise in medicine. It is of little use to demand our individual rights in detail; our voice is not heard. Societies must be met by societies; and perhaps the most practical way of forwarding the cause of scientific liberty within the realm of medicine, would be that the members of each university or college should form societies, whose object should be to bring before their respective universities or colleges the result of their own investigations into the new system of therapeutics. How could any university or college well refuse to listen to testimony given by its own members?—men, of whose competence to practise they themselves have certified, after a test-examination. A well drawn up statement of the experience of a number of the members of universities or colleges should be prepared, and formally brought under the notice of each university or college by its own members, and a commission of enquiry and investigation should be asked for. If this proposal be accepted (and I do not see how it could be refused without a grave dereliction of public duty), then the medical societies could no longer close their doors to those men whose practical knowledge of the subject alone enables them to discuss it scientifically.

Further, I would suggest combinations of the men of each separate medical school. Let the former students of each school form societies, to bring before their alma mater the result of their subsequent investigations; and let each society ask of its own hospital authorities, that a practical investigation into the facts they are able to adduce should be conducted within the walls of the hospital to which they owed their first insight into medical practice. The members of each university, college, medical school and hospital have a right to claim a hearing from the bodies of which they are members, and the time has come for us to claim these rights, in the cause of our common humanity. If these bodies refuse to listen, we must then, relying on our still wider rights as English citizens, appeal to the Fourth Estate—the Press; and a free discussion before the public cannot fail, in the end, to obtain us that which we seek solely in the interests of the public weal. But let us first proceed cautiously, patiently, but firmly, each dealing with his own college. I believe I am right in stating that sixteen of the members of the Royal College of Physicians of London, having experimented into the practice of homœopathic therapeutics, have openly adopted this system into their practice. I cannot but think that, if these sixteen men were to draw up the results of their investigations, and to bring them before their college, that such a course would be fraught with much advantage to their own college and to the public; and would tend, more than any mere individual protests, to end the unprofessional conduct of certain other members of the college who refuse to meet any physician who has added a knowledge of homœopathic therapeutics to his practice. It is their ignorance of homœopathy and of its teachings, it is their misunderstanding as to its principles and practice which underly half, if not the whole of the unprofessional and unjustifiable attitude which the majority of the allopaths hold toward those physicians who, having in all other respects equally high qualifications with themselves, have proceeded further than they have themselves gone in therapeutic investigation.

C

It is not to be credited of a body of English gentlemen (and the majority of the medical profession justly claim a right to that title) that they would willingly continue to practise an injustice or a meanness toward an opponent, and still less toward their brethren, men of equal attainments, holding similar degrees, of as high a sense of honour and probity as themselves. We are therefore bound to assume that the present attitude of the allopaths towards those physicians who have gone a little further into the field of therapeutic research than themselves is founded on misunderstanding, and we ought, if possible, to remove this misunderstanding, not only for our own sakes, but to save the profession from impalement on the horns of a dilemma, prejudice being the one horn and injustice the other.

Before concluding, I ought to say a few words on our efforts to establish courses of lectures in London, which, if supported, as we hope they will be, may lay the foundation for a school of homœopathy in England. At present we confine ourselves to courses of lectures on Clinical Medicine, by the physicians and surgeons to the London Homœopathic Hospital, and to lectures on Homœopathic Therapeutics and Materia Medica. During our first session Dr. Hale delivered a course of four most interesting lectures on Clinical Medicine, Dr. Dudgeon gave two lectures on the History and Principles of Homœopathy, and Dr. Richard Hughes gave a long and very instructive course of lectures on Materia Medica and Therapeutics. These lectures will be published in due course, and the medical profession will have a further opportunity afforded it of correcting its misconceptions and of studying the science of homœopathy in its varied aspects. It is proposed to recommence these courses of lectures next October, on the first Thursday (the 7th), and to continue them on each succeeding Thursday, at 5 p.m. These lectures are designed wholly for the profession, and are open gratuitously to all members of the medical profession and to medical students, but are not open to the public, and are not " popular " in the ordinary sense of the word. The demand on the part of the public for homœopathic practitioners is so far in excess of our power to supply it, that it is to be hoped that the knowledge of homœopathy, which these lectures are calculated to spread, will provoke such spirit of enquiry as may lead to a further practical examination of the subject by many fully qualified men. Our experience hitherto has led us to the conclusion that to "enquire into" the practice of homœopathy is "to adopt it." It is those who deny it such practical test who oppose it.

To this and to all other efforts tending to remove the misunderstanding which leads to the opposition of the majority of the medical profession to homœopathy, and to diminish human suffering, we must all give our heartiest support; remembering reverently that, in so doing, we are humbly following in the footsteps of Him who "Himself took our infirmities and bare our sicknesses;" who, in the beneficence of His care for the bodies as well as the souls of men, caused the blind to see, the lame to walk, the lepers to be cleansed, the deaf to hear, and who even raised the dead to life; charging His disciples also in nothing more strongly than that they should continue and complete this physical regeneration of mankind. The full meaning of this carefulness to heal the sick —to cure the diseased—is by none more thoroughly appreciated than by those thoughtful physicians who know how many mental and moral aberrations are the natural sequence of bodily derangements; and thus, in religiously following out our Lord's injunction to "heal the sick," our piety and our devotion to His cause binds us with all the firmer bonds to do so to the best of our ability, following that system which we believe to be true, undeterred and unswerving from the strict line of integrity, whatever may be the immediate consequences to ourselves. How infinitely small does the ostracism of a prejudiced majority of the profession appear to the man who is but following the strict and single line of his duty to his God and to his neighbour. Time-serving is never even good policy. "For what is a man profited if he shall gain the whole world and lose his own soul? or what shall a man give in exchange for his soul!" Therefore let the physician practising homœopathy, while ever courteous and ready to communicate, yield no single foot of the ground of truth whereon he stands; and where it is his duty to do battle against error, let him enter into no compromise, but fight on manfully, keeping ever steadfastly before his eyes that admirable maxim of the wisest of Hebrews: "Whatsoever thy hand findeth to do, do it with thy might."

A SCIENTIFIC PRINCIPLE FOR TOXICOLOGY.

By William Sharp, M.D., F.R.S.

"Sometimes it is better for us to believe that a thing *is* done, leaving the question of *how* it is done to the omnipotence of God."—
ERASMUS.

"I frame no hypotheses."— Sir Isaac Newton.

The physician's field of knowledge is vast and varied; his duty is serious, but simple and soon told—to ward off, to remove, or to abate sickness.

Sanatory measures may ward off disease; to remove or mitigate it other means are required.

Among these means the most ancient, and the most universally employed, is the administration of medicines.

That medicines may be given with confidence and satisfaction, a knowledge of their action, much more distinct and clear than any we have hitherto possessed, is required.

To help towards such distinct and clear knowledge, and thereby to increase our confidence and satisfaction in the use of medicines, has been the object of former Essays. It is also the object of the short Paper to which I have now the pleasure of inviting your attention.

The words "medicines" or "drugs" are to be understood to include all substances, whether mineral, vegetable, or animal, which are not food, which do not make blood, which do not afford nourishment to the living body of man. If any exception is to be made to this comprehensive statement, it will be in favour of alcohol, and the articles which contain it. In this case these may be classed separately as pure stimulants.

Drugs or medicines belong to the class of causes of disease. Like other causes of disease their action in health is always more or less injurious. They differ from other causes of disease in this, that in certain comparatively small doses, their action in disease is curative.

In former Essays on the action of drugs, the following propositions have been maintained; and it will be observed that these propositions are not hypotheses or speculations of the mind, but facts capable of direct proof.

I. *On the seat of the action of drugs.*

· The action of drugs, as regards its *seat*, is local or partial. Each drug selects certain organs, or parts of the body to act upon; or, in other words, each organ or part of the body appropriates certain drugs and is affected by them.

This is a universal or general fact. If any one doubts it, let him name any drug the action of which is not local; that is, not by preference more on some parts of the body than on others.

This peculiar action would be surprising to us, if we were not so familiar with it. It is entirely inexplicable to us. It is always injurious in health; and, if we reasoned *à priori* from this, we should conclude that it must be still more injurious during the morbid excitement of disease; but, on the contrary, it is found to be beneficial, to be frequently even curative. This is a fact, happily of every day occurrence; but we are as entirely without explanation of it as we are of the deleterious action of drugs in health.

The local action of drugs is so fixed and characteristic, that it affords a stable foundation on which to classify and arrange all medicines. The only classification which is of any use to the physician. Each organ or part of the body, solid or liquid, may be taken, and to it may be attached a list of drugs which have their first or strongest action upon it, or upon some parts of it. Other organs may also be so arranged as to show a subordinate action upon them. These tables will be found of the very greatest practical utility to the physician, as he daily prescribes the various articles of the Materia Medica as remedies. For

Organs appropriate the same drugs in disease as in health. Unless this were so, the testing of drugs in health would be of little value. But being so, experiments made with drugs in health become of the highest value. The usefulness of accurate diagnosis is also greatly increased by this fact.

When a rule has no exceptions it may seem superfluous to mention examples. But it may not be quite without interest to you to be reminded that opium acts upon the venous circulation of the brain, whether that organ is sound or apoplectic; that arsenic goes to the stomach, alike whether it is healthy or inflamed; so cantharides affect a sound or a diseased bladder; so the bichromate of potash visits the nose; belladonna and physostigma the iris; and aconite and digitalis the heart.

This branch of science—the study of the local action of drugs—has been named *Organopathy*.*

II. *On the kind of action of drugs.*

Drugs have many kinds of action. What these actions consist in is hidden from us. How they are brought about is unknown to us, and is, probably unknowable. But with the effects of many of them on the living body, both in health and disease, we are very familiar.

The action of drugs, as regards its kind, is dependent upon the *dose*. Each drug has its own doses, and each dose has its own specific action.

Moreover the various organs of the body have not only their own drugs for the seat of action; but also their own doses of these drugs for the kind of action.

From these considerations it is evident that the question of dose is a very complicated one. It is not surprising, therefore, that it has hitherto remained in great darkness; and that the notions and opinions which have been formed and expressed upon it, have been confused and contradictory.

Two years ago, at the Congress at Leamington, I had the great pleasure of announcing to you the discovery, I believe, of a universal or general fact of great value, namely :—

> *The kinds of action of comparatively large and small doses of the same drug are opposite, or in directions contrary to each other.*

Proof of this fact was given in a series of experiments upon myself and others.

That large doses and small doses of the same drug have actions in contrary directions is not hypothesis but fact. Of this fact no explanation has been offered, but it has had given to it the name of *Antipraxy*.

Suffer me to repeat. One range of doses of every drug has an action on the living human body, whether in health or in disease, the tendency or direction of which is contrary to that of another range of doses of the same drug. The larger doses act in one direction, the smaller ones in the opposite.

---

* *Essays on Medicine*, 10th Ed. 1874, page 409, and Essay XVII.

It is not meant to imply that there are not other causes which will interfere with, and more or less change, either of these directions, after the manner of a composition of forces; but, for the present, these interfering influences are put out of sight, for the sake of obtaining a clear notion of the action of different doses of drugs. It is best to study one problem at a time, and in its simplest form. The present problem is the kind of action of different doses of the same drug.

The kind of action, or its direction, is, for each drug, twofold, according to the dose. This twofold action of large and small doses is always of an opposite kind, or its tendency is always in the contrary direction.

It may, perhaps, be permitted me to remind you of a few examples of this action in opposite directions, of doses of the same drug which are to each other comparatively large and small:—

Large doses of *opium* stupify the brain; small doses excite it.

Large doses of *aconite* quicken the action of the heart; small doses retard it.

The action of *digitalis* on the heart is the reverse of that of aconite; large doses enfeeble, small doses increase its action.

Large doses of *veratrum, rhubarb,* and many other drugs produce diarrhœa of various kinds; small doses of these drugs cause constipation.

While doses of *opium, lead,* and other drugs act reversely; so that large doses constipate, and small ones open the bowels.

Some drugs, as *squills,* and *turpentine,* in large doses increase the action of the kidneys; and in small ones diminish it.

While others, as *aconite* and *digitalis,* act reversely on these organs; large doses diminishing and small ones increasing the secretion.

Some drugs, as *sabina,* and *ruta,* in large doses increase the catamenia; in small ones diminish them.

Belladonna applied topically to the eyebrows in large doses dilates the pupil; and in small ones contracts it.

While *Calabar bean (physostigma)* acts on the pupil in the reverse order; large doses contracting the pupil, and small ones dilating it.

These examples of the contrary action of different doses

of the same drug in *health*, will suffice to illustrate the kind of proof the proposition admits of. Every medical man, if he will experiment upon himself, may add to the number.

In the Essay on this subject[*] some facts were given, which show that other branches of natural science are not without analogies or examples of this contrary action of different quantities. Perhaps a few remarks may be permitted on the facts so mentioned.

In the Essay referred to, one of the examples from analogy is taken from chemistry, and deserves a few words of explanation. The facts stated are the combinations of *manganese* and *oxygen* in different proportions. The compound containing a small quantity of oxygen being a base which combines with *acids* to form salts; and that containing a large quantity of oxygen being an acid which combines with *alkalies* to form salts. The notation of these combinations was given in the language used twenty years ago, because this was most familiar to me; but the facts are equally true if stated in the terms used to-day. The present formula is as follows:—

$$MnH_2O_2 \ = \ \text{an oxide or base.}$$
$$MnH_2O_4 \ = \ \text{an acid.}$$

Here we have the same number of equivalents of manganese and hydrogen in both compounds; but the oxygen is doubled, the acid having twice as many equivalents of this element as are contained in the oxide. The opposite characters, therefore, of the base and the acid appear to be due, not to the absence of hydrogen, in the one case and to its presence in the other, for it exists in both, and in the same proportions in both, but to the less quantity of oxygen in the one, and the greater quantity in the other.

Another example might have been given which in one respect is better. Manganic acid has not yet been isolated, and is known only in combination as existing in salts. The *oxide of chromium*, which forms salts with acids; and *chromic acid*, which forms salts with alkalies, are both well known as separate bodies. Their contrary properties are connected, in some way unknown to us, with the different quantities of oxygen which are respectively contained in them.

[*] *Essays on Medicine.* Essay XXIV., On " Antipraxy."

It is to be remembered that these and other analogies were not given as proofs. Analogies are not proofs. Even if correct, they are of no value in this sense; and if erroneous, they are not damaging. Their use is to facilitate the conception of a new idea, and sometimes to render its truth probable.

To return from this digression :—

Suffer me to call your attention to the fact, that this contrary action of different doses of the same drug is quite distinct from those effects which have been called *primary* and *secondary* actions of drugs. It may, or may not, be true that *each dose* has these two actions in contrary directions, but this contrariety or opposition is not what is meant by Antipraxy.

It is worthy of notice that Antipraxy, by which, in one word, it is intended to express the universal or general fact of the contrary action of great and small doses of each drug, is an induction from experiments with drugs only, and with their action upon the healthy bodies of men. There may be some phenomena in the actions of the imponderable agents or physical forces of nature on living beings which are analogous to these actions of drugs, but they cannot be adduced as proofs of them. Moreover, the actions of these forces—of electricity for example— are so varied, so complicated, and so little understood by us, that they must be left to be further investigated for a long time to come, before any general conclusions can be drawn from them in reference to the treatment of disease.

Let it also be noticed that this contrary action of large and small doses is a higher induction, or a wider generalization than homœopathy. This will appear from the consequences or deductions which flow from it. We shall find that homœopathy is one of them.

We proceed, therefore, now to consider, very briefly, the

Deductions from Antipraxy.

1. A law for the choice of the Dose.

The first consequence or deduction from the contrary action of large and small doses is a law for the dose.

In the Address already referred to, the law was thus stated :—

" When a drug is prescribed as a remedy for a diseased

organ, upon which it acts when taken in health, and for the kind of diseased action which, in certain large doses it produces in health, the dose must be small enough to be within the range of an action in the opposite direction."*

Suffer me to offer a few remarks upon this law :—

It is a fact, not a speculation, nor hypothesis, nor a transcendental imagination. It is a fact easily verified; any medical man of ordinary powers of observation may prove it upon himself. No hypothetical explanation of it is offered.

It is simple and easily understood. The youngest student of medicine can have no difficulty in apprehending it.

It is of the most practical importance. Every prescription may be governed by it, and with great facility. If a dose of a drug is known to excite the brain, another dose of the same drug will soothe it. If a dose of a drug quickens the action of the heart, another dose will slow it. If a dose of a drug increases the secretion of the kidneys, another dose will diminish that secretion. If a dose of a drug acts as an aperient, another dose of the same drug will act as an astringent. If a dose of a drug produces spasms of the muscles, another dose will tend in the opposite direction, or towards paralysis. If a dose of a drug dilates the pupil, another dose will contract it. This is practical knowledge which admits of daily application. It is to be remembered that the remedial action of each drug is that of the small dose, not that of the large one.

2. A law for the choice of the remedy.

The second deduction from the contrary action of large and small doses is homœopathy. You know that homœopathy is the giving of a small dose as a *remedy* for a disease which arises from another cause, but which resembles that which a large dose of the same drug produces. The disease in its seat is the same as, in its kind is similar to, that of the action of the drug in large doses; the cause of it is different. To this method of treatment Hahnemann applied the motto *similia similibus curantur,* and gave the name of homœopathy. The action of small doses being in the opposite direction of that of large doses, it is evident that the motto *contraria*

* *Essays on Medicine.* Essay XXII.

contrariis curantur, and the name of antipathy may with equal justice be given to it. This system of therapeutics may be received as a direct inference, consequence or deduction from antipraxy.

Allow me to remark upon this law for the choice of the remedy that, taken in this light, and free from any hypothetical explanation, it is, like the preceding law of the dose, a fact, not a speculation. It is also, like that law, a fact easily verified; every medical man may test it in his own practice.

Like that law it is simple and easily understood. Every practitioner may without difficulty, though not without labour, learn to obey it in his daily practice.

Like it also it is of the highest practical importance. Every prescription may be governed by it, and with great satisfaction.

It is very easy to invent hypotheses; it is very difficult to establish a law of nature. Hahnemann attempted both. He succeeded in introducing a new method of medical treatment, and in setting up a new sect of medical practitioners; but his hypotheses are already almost universally rejected; and his attempt to establish a law of nature has not succeeded. It is to be hoped that success will crown the labour of some other man.

3. *A law for the choice of the antidote.*

Your attention is now called to a third deduction from the contrary action of large and small doses. *Small doses are antidotes to the injurious effects of large ones.* Here, not only is the disease the same both in its seat and in its kind, but the *cause* of the disease and its *antidote* are the same also.

The subject belongs to toxicology; and this is a principle upon which toxicology, as a branch of science, may in future rest.

The thought was expressed in the address at Leamington two years ago, in the following words :—

" For a drug to be a medicine it must have two actions in different doses; the action of the small dose must be contrary to the action of the large dose. This suggests the idea that for the virulent poisons, such as *snake-venom, arsenic, opium,* &c., for which no antidotes are yet known, the best antidote *may be* very small doses of itself. The only opportunity I have yet had of putting this thought (an hypothesis in the useful sense) to a practical test is in respect of mercury. In a case of poisoning by this metal the third trituration of itself (the millionth part of a grain) was manifestly beneficial." *

For this I was rebuked at the Congress last year in London. It had been expressed the year before merely as a suggestion or hypothesis.

Now, it is repeated, not as a suggestion but as a consequence or deduction from the contrary action of different doses. It is given, not to form a new chapter in the science of toxicology, but to be the foundation of the science.

It is a principle by which the use of medicinal antidotes may be regulated. This does not exclude other methods of treatment in cases of poisoning—such as the use of *chemical* antidotes where these are known, sulphate of soda or of magnesia for sugar of lead, chalk or magnesia for mineral acids, albumen for corrosive sublimate, common salt for nitrate of silver; or such as the use of *mechanical* means of relief, the stomach pump.

This principle is not the same as the principle of homœopathy, nor is it opposed to or inconsistent with it. It is a a new groove of experiment running parallel with the groove of homœopathy. One belongs to therapeutics, the medical treatment of disease; the other to toxicology, the antidoting of poisons.

Neither is it identical with what has been called isopathy. This, so far as I am acquainted with it, seems to consist mainly in the use of the products of disease as remedies, and which, I think ought to be rejected.

As a principle of toxicology it has been learned by reasoning. It is a deduction from the general fact, that the action of large and small doses of the same drug are contrary, which has been called antipraxy. There remains the duty of verifying it by experiment.

These experiments have been begun, and I have no doubt that, before any considerable time has passed, a sufficient number of proofs will be made known, and the principle now expressed will be established, not only as a necessary consequence of a previous induction, but also as a practical fact.

* *Essays on Medicine.* Essay XXII., page 733.

In the early part of last year (1874) I wrote to Dr. Mahendra La'l Sircar of Calcutta, the Editor of " the Calcutta Journal of Medicine," requesting him to test the hypothesis suggested at the Leamington Congress in 1873, by experiments with snake poison. This suggestion was immediately acted upon by him, but his experiments were interrupted by a serious illness which compelled him to leave Calcutta for some time.

In the number of the " Calcutta Journal" for June and July, 1874, a report of these experiments is given, entitled " Pathogenetic action of the Cobra poison." (Vol. VII., p. 230.)

Referring to my letter he quotes this sentence from it, " I do not think that experiments with animals are justifiable or useful as a rule, but perhaps this subject is an exception." And he adds, " We heartily concur with this expression of opinion on the now much disputed question of the advisability and justifiability of experiments with the lower animals, so as to entail suffering or loss of life or both. We think it is nothing but impatience, a mistaken idea of progress, a vain desire to advance knowledge, which spurs us to do many things which we ought not to do. Experiments on living animals, however carefully conducted and performed with the aid of anæsthetics, cannot but inflict pain and shorten the duration of their lives. Such experiments should, therefore, never be wantonly resorted to. They are only justifiable when the object is not the mere advance of knowledge, but of such knowledge as will lead to the alleviation of suffering much greater than we inflict, and the saving of many more and much more important lives than we destroy. In their performance we should observe the strictest economy as regards suffering and loss of life."

Dr. Mahendra La'l Sircar refers to former experiments of his own with the cobra poison, and also to those of Dr. Fayrer and Dr. Lauder Brunton, which, however, had no reference to the enquiry now instituted, and afterwards he details seven new experiments.

In a letter written to me in January of this year (1875), after alluding to his long illness and consequent weakness, he says he has resumed the experiments, but in consequence of the snake-man absenting himself, he has not been able to make much progress. After referring to some of these experiments he describes the following :—

"In one of these experiments recently made (with the *daboia*), different degress of bite inflicted upon the same animal at short intervals appeared in one particular to be antidotic. A daboia was made to bite a full grown cock. It appeared to inflict the bite, but the cock was unaffected. A few minutes after the first ineffectual bite, the snake was made to bite again, and it did so twice, after which the bird dropped down dead. In the autopsy made the following day, the blood was found *coagulated* instead of fluid, as is characteristic of *daboia* as distinguished from *cobra* poisoning. The only explanation I can offer of this anomaly is, that the first bite was too trifling to cause death, but was antidotic, so far as the condition of the blood was concerned, to the second bite which, from the quantity of the poison injected, proved fatal. Further experiments are needed to confirm or nullify this hypothesis, which is in principle the same as yours."

Other experiments might be mentioned, but the time allowed me has been exceeded. Suffer me, however, to give one, for it and the comments upon it are remarkable and very interesting in reference to this subject. It shows, I think, that snake-venom is subject to the law of antipraxy, and, therefore, may with propriety be experimented with as an antidote to itself.

In the "Proceedings of the Royal Society" for Feb. 18, 1875,* is given a Paper "On the nature and physiological action of the *crotalus*-poison as compared with that of the *naja tripudians* and other Indian venomous snakes," &c., by T. Lauder Brunton, M.D., F.R.S., and J. Fayrer, C.S.I., M.D. From this paper the following sentences are extracted:—

"From observations which have been made by Mr. Richards and ourselves, we have arrived at the following conclusions.

"The blood appears to remain *fluid* after death under the circumstances noted below:—

"1st. When *a large quantity* of the cobra poison has been directly injected into the circulation, as, for example, into an artery or vein.

. . . . . .

"The blood undergoes either partial or complete *coagulation* under the following conditions:—

* Vol. XXIII., No. 159, page 261.

"1st. When *a small quantity* only of the cobra-poison has been injected into a vein or an artery.

. . . . .

"Why the admixture of a large and quickly fatal injection of the cobra-virus into the circulation of animals should produce comparatively permanent fluidity of the blood, or interfere with its ordinary coagulability soon after removal from the body or after death, and why the injection of a smaller and more slowly fatal quantity should interpose no obstacle to its speedy coagulation, are questions extremely difficult to account for or explain. We can only state the fact that, in the one case, co-agulation occurs speedily, and in the other this coagulation is retarded or altogether prevented by some cause at present unknown."

Here is a special case, and its difficulties, and they are stated by the two men who are at present the foremost in these researches on the physiological action of serpent-poisons. If you have followed me in the observations and reasonings of this Essay, you will, I think, see clearly that the facts here given by Drs. Brunton and Fayrer, are but illustrations of a general law, being individual in-stances of the contrary action of different doses of poisons. Moreover, I think you will agree with me, that we can avail ourselves of this law in this, as in other instances, in the most practical and useful manner in the discharge of our professional duties, notwithstanding that we have no explanation of it; and I trust that you will also agree with me that it is wise to be conscious that we have no explanation, to acknowledge this frankly, to wait for the discovery of it, and, in the mean time, to abstain from the folly of inventing an explanatory hypothesis.

These Essays were begun nearly twenty-five years ago, by quoting an old Sanskrit proverb :—

"It has been heard of old time in the world,
That poison is the remedy for poison."

The former Essays have been devoted to the task of showing how one poison may be a remedy for another. In this has been commenced an attempt to show that sometimes a poison may be a remedy for itself.

It is an old proverb :—

"Etiam aconito inest remedium."

To this in the future may a new one be added :—

"Aconitum aconito sit remedium !"

Let it be permitted me to say in conclusion, that I have been too much an invalid this year to be in a condition to try experiments with reference to this subject upon myself, or I should have been glad to do so, using for this purpose some of the drugs which furnished me with the experiments reported to you two years ago. If I may again have health I hope to undertake them, and, if God will that I live, it will afford me great pleasure to give you an account of them at your next Congress. Will any one help me?

NOTES ON UTERINE THERAPEUTICS.

By R. Ludlam, M.D.,

Professor of Midwifery, Hahnemann Medical College, Chicago.

It is a remarkable fact that, in the treatment of the ordinary diseases of women, although the opportunity for observation by the medical men of our school of practice has been very extensive, the recorded results of that experience are comparatively limited. We re-present a system of cure that is believed to be especially adapted to the treatment of this class of disorders, and *nolens volens*, must prescribe for them. Three-fourths of a century has elapsed since this experimentation began. In that interval not an hour has passed in which some physician, had he been competent and so disposed, could not have noted a clinical fact that would have multiplied our resources, and helped to develop an available system of uterine therapeutics.

I apprehend that the reasons for this singular anomaly in medical literature are worthy of consideration. Why is it that, while nearly one-half of our patients are women, whose diseases are more or less modified by the crises through which they are constantly passing, not one page in a hundred is devoted to their clinical history? And, among the records that have been made in this depart-ment, why has so small a proportion of them been con-tributed by our older and more experienced practitioners? How shall we explain the fact that men who have achieved results which have made them famous is so many families have gleaned so little for our libraries?

I. Homœopathy and gynæcology are both of them comparatively new. In the remarkable development which they have undergone, each has been subject to a peculiar bias. Those who cultivated the former very naturally, and very fortunately, devoted their attention to the Materia Medica; while those who contributed to the latter, confined their researches to a limited depart-ment of Pathology. Each worked his vein in his own way; but neither party has accomplished what their combined labours only can perfect.

The inference is a just one that, when applied to the

D

treatment of the diseases of women, our therapeutical resources are incomplete because we have been so intently and so exclusively occupied with another branch of medicine, as practically to have overlooked the fact that a new and kindred specialty has been developed meanwhile, and has therefore escaped the attention which it merits at our hands.

The growth of gynæcology has been equally one-sided. Uterine diagnosis and uterine surgery are rapidly approaching perfection; but the leaders in this department are confessedly ignorant of uterine therapeutics. Practically, they know as little of the adaptability of remedies *per se*, and of their curative capacity within the range of this specialty, as Hahnemann did of the clinical thermometer. For the best of them omit all internal medication, or nearly so, and trust exclusively to empirical expedients of various kinds.

These unilateral defects are obvious. A system of therapeutics that takes little or no cognizance of the peculiar clinical history of woman is equally imperfect with a system of gynæcology that rejects our provings and despises the law of similars.

Every woman who is to survive the climacteric must wage a thirty year's warfare in which her physical experiences will be as distinctive as they are dangerous. And it would be unreasonable to suppose that nature disregarded this fact when she endowed our drugs with their curative properties. Although they are not convertible, each of these branches, therefore, has its counterpart in the other.

We do not need a Materia Medica for this class of patients especially; but there *is* a demand for such a modification, improvement and adaptation of the old one as will include the whole gamut of their toxical susceptibilities through puberty, menstrual life, pregnancy, the parturient and the puerperal states, lactation and the mènopause. Moreover, it is requisite that we should institute provings upon women who have first been declared by competent examination to be healthy; that the symptoms gleaned shall have been subjected to the scrutiny of experts in this specialty; and that the clinical deductions drawn from the use of these drugs shall be stamped with the authority of those who have had an abundant experience in their employment.

It may answer to treat our domestic animals on the basis of provings that were made upon other creatures, and to come as nearly as possible to curing them with an approximate chart of their susceptibility to drug-action. And it may be allowed that the veterinary surgeons shall arrange and adapt a Materia Medica to the best advantage of their patients. But I submit that a *woman* deserves better treatment at our hands than either a dog or a horse!

II. I beg to offer another thought in explanation and in extenuation of the unfortunate defect referred to. Being "a new departure" in medicine, homœopathy must first pass through a *controversial* period. And, whatever doubts we may entertain with regard to the waste of words and of precious time in further support of a form of truth that ultimately will prevail, we shall agree that the blood of the martyrs does not contain *all* of the elements of growth and of prosperity. Our being compelled to fight for a foothold has not only served to drain away our practical energy, and to dwarf our productive capacity, but it has placed us, and kept us in an attitude of antagonism with the claims of other branches of medical science.

Moreover, in view of the diversity of our gifts, and however skilful and successful our physicians have been in the general practice, it is manifest that only a small proportion of them are adapted to work efficiently in the department of Materia Medica. The consequence is that, as a rule, whenever these gifted persons have been diverted from their proper function, to the defence of our doctrines, the dignity and value of our literature have suffered in a corresponding degree.

And, furthermore, those in our own ranks who may have had a special genius for the study of uterine therapeutics, and who might have given us the fruit of their labours, have been prevented, discouraged, and kept in the background by the smoke and din of the conflict. And what is true of this branch is true of all. Indeed, with noteworthy exceptions, the remark is equally applicable to the literature of separate diseases of whatever kind.

To attempt a verification of these facts would be to reflect upon the intelligence of this honourable body. If our literature is not so practical and creditable as we could have desired, it behoves us to recognize and to remedy its defects. If its first period has been of necessity controversial, its second should be clinical and demonstrative. If we would condense our records to "the posterity point," we must bring a larger share of the gleanings of actual, varied, and intelligent professional experience into view, and into use.

III. Most of our knowledge of subjects connected with the diseases of women is derived from researches that have been made within the period of the present generation. Ovarian physiology and pathology; the whole philosophy of uterine lesions, whether acute or chronic, direct or remote; the contingencies of pregnancy and of childbed; and the etiology and differential diagnosis of the puerperal diseases, have been studied as they never were before. The increased means of physical exploration, the disclosures of the sound and of the scalpel; the revelations of the microscope, the results of hygienic prophylaxis applied to this specialty, and the remarkable contributions of clinical thermometer and the aspirator, are not to be despised.

A few years ago meteorology and botany were studied separately. It was not even supposed, that they had any especial relation to each other. In our day their union has furnished the practical and indispensable science of botanical geography.

It is said that the best quality of steel is made from a combination of several different kinds of iron, which have been brought from as many different countries. Certain it is that a bundle of wires will sustain a bridge which no single bar of iron, however large it may be, will support.

There is little doubt that the time has arrived when all physicians should avail themselves of whatever improvements have been made, or are making, in the realm of medicine and of surgery. If our friends on the other side of the fence, or rather in the next field, pay us the compliment, and are pleased to adopt or to adapt the whole, or any part of our Materia Medica (with or without acknowledgment), it shows that they are progressive. We have no exclusive claim upon the writings of Hahnemann, of Hering, of Hughes, of Dunham, of Hale, or of other eminent workers in that department. If we make a good wire and they want it, to help humanity over the rapids, *let them have it.* And, if they can furnish us one in exchange, *let us take it and use it properly.*

Because we accept the pathological views of Rokitansky or of Tilt on ovarian irritation and inflammation; or those of Scanzoni, or of Gallard on sub-acute metritis; the ideas of Bernutz on inflammation and abscess of the broad ligament; of Thomas on areolar hyperplasia of the uterine cervix; or of Hervieux, or of Barker, on the puerperal diseases, it does not follow that we are committed or restricted to their clumsy therapeutics. An intelligent idea of the disease that is to be cured is fundamental, even although it does not, and can not furnish an exclusive basis for the selection of a remedy. By keeping these cardinal views in mind, testing them cautiously, and confirming them in our own observation, we shall be able to place a fixed and determinate value upon our curative resources, to do more good to our own patients, and to help those who shall come after us.

It is undoubtedly true that such lesions have sometimes been cured unwittingly. For, under certain conditions, a medicine may act more directly, and more faithfully too, than the doctor himself. But, where is the record of this experience, and what is it worth, if it is not seasoned with a discriminating knowledge of cause and effect. Unless it is based upon a proper and thorough appreciation of all the points involved, such an experience brings little or nothing into the storehouse, and will only cripple our literature.

Indeed, in gynæcology, the sources of fallacy are more numerous than our well-authenticated clinical facts. And, so long as a majority of the symptoms of uterine and ovarian disease are remote, reflex, symptomatic, and sexual without being objective and intra-pelvic, it can hardly be otherwise. It would come within the province of uterine therapeutics to weigh and establish the significance of these individual symptoms, both as they relate to the disease in question, and to its remedy. And, what is more, such a system would consider the modifying influences of the menstrual cycle, of each and all the crises peculiar to women, and especially of the hysterical diathesis.

IV. The proper management of these diseases is, therefore, very difficult, and should not be dismissed without careful consideration. With due deference to those who confide implicitly in what are called the "key-note," or "characteristic" indications for our remedies, I fail to see how these indications can be made to cover so wide a range of morbid possibilities as are included in the diseases of women. The truth appears to be that, while there are so few *pathognomonic* signs of disease, there are just as few really *characteristic* symptoms of drug-action. And I apprehend that a forced extension of the meaning of either of these classes of symptoms (which are the natural and necessary counterparts of each other) is impracticable and mischievous.

To limit the range of indication of such a remedy as *apis mellifica* in ovaritis and cellulitis, to one, two, three, or even to ten symptoms, would be an injustice to the women of this, or of any other community. And so likewise of *calcarea carb.*, of *sepia, belladonna, ignatia, alumina, helonine, gelseminum*, and of all the uterine polychrests. Such a restriction of their employment would narrow the range of their application; for we might be called upon to treat a great many cases of leucorrhœa, for example, before we could match one of the unified, isolated, key-note (shall I not say *arbitrary?*) symptoms which are said to indicate these invaluable, every-day remedies.

And, beside looking toward the past, when a cathartic, an emetic, or venesection covered all the requirements of practical medicine upon a single indication, this plan of prescribing puts an extinguisher on the further development of special therapeutics—at least in so far as the old remedies are concerned.

It certainly is desirable to know upon what data we may rely, and to be able to select our drugs from among those symptoms, whether pathogenetic or clinical, which are trustworthy. In no department of the practice is this end more desirable than in the treatment of the diseases of women. But, in perfecting our special therapeutics, we should proceed very cautiously, and with a full recognition of the possibility of finding newer and more valuable treasures than have yet been discovered in the Materia Medica. For we may depend upon it that, as the study of pathology develops from the general to the special (which is inevitable, if it continues to grow), and as this branch is raised to the dignity of a separate science and pursuit (which is already more than half accomplished), the demand for a thorough and complete record of drug-symptoms will be much greater than it is now. In this view, I hail the good work of my American brother ALLEN.

V. With the reaction that is setting in against an exclusive reliance upon the more popular resources of uterine surgery, we should be careful not to "lose our heads," and go to the opposite extreme of theory and practice. For, even in the light of the brilliant results that have already been obtained by internal and local treatment, it is unquestionably true that certain diseases of the female organs will always require to be treated by manual operation. We may perhaps lessen the number of these diseases, but there will yet remain those which will demand a resort to the knife accessories.

That the general profession will one day, and very soon, concede and decide, that the cauterization of the neck of the womb for ulceration is quite as indefensible and harmful as the cauterization of the throat and larynx in diphtheria, I have no doubt. In the study of uterine lesions, we are learning that its disorders of place most frequently depend upon avoidable causes, and that they are more amenable to proper internal and hygienic, than to mechanical treatment. As a consequence of this increased knowledge and experience (but not of prejudice or abuse), the pessary bids fair to become as extinct as the dodo. In fact it never was anything but a crutch, and yet I fancy that we are not quite ready to throw it away.

The success of homœopathy in the treatment of the diseases that are incident to the puerperal period is acknowledged by every one, who is acquainted with the subject. And, bearing in mind the remarkable analogy between these conditions and those of surgical fever, so well portrayed by the late Professor Simpson, it is obvious that this system of cure should be equally useful in the after-treatment of cases of gynæcological surgery. And so it is.

Upon this part of my subject there is great danger of an excess of enthusiasm. Our achievements in this line are comparatively new and fresh. For it is but a few years since we began to do for ourselves the more serious work that pertains to this department of surgery. But experience already warrants us in believing and in teaching that the risks and calamities of ovariotomy, and of kindred operations, have been greatly lessened, and will be still more decidedly reduced in the future, by the proper employment of our remedies in their after-treatment.

The rivalry for success among eminent gynæcologists has hinged upon all sorts of expedients, of experiments, and of improvements in the mode of operation ; and the outcome has been productive of the happiest results. The rate of mortality has already been reduced to a figure which is comparatively low ; and all that is lacking is to bring the resources of our therapeia to bear in a rational way upon the prevention and cure of the ills that more especially beset these cases after the operation has been concluded.

ON THE DIFFERENTIAL DIAGNOSIS OF ULCER AND CANCER OF THE STOMACH.

By J. Meyhoffer, M.D.

There is, perhaps, no physician who has not been made .ware, at the very beginning of his professional career, ·f the want of harmony existing between the symptoms of ᴸ disease as brought under his notice and descriptions of ᴛ, in standard works on pathology. It would appear that .he authors of the latter have taken as models the works ɔf jurisprudence, rather than the human being exhibiting morbid manifestations of life. Hence the frequent errors in diagnostics, the differences of opinion and the variety ɔf terms used to describe one and the same disease.

Perhaps none of the "ills" which "flesh is heir to" give rise to so much hesitation and doubt in their diagnosis as do ulcer and cancer of the stomach. They have so many analogous symptoms; both are sometimes equally fatal; while, in some instances, *post-mortem* examination alone has revealed the real nature of the disease.

It may, therefore, not be superfluous to point out a few of the symptoms which are characteristic of these two maladies.

The following extracts are from the records of 19 cases of cancer and 7 of ulcer of the stomach which have come under my personal observation; not counting, of course, such patients as I have only seen once in consultation.

Types of Cancer.

I.—A German woman, of 46, who had been suffering ᶦor eight months, presented, May 14th, 1868, the following symptoms:—Her skin was of that peculiar pale, yellowish colour, considered so characteristic of cancerous ᴄachexy, and she had vomited nearly every day for several months. She habitually ejected food, and occasionally a mucous, slimy fluid. Emaciation had made great progress. Within the last three months the nauseated patient had taken food with the greatest repugnance, and then it gave rise to great weight at the stomach. Pressure on the epigastrium was painful, but there was *no* corresponding *pain in the spine*, neither was any induced by pressure, nor had there ever been any, as I was repeatedly assured by the patient. The most careful palpation could not detect any induration or swelling; the dimensions of the stomach were rather reduced than otherwise. The patient died after having been five months under treatment. The vomiting increased in frequency, though food was only given in a liquid form; towards the end the ejected matter assumed the colour of coffee-grounds. *Post-mortem* examination was not permitted.

II.—A French officer, aged 67, came under my care Jan. 6th, 1863, when he declared himself to have been suffering for nearly a year. He was reduced almost to the appearance of a skeleton covered with a dry, straw-coloured skin. Though his appetite was fair, he complained of indigestion, great weight and dull pain at the stomach after taking food, which increased gradually with each meal until he vomited, which he did about every third or fourth day. He then threw up an enormous quantity of pulpy matter, of very offensive and acrid odour, mixed with *sarcina ventriculi*. Sometimes he had very violent, spasmodic pain in the stomach, lasting from a few minutes to several hours. This pain *never* corresponded with any *pain in the back*, nor was the spine, at any place, sensitive to pressure. Local examination ascertained the presence of a smooth, hard tumour, on the right side of the epigastrium, of the size of a small egg. The stomach was extremely dilated, as was demonstrated by the particularly deep, tympanitic sound, so distinct from that of the intestines. The exclusive use of milk diet, with the occasional addition of a teaspoonful of brandy and the application of ice-bags, relieved him considerably from his indigestion and gastralgia. He died during the following summer in the North of France.

III.—A tailor, of Nice, aged 62, of sober habits, complained, March 9th, 1873, of *vomiting a mucous matter every morning before taking any food;* this had existed for about six weeks, within which time he had also grown considerably thinner. What brought him to ask for advice was, that he had began to eject his food after each meal. He had relatively not much pain in the stomach, and yet pressure on the epigastrium was very painful, and there could also be felt a tumour, of an unequal, knotty surface, about the size of a small child's fist. He remembered having had *feverish attacks* even before the mucous

vomiting had set in; but *no pain in the back*, either spontaneous or on pressure. When I first saw him his pulse
varied between 100 and 120; the latter rate was in the
evenings, accompanied by increase of temperature, with
profuse perspiration during the night. In April he began
to vomit blood, retained nothing on his stomach, and by
the end of June—less than four months from the beginning of the vomiting—he had breathed his last.

Types of Chronic Ulcer of the Stomach.

I.—A chambermaid, aged 26, very chlorotic, disposed
to hysteria and complaining frequently of gastralgia, was
taken in June, 1874, with profuse hæmatemesis, nearly
filling a large bowl with dark blood. This hæmorrhage
was inaugurated by acute pain in the epigastrium, extending to a *part of the spine* on the *same level*. The
patient described the pain as a feeling of the flesh being
torn and lacerated. Pressure near the xyphoid process
was extremely painful; the spine was free from any
morbid sensation on pressure. Appetite fair, tongue
clean, bowels costive, menses regular but scanty, pectoral
organs sound, ænemic murmur in the large blood-vessels.
The treatment presented no difficulty; iced milk for food,
an ice-bag on the the epigastrium, *arsenic* and *iron*, rapidly
restored the health of this patient.

II.—Another female, aged 34, in easy, independent
circumstances, of a placid temperament, regularly menstruated, had suffered for about two years from indigestion,
gastralgia, and pain in the spine. On the morning of
May 15th, 1871, after taking her breakfast as usual, she
was seized with violent pain in the stomach and back,
and, after a time, vomited all the food she had eaten.
From that day forth she was unable to take nourishment
without vomiting; after some delay, part or all of the
food taken, or, less frequently, only a bilious liquid was
vomited. On the 22nd of the same month she came to
see me. Her general nutrition was unimpaired, but, as
the suffering had become more or less permanent, her
features looked drawn. The pain was just under the
xyphoid process, limited to a space not larger than a
sovereign, and extremely sensitive to the touch, so that
she could not bear the pressure of her clothing. The
pain extended from the epigastrium to a corresponding

point in the spine, where pressure aggravated it. The suffering became more acute the longer the vomiting was delayed, lasting sometimes the whole night. The pain was described as burning, shooting, and gnawing. *Nux vom., argent., nitr.* and *arsenic*, with milk diet, restored her, and she has not suffered any relapse.

III.—An American gentleman, 39 years old, came to me for advice on October 29th, 1869. Until within nine months of that date he had enjoyed perfect health, when, one evening, after his usual dinner, he threw up his food. The following evenings he ejected part or all of his dinner. He did not remember feeling any pain at that period; but, about a month later, he, one day, vomited a bowl full of blood, experiencing at the same time an acute pain in the epigastrium, extending to the *first and second lumbar vertebrae.* He compared this pain to a grinding of the textures. Under the action of milk diet, *nux vom.* and *phosphor.* every symptom vanished within two months, and he left Nice in the Spring of 1870 without having had a relapse.

We have in these cases two very distinct types of invalids before us.

The first complain of their stomach alone, and have no pain in the back: their suffering, though sometimes very great, never extends to the spine. Moreover, in the great majority of instances they begin to *emaciate* before they complain of gastric disorder. A no less important symptom, mentioned in no medical work on the subject, is *fever;* it existed in 14 out of the 19 cases. This fever, in the earlier stages of the disease, appears in the form of ague. The attacks are intermittent, but not always regular in their periodicity. Sometimes they consist only of a slight shiver, cold hands and feet, without being followed, appreciably, by heat. These feverish attacks are sometimes so slight as not even to attract the notice of the patient unless his attention be directed to them. In the majority of instances, however, there is a regular shiver, followed by heat and perspiration. We have seen these feverish attacks occur long before any cancerous disease could be suspected. An English lady came under my care, sent with a letter from her physician, saying that she had repeatedly suffered from intermittent, feverish attacks, which had given way to *cedron.* She then presented simply the symptoms of gastric catarrh, and only vomited

.fter having eaten fat or heavy food. In the course of the winter she had, now and then, a return of feverish attacks, but left Nice in the following spring apparently much better in health. Pressure on the epigastrium had always been painful, but no swelling could be detected. She returned the next autumn to Nice in the last stage of cancerous cachexy, being unable to keep down any food whatever. She had a large tumour in the epigastrium.

These feverish attacks, so common in the earlier stages of cancer of the stomach, are not to be confounded with the cachectic fever of its ultimate stage; the latter is permanent, with tendency to exacerbate.

When, therefore, a patient who has never been under the influence of malaria, exhibits intermittent, febrile symptoms, and grows thinner while no other lesion can be discovered except gastric catarrh, the physician will do well to be very circumspect in his prognosis. The latter will become still more serious, I should say *pessima*, when the patient begins *to vomit* a slimy mucous matter *in the morning before breakfast*. This symptom in itself is very characteristic, when happening to an individual past middle life and of sober habits; while, if associated with emaciation, there can be no doubt as to a cancerous condition.

Another not less valuable element of diagnosis is the age of the patient. According to statistics, in the large hospitals of Hamburg, Breslau, and Vienna, the largest numbers of ulcer of the stomach occur between the ages of 20 and 50, *i.e*, 75 per cent., whereas cancer is, at that time of life, comparatively rare, *i.e.*, 25 per cent. These numbers have only to be reversed for persons after 50 to show that cancer of the stomach follows on the decline of life.

The second type, suffering from ulcer of the stomach are subject to more acute and permanent pain than the first—this pain extending to a corresponding point in the spine, where it is sometimes quite as acute as at the epigastrium. Moreover, the pain in the vertebral column is not only spontaneous, but is also habitually aggravated by pressure. Permanent pain at the xyphoid process, pain in the spine, and violent gastralgic attacks, are characteristic of ulcer of the stomach. These patients show no signs of emaciation unless arising from habitual vomiting of their food, frequent hæmatemesis, or other diseases independent of the gastric functions.

Ulcer of the stomach affects more generally individuals under the age of 40; after that period its frequency diminishes rapidly, while cancerous products increase in the same ratio.

Unfortunately, all cases are not of equal simplicity, as will be seen by the following instance of ulcer of the stomach simulating cancer:—

A lady, aged 49, still regularly, though scantily, menstruated, came under my care in the beginning of December, 1872; the winter previously she lived in besieged Paris, and went through the horrors of the Commune. During the siege she began to suffer from her stomach, and for some time had vomited, besides her food, black matter. She was much emaciated, hollow-eyed, her skin presenting the appearance of dirty parchment. A little above the navel there was a nodulated tumour of the size of an egg, which was not painful on pressure. The stomach was dilated. The patient related that, about four months previously she had felt a violent pain in the stomach, and since then had begun to vomit, at first only her food, and soon afterwards the black matter abovementioned. The pain, originating in the epigastrium, extended in a *straight line to the spine,* and had increased sometimes to an unbearable degree. It was described as burning, but, when more acute, as shooting, cutting as with a knife, and lacerating. The slightest pressure under the xyphoid process was extremely painful. She had never had any febrile symptoms. The treatment to which I submitted this patient consisted of small doses of milk every two hours—every other kind of food was prohibited—and *arsenic* 6th, one drop every four hours.

For the first five days there was no change; she ejected the milk, mixed with black matter. I next applied a small ice-bag to the epigastrium every day for several hours; same medicine and milk. She still continued to vomit, but no longer after *each* portion of milk or medicine; and, a few days later, only threw up her milk, mixed with mucus, without any blood.

The application of ice was persisted in for several months; vomiting occurred less frequently, and ultimately entirely ceased. The medicines most useful in this case were *ars., argent. nit.,* and *phytolacca.*

Now, after three years, this lady is living, without suffering, and in a better state of nutrition. The tumour still exists, though diminished, and she is obliged to content herself with liquid food. It is almost superfluous for me to say that, notwithstanding the *characteristic pain in the spine,* and the *absence of febrile symptoms,* I considered this case as one of cancer of the pylorus when it came into my hands. There was the tumour, the peculiar colour of the skin, and the black colour (like coffee-grounds) of the matter ejected from the stomach. The favorable course of the disease alone convinced me of my error by revealing its true nature, *i.e.,* ulcer of the pylorus, and confirmed the great diagnostic value of spinal pain in this disease.

Post mortem examinations published by Cruveilhier, Lebert, Virchow, and Revillout have shown that simple ulcers of the pylorus sometimes cause considerable hypertrophy and stricture of this part of the alimentary canal, simulating thus, during life, all the symptoms attributed to cancer. Though such cases are rare, they may recur, and it will be well then to remember that the presence of *spinal pain,* and the absence of *intermittent febrile symptoms* will enable us to give a more favorable opinion of a patient than indications of confirmed cancer would allow us to do.

The prognosis of chronic ulcer of the stomach depends on the organic alterations which it may have induced, as well as on its treatment.

Stricture of the pylorus necessarily leads to imperfect nutrition with all its consequences. The more active the treatment, the less chance has the patient of recovery.

The treatment which I recommend as the most satisfactory is, 1st, Exclusive milk diet; 2nd, Ice-bags applied to the epigastrium, when there is a tendency to hæmatemesis and great pain; 3rd, As principal medicines, *arsenic, argent. nitr., phosphorus,* and *nux vomica.*

ON DIPHTHERIA.

By W. BRYCE, M.D.

As the treatment of Diphtheria has been so ably discussed, within recent years, by several of my colleagues, I shall attempt, in these few notes, to bring forward only one or two points, which may perhaps help to make more exact the treatment of this disease, always a source of much alarm to the public and anxiety to the medical attendant. The time at my disposal to-day is so very limited that I can make only a very few general and preliminary remarks in a very imperfect and sketchy way, without attempting to adduce much of evidence or argument in support of them. I can do nothing more than throw into a few fragmentary statements the ideas that have occurred to me from time to time, hoping they may be sufficient to indicate what I mean, and elicit the opinions of those present. I can give, as it were, only a few detached links, because want of time prevents my giving anything approaching to the whole chain of evidence. For the sequel, however, I consider it necessary to say—

First, That, as far as my observations have gone, I have seen no evidence for the statement that the disease is very infectious. I shall afterwards try to show that there is another form of the disease, possibly communicable from one person to another through the medium of the intervening atmosphere, which to all outward appearance is the pure disease, but in reality is not, and requires a different treatment.

Second, That the disease is capable of originating spontaneously by the operation of some specific and as yet unknown—miasm, generated either in a local atmosphere vitiated by the neglect of proper hygienic arrangements, or in a peculiar condition of the general atmosphere of the place.

Or, again, that the disease may be produced by the effects of such states of the general or local atmosphere on an organism predisposed, or much subjected, to the deleterious influence of such conditions, whereby the system becomes poisoned and specific asthenic disease is the result.

One or two illustrations on each of these points must suffice.

In my frequent experience several members of a family may be attacked simultaneously, and the disease spread no farther in the household; or, there may be only one seized in a large family, or in a boarding-school.

In most of my cases there could be no exposure to infection traced. In one outbreak I calculated from report that a very great many seizures must have taken place simultaneously, or at most within a day or two of each other, at widely distant places. On this occasion I myself was called, on the same morning, to seven cases at distances varying from one mile to five, one locality at least having been long exempt from the disease. Three of these cases were on the outskirts of the town; one was in a large roomy house on the top of a hill; and the three others were in a large country house situated on a rising ground and sparsely surrounded with trees. This outbreak—and it was a very extensive and a very fatal one, though I was fortunate enough to lose only one patient— was preceded, for several weeks in the month of June, by a heavy, humid and enervating state of the atmosphere, with a dense covering of thick clouds close overhead, but no rain falling, except a few drops now and again when the clouds were overcharged.

We have long been familiar with the fact that certain states of the general or local atmosphere tend to the production of diseased action by their insidious and poisonous workings on the delicate organs which, by harmonised union, make up the sum-total of the human sufferer.

The disease-producing effects of humidity combined with heat we see on a large scale in the extensive prevalence of abdominal complaints in summer and autumn. To take an illustration from the vegetable kingdom, we know that the potato blight has always been preceded by the prevalence of warm humid weather. Everyone knows that typhus originates from over-crowding. A very remarkable instance of the spontaneous origin of specific disease occurred to me three years ago in the case of a lady, who spent the greater portion of the first four days she was in town, after coming fresh from the country, in the house of a deceased relative, an aged lady who abhorred fresh air. This house had been closely shut up for some months from the time of the old lady's death, and for years before that event had not known an open window. This lady was soon after attacked with typhus

E

of a bad type and died on the fifteenth day. There had been no exposure to infection.

Finally, I think evidence is against the supposition that the disease is produced by bacteria or other minute organisms. If so, few cases, I should think, would recover. Blood-poisoning after a surgical operation we may look upon now as most probably caused by these organisms, but when do we find such cases recover? The presence of these bodies in the exudation of diphtheria is, I consider, no valid reason for supposing that they are the cause of the disease. They are the result, and constitute a symptom of the asthenic condition of the patient, but are not necessarily the cause of that condition. I am inclined to account for their presence in the exudation on the throat during life to the fact of the exposure of that part to the external air. The exudation, though within the substance of the mucous membrane, is, as it were, no longer a part of the living body, and being of low organization, soon tends to putrescence. Hence the presence of these bodies.

In the following notes I shall speak of the disease in three stages. The division is arbitrary, but I make it for the sake of brevity in dealing with the treatment. In what follows I speak only of the dangerous form of the disease. I feel I cannot state too strongly that a case may be attended with great danger though the early symptoms may be only slightly marked—in this resembling scarlet fever. The more violent or inflammatory form is not attended with much danger, though often followed by great prostration of strength.

The first stage is seldom seen. When it is I have found a few hours of *aconite* useful.

The second stage is that in which we generally find the patient at our first visit.

Here my first medicine has always been *belladonna*, which I have invariably given in the first decimal. I rarely continue it longer than twenty-four hours, and often not more than twelve. I have always found it do great good.

Muriatic acid

to follow *belladonna* on the second day was my medicine-in-chief when I first attempted the homœopathic treatment of diphtheria nineteen years ago. I gave it internally in the first decimal dilution. As I was just then emerging from old-school routine, it was pleasing to my old ideas and habits to brush the throat every three hours with glycerine to dissolve the false membrane. This operation over I applied with a camel-hair brush some of the same dilution of the acid. I fancied that my success with this treatment entitled me to look upon *muriatic acid* as an undoubted antidote to the poison of the disease. I tried this treatment faithfully for some years, but eventually some deaths, but more especially one case of partial paralysis which recovered, and one case of progressive that died, led me to see that in this view I was in error. The torture given to the little sufferers by the local treatment helped on the relegation of this remedy to neglect. Still I am not quite sure if it is perfectly wise to abandon it in all cases. I tried *mercurius solubilis* and *corrosivus*, but with no good result.

The following case will give an idea of how I was led to place some confidence in the early stage of the disease in the

Mercurius biniodatus.

Miss M—— I found necessary to treat for the whole of the first day with *belladonna*. On the morning of the second day, finding the tongue white, thickly coated, and mercurial-looking, and no further good to be expected from the *belladonna*, I prescribed two grain doses of the *biniodide* third decimal trituration every two hours. On entering the bed-room at my evening visit on that day I found the patient with her head over the side of the bed, and a basin set on the floor to receive the water that was running from her mouth. I, of course, stopped the medicine ; the salivation gradually subsided, and in a few days she was up and about quite well, no other medicine having been given for the disease. Here we must, of course, grant the existence of an idiosyncrasy, but at the same time I think we must allow that the medicine manifested a wonderful power over the disease in this instance. I may mention that when I first saw this case I gave a very guarded prognosis. To all appearance it was quite as bad at this stage as another that died that same day with all the worst symptoms of blood-poisoning, the fatal issue being preceded by vomiting and diarrhœa, and finally by melaena. Now and again I find it necessary to continue the *belladonna* longer than twenty-four hours, and when I do I find it answer quite well to alternate the *biniodide* with it.

In the non-malignant forms of the disease I seldom prescribe any other medicine than *belladonna* followed by the *biniodide*, finding these sufficient to combat the whole attack. The action of the *biniodide* in these cases, and the decided effect produced in the case of Miss M——, give me confidence in it in this stage of the severer forms, unless there are very decided indications for the employment of some other remedy, such as

Kali bichromicum,

which I have used several times in some of the milder types, but only in one anxious case, and in all these this medicine alone has been sufficient to remove the disease. It was selected solely on account of the presence in them of the characteristic yellow-brown fur on the tongue. In these cases, as in all others of any kind in which this remedy is decidedly indicated by the above condition of the tongue, it acts with wonderful rapidity and power.

In addition to the internal remedies I frequently order a gargle made by adding the tincture of *phytolacca* to glycerine. If the child is too young to gargle, I order it to be applied to the throat with a brush. I have sometimes used the *permanganate of potash* as a gargle, and now and again *muriatic acid* spray.

Hepar sulphuris

I have never used for the disease, but I always prescribe it during convalescence, and with marked benefit to the throat.

Though *belladonna*, the *biniodide, muriatic acid,* and *phytolacca* are useful in their own spheres, and though the *permanganate* and *chloride of lime*, both of which I have also used, may act with decided benefit as superficial disinfectants in preventing re-poisoning, yet they all so often fail in the malignant form of the disease as to force upon me the conviction that as yet we have no real specific for this malady.

In all the fatal cases among my own patients, excluding the laryngeal variety, there has always been within the first few days a very decided improvement in all the symptoms, but before the end of the first week a re-poisoning or re-infection has taken place, and after that a rapid retrogression, and a free and fresh invasion of the throat. I have therefore chosen to call this

The Third Stage, or Stage of Relapse.

For some years I have had no faith in any remedy for this stage, though I have tried *phytolacca, permanganate of potash,* and *chloride of lime.* The only remedy I have faith in now is removal of the patient from the poisoned atmosphere of the house to as pure, dry, and cold air as possible, that it may effect the destructive oxidation of the noxious materials against which we are contending.

I went one morning during the outbreak in 1866 to perform tracheotomy in a bad laryngeal case. The house was so bad that I thought the child would have no chance in such a place. I therefore sent it off at once to Edinburgh to be operated on in a large roomy ward. It was so much relieved when it reached Edinburgh, or rather by the time the surgeon saw it, that he did not think it necessary to operate. In a few days it was brought home quite well. This case made a deep impression on me. Dr. Hilbers, I believe, advises removal. I became aware of this through Dr. Hughes's writings; but I am now speaking of events that led me to a similar treatment before I could be áware of Dr. Hilbers's view, as Dr. Hughes's book had not then appeared.

In the following case I put this treatment to the test.

Miss L—— and her two brothers were attacked at the same time with diphtheria in a severe form. On the fifth day all three were much improved, the girl especially, who was feeling so much better that she could not be kept laying down, but insisted on sitting up in bed to arrange wools for some canvas work. Sixth day, stationery. Seventh day, not so well. Eighth day, decidedly much worse. Ninth day, getting rapidly worse. On the second day of her relapse I found symptoms of re-infection showing themselves in both her brothers, who, during the next two days, got steadily worse. After the relapse I changed to the *permanganate* internally, and made into a gargle. The condition of the girl on the tenth day at noon was this:—Pulse 170; fresh invasion of the throat and the voice now gave evidence that the exudation had invaded the larynx also; the skin presented the dark, dirty look of severe blood-poisoning. The patient could not be prevailed upon to taste food, and had taken nothing since the relapse. Too frequent and sad experience of such cases compelled me to predict not only the worst, but that I feared death must take place within twenty-four hours or forty-eight at most. I fortunately, however, remembered the happy effects of the accidental cure by the removal of the child to the Edinburgh Infirmary. I therefore had all the three patients wrapped up and removed to the seaside, where we found an empty house. The girl I enveloped in blankets and placed in a chair, during the hours of daylight, at a large open window, with a crisp, cold, and very keen east wind blowing full upon her. The next day there was a wonderful change in her condition; and after that she gave me little anxiety. They all made a good and perfect recovery, though the girl was long in regaining her voice.

Perhaps it was unnecessary to go the length of this sudden and extreme exposure to so cold and dry a wind; but it must be remembered that the case was *in extremis*, and that therefore some rapidly-acting remedy was necessary to give her a chance of life. Curiously enough she did not contract even a cold in the head by this sudden change from ten days in bed. It seemed necessary to give the remedy a fair trial, and to award to her the full benefit of the ozone we had providentially supplied to us, in abundance, at the opportune moment.

The good effects of the removal in the cases of these three patients was so very decided, and the recovery after it so rapid, that since then I endeavour to *ward off* the third stage. If the case is not improving satisfactorily by the third or fourth day, I send out the patient in an open carriage once or twice a day for a lengthened drive, if circumstances prevent complete removal, as they often do from the difficulty of getting any one to consent to take such patients in. In cases of post-diphtheritic paralysis removal, especially to the seaside, is almost indispensable. Why, then, should we not ward off all by an earlier change. I have not seen any injury to the patient by sending him out on the third or fourth day of the disease.

I have recorded how an accident led me to see the good effect produced by the removal of the patient to a pure air. I shall now bring these notes to a close by relating very briefly the history of two characteristic cases which may help to a more correct treatment in some instances. For some years before this I had often thought over the relationship that appeared to me to exist between scarlet fever and diphtheria : the albuminuria, generally temporary—the parts of the body generally invaded—but in particular the great tendency in both to a special localization of the eruption, and its peculiar product, on the throat. Is not the odour also of the breath similar to that of scarlet fever and rötheln ?

I was called to visit R. L. on the 6th. His illness had set in a day or two previously with some fever, accompanied with vomiting and swelling of the cervical glands. To all appearance it was now a case of diphtheria in its malignant form. No eruption could be discovered. The throat and fauces were extensively involved, not with the superficial croupous exudation often seen during the progress of a case of scarlet fever, but with the special product of diphtheria deeply imbedded in the mucous membrane. My first feeling was that I had before me a case combining the two diseases. Influenced, however, by the opinion of medical friends, I had not the courage to treat the case as one of scarlet fever. The remedies most in favour with me for diphtheria were tried, but made no impression on the disease, and the case ended fatally on the 8th, or the third day of the treatment.

The only other case that I shall relate is one which I regard with special interest. It came under my care not long after Mr. Pope's paper on the *Ailanthus Glandulosa* was published—in 1867—and soon after a fair trial had shown me that this medicine was destined to be our sheet anchor in scarlet fever.

I was called to visit J. G. on the 10th. This case was in every respect similar to the fatal one just recorded. Had some fever, accompanied with vomiting, on the 7th, but no history of any eruption. Now, the fourth day since the seizure, no trace of eruption on the skin, and scarcely any fever, but the throat extensively invaded with diphtheritic exudation.

On careful enquiry I found that, during a short absence from his mother's house, he had been within the circle of a local outbreak of scarlet fever. I ordered the patient to be carefully and warmly wrapped up in bed, and to have three drops of the mother tincture of *ailanthus* every halfhour. On the second day of the treatment an eruption, scarcely possible to recognise as the pure scarlatinal, appeared on the lower part of the body. I have known the eruption appear only on the legs, and hence it may often be overlooked. On the third day I was able to say that all danger was past. In the treatment of scarlet fever by *ailanthus* I always look for marked improvement by the third day, when the medicine has thrown the eruption well out on the external skin. The recovery was rapid and complete. No other medicine was given, and no other treatment employed, save keeping the patient in bed till desquamation was effected. There were no sequelæ.

Your time does not permit of my adducing farther proof of the existence of this form of the disease; I consider, however, that the two cases given above will be sufficient to justify the statement already made, that there is a disease, possibly infectious, which passes for diphtheria, but which is in reality what I am disposed to call SCARLATINAL DIPHTHERIA. The existence of an offensive odour would of itself incline me to suspect that the case was one of this variety. It is not so decidedly infectious as to incline me to look upon it as a form of undeveloped scarlet fever. I prefer to look upon it as a hybrid caused by the simultaneous operation of the poisons of both scarlet fever and diphtheria. In analogy with this we have rötheln, a disease produced by the combined action of the poisons of scarlet fever and measles. In measles the eruption tends to develope more on the external than on the internal skin, and hence its milder form and greater immunity from grave sequelæ; while in scarlet fever, though more nearly balanced, there is rather a greater tendency to develope on the internal. We have thus a hybrid in rötheln, with a predominance of measles externally, while the throat is more that of scarlet fever. The eruption in diphtheria is thrown entirely on the internal skin, with concentration for the most part on the throat; and when conjoined with scarlet fever, though there is a slight eruption externally, the great force of the eruption in the hybrid—scarlatinal diphtheria—is cast upon the mucous membrane, with a great tendency to have its special product localized on the throat; hence its malignity.

For many years past, when called to visit a case of diphtheria, I have always made careful enquiry, even before the above cases occurred, with the view of finding out whether the attack set in with vomiting along with the fever, and whether there was any history of exposure to scarlet fever infection. On finding these conditions to exist, I have always prescribed *ailanthus*.

I ought to mention here that I should not be inclined, however, to order the removal of a scarlatinal case as I do one of the pure disease.

Had I time to give all my experience of later years, particularly in Edinburgh since my removal here in 1869, it would be found that the whole of that experience supported the conclusions already stated.

It is with diphtheria as it was with scarlet fever up till the time of the *ailanthus*—we have as yet no medicine that excites a condition analogous to that produced by the diphtheritic poison. Till some fortunate accident reveals to us such a remedy we must content ourselves with meeting, as best we may, the separate conditions presented to us in this dire disease.

TRANSACTIONS

OF THE

BRITISH HOMŒOPATHIC

CONGRESS,

HELD AT BRISTOL,

On THURSDAY, SEPTEMBER 21st, 1876.

T. HAYLE, ESQ., M.D.,

PRESIDENT.

𝔓ublished by 𝔄uthority.

LONDON:

E. GOULD & SON, 59, MOORGATE STREET, E.C.

1876.

Price One Shilling.

CONTENTS.

———

PREFACE.

THE Annual Congress of medical men who practise homœopathy was held this year at Bristol, under the presidency of Dr. Hayle, of Rochdale, whose admirable address is here published.

The Papers of Drs. Sharp and Nicholson are valuable, especially as they attempt to explain the rationale of homœopathic cures, and are very suggestive of further research in the same direction. The discussions have been published for the first time.

Ample time was afforded for the discussion of a series of propositions bearing on the subject of the School of Homœopathy, and the general interest awakened by the debate augurs well for the success of the undertaking. The November number of the *Monthly Homœopathic Review* contains a full report of this part of the proceedings.

The members decided, by a large majority, that the next meeting should be held at Liverpool, on the second Thursday in September, 1877. A List of officers will be found on the next page.

J. GIBBS BLAKE, *Hon. Sec.*

December 1876.

THE MEDICAL WORLD;
ITS PARTIES, ITS OPINIONS, AND THEIR TENDENCIES.

GENTLEMEN,—I think we have arrived at a period in our history as a party among the practitioners of medicine, at which we are able to take a review of our position in a calm and unprejudiced way. As regards our opponents, the heat and animosity of active persecution is over, the policy of masterly inactivity and strict blockade has nearly been played out. Prejudice and party spirit are beginning to grow weak under the influence of more accurate information and better feelings; and the appeals of justice are beginning to have a chance of being heard. Refusals to meet us have ceased to be bitter, are often indeed apologetic; and gentlemen feel sore at being tied up by a set of arbitrary rules, laid down during the prevalence of excited feelings, in which they have ceased to share, perhaps have never partaken. I may add that many now disregard these rules, and will not be bound by them.

So much as regards the outward aspects and external relations of the opposition. The signs are still more favourable when we look within. The pernicious and destructive practices of blood-letting, purgation, and salivation have passed away. The time has passed when violence done to the human frame could be called in any sense heroic. Yet it is hardly sixty years ago when a princess, the next in succession to the throne, and the hope of the nation, was bled and reduced by way of precaution—prophylatically, I may say—till she sank under a natural process, which the poorest cottager in the realm, left to the mercies, and even the inclemencies of nature, passes through with small help and little risk,—certainly with no prophylactic treatment.* It is but fifty-six years ago since her father, George IV., was bled by the order of one eminent physician to eighty ounces, and as if that had not been enough, by the order of another distinguished physician to fifty ounces; which

---

* I was told by an old lady friend that in her time ladies were bled in pregnancy, to prevent abortion. Possibly the buffy coat of the blood in pregnancy may have had something to do with it.

B

latter bleeding, says Greville, " certainly saved his life, for he must have died if he had not been blooded." This, however, was not, it seems, enough, for in a day or two twenty ounces more were taken, with the view, I suppose, of improving his condition, his life having been already saved by the second bleeding. A short time after, the unfortunate Queen Caroline, in her last illness, was bled to sixty ounces, but unfortunately succumbed to the disease —not, of course, to the bleeding—before her life could be saved by the abstraction of forty ounces more, which Lord Brougham said had been intended. These things are not done now ; indeed, if done, would be encountered by suits at law, and the penalties of malpraxis. The times are changed ; the seasons—not the physical, but the intellectual—have altered ; and it is hard to find a young physician of ten years' standing who has ever seen a patient bled. One who passed in 1871 assured me he never had.

One admires the simple faith, the depth of the convictions which carried the practitioners of the time through these sanguinary practices. One hundred and fifty ounces of royal blood on one's hands is a serious matter, to say nothing of its being human. There is a *naiveté* about the whole procedure which is quite touching and really instructive. For these were not experiments made by young practitioners *in corpore vili*, for whom a Vivisection Act might be needful—experiments made on obscure persons, whose fate would make no noise ; they were practices sanctioned by the highest wisdom and greatest experience of the profession. It was the Baillies, the Henry Halfords, and the Matthew Tierneys of the day who thus dealt with the highest and most valued people of the realm. We all recollect the interest awakened by the recent illness of the Prince of Wales ; how a nation held its breath until he was pronounced out of danger. Well, this was but a faint emotion, compared with that with which the announcement of the death of the Princess Charlotte was received—the young wife, the young mother, the hope of the good, who had anticipated in her the purification of a polluted and desecrated court; a hope now happily realized in our present beloved queen.

What an assurance of being right, what a conviction of their own infallibility must these men have had, to have ventured upon such practices upon such persons ! How

ignorant are those who do not know their own ignorance!
Fancy a man in the dark, who thinks he sees! What colli-
sions and sore places may we not expect for himself and his
friends. And these infallibilists were the first authorities
of their day! How are they looked on now? How are
they regarded by the infallibilists of the present day, their
successors ; the men who, in the face of these facts, dare
to proscribe the exercise of free thought and practice
among their contemporaries, under penalty of excommunication? Well may we say with Talleyrand, when
asked what he thought of a *gaucherie* of William the
Fourth's, " *C'est bien remarquable.*" Let us carry the
inquiry a little further. What will be thought of these
authorities, who deal in excommunication, by the next
generation? Are we sure that the hypodermic injections
of morphia or atropine daily used, the habitual use of
large doses of chloral, of bromide of potassium, and other
drugs, without a knowledge of the peculiar changes in
their action when given in different doses, and of their
general action on the system, as brought out by provings
on healthy individuals of different sexes and at different
ages, will be considered a generation hence as fair play to
the human system, or the acts of prudent and wise
men? Will alcoholism be considered scientific? or poly-
pharmacy?

These lingering relics, however, of the animal impulse
to do things with the strong hand, as manifested not only
in the treatment of disease, but of so-called heresy, are
gradually fading away before the influence of scientific
training. The infallibilists of the present day are not so
consciously infallible as their predecessors. They do not
commit such atrocious outrages on the human body,
though there is much room for improvement even now.
They are not so intolerant of free thought and practice ;
and would be even less so than they are, if they dared.
Patient observation, and a desire to know more thoroughly
the nature of the remedial agents they employ and their
effects on the organism, and a more conscientious appreciation of consequences, are gradually taking the place of
the combative instincts, and diseases as well as differences
of opinion are more respectfully treated. A most hopeful
feature, to my mind, is the consciousness now widely felt
among medical men, of their knowing little about the physiological action of drugs, and of the necessity of such

B 2

knowledge before they can be used scientifically or conscientiously in the treatment of disease. Our first position, therefore—the necessity of proving a medicine on the healthy body, to get at its physiological action as a basis for use in disease—is conceded. This is the thin end of the wedge, and all the rest must necessarily follow. An accurate knowledge of the action of drugs, including their twofold and opposite actions—the antipraxis of Dr. Sharp —must inevitably lead to the acknowledgment of similarity between the symptoms produced by the large dose of the medicine and those of the disease as the principle of selection ; while the aggravation produced by its use in a large dose will infallibly necessitate a diminution of the dose to the point at which its curative action begins. This of course implies the reception of the small dose in the treatment of disease.

At present, whenever an allopathic writer warns us against the use of this or that remedy in the treatment of this or that disease, in consequence of its producing aggravations, we take it as an indication for its use in our doses, knowing as we do—what he does not yet know— that if we diminish the dose to a certain extent, we get curative action.

This fact has been taken up and brought prominently forward by our esteemed colleague Dr. Sharp, who has opened out a rich vein of research for all who wish to be useful in the interesting investigation of the point in the dose of each drug from which its opposite actions diverge. This change of action is of course due to no change of properties in the medicine, but entirely to the tone of the nerves acted on. A medicine, from a minimum dose upwards, stimulates and causes an increased display of action of the nerve-power, upwards, up to a certain point; and then gradually or suddenly (a point not yet, I think, experimentally inquired into), but it is to be supposed gradually, as nature rarely does anything *per saltum*, opposite effects are produced, ending in paralysis of function. The range of each kind of action will vary, within limits, to some extent in each individual, largely in the different temperaments. Idiosyncrasy, we know, as in the case of *ipecacuan* or *musk*, extends the range in the direction of a minimum very largely. In the direction of the maximum dose which can be borne, as in the case of alcohol, there are also considerable differences. These differences, however, will never affect the advantage to be derived in practice from a knowledge of this opposite action. We shall always be able to find a medium dose on either side of the turning point, which will suit the great majority of constitutions.

But now a very important question arises. The preceding observations apply to nerves in a healthy state; how do medicines act on them when in a diseased state? and how does that action stand in relation to the hypothesis of the selection of the remedy on the homœopathic principle but its use on the enantiopathic principle? Here we are met with the fact, that in order to cure symptoms similar to those produced by the small dose of the remedy, viz., those of stimulation, we dare not give the large dose, or the dose which produces depression of function tending to paralysis—that is, we dare not act on the enantiopathic principle. Let us hear what that industrious worker, Dr. Hale, of Chicago, says:—*

" For primary symptoms," he says, " the smallest possible dose is best indicated. Who would dare to give *nux* in doses of the crude drug, or even an attenuation below the 3x, in cases of uterine spasm depending on spinal congestion? Who would select appreciable doses of *nux* for angina pectoris, cardialgia, or other tetanoid affections of the viscera? What dose would be safe in cerebro-spinal meningitis, myelitis, or other congestive or inflammatory affections of the cord? In looking over," he goes on to say, " the reported cases of cures by *nux vomica*, I find that the most brilliant cures were made by the high potencies, when they were primarily indicated."

Now, are these enantiopathic cures? Certainly not. They are homœopathic cures; cures made by a medicine selected for its homœopathicity, and administered in a dose acting homœopathically; cures made by medicines acting in the same direction as the morbific agent. In the cases before us the morbific agent stimulates the morbid parts, and the curative agent also stimulates the same parts. One thing, however, is noteworthy: the stimulating power of the curative agent is much inferior in degree to that of the morbific. If it were equal to it, or nearly equal to it, it would aggravate and intensify the symptoms. This fact it was which led Hahnemann to

* " Primary and Secondary Symptoms of Drugs as determining the Dose."—*N. A. J. of Hom.*, May 1876, p. 556.

reduce his doses below the aggravation point; and he found the diminution might be carried to an inconceivable extent, without diminishing the extent and durability of the curative results.

How to explain these results I dont know. It's like damning a man with faint praise, to take the conceit out of him. My predecessor in this chair, in his able address, adduced the instance of the curative action of alcohol in relieving fatigue, as an illustration of what happens in the case of the small dose, homœopathically chosen. " The sphygmograph," he says, " shows that the small dose of alcohol has power to restore arterial tonicity when it is administered to a patient in whom there is a want of this tonicity, caused by fatigue." The case before us is a different case. Our case is a case of increased tonicity amounting to disease, relieved by a smaller dose of a similar agent acting in the same direction. It is not a case of enantiopathic action; it is a case of homœopathic action; and an explanation drawn from the opposite actions of different doses of medicines does not apply. The case, however, is one of real occurrence, and can be reproduced by any experimenter. I do not think we need wait for a case of natural disease for our experiment. An artificial disease can at any time be excited by small but appreciable doses of a powerful medicine;—an artificial disease presenting the stage of excitement; and that can be treated by a sufficiently small dose of a homœopathically-selected remedy—a plan, by the way, which will much increase the interest and utilize the value of our provings. The truth of the homœopathic law can thus be verified in a scientific way. We shall be able to try the issue, not on the ever-shifting field of natural disease, encumbered as it is by a thousand different complications, but on a field of our own choosing—in conditions of our own selection—with an immensely greater probability of ensuring results. Nay, more! we shall be in a position to experiment on the dose, and so to put it on a scientific basis; we can vary it to any degree and in any mode, and ascertain what dose and what time or mode of administration produces the best effects. In fine, by gaining the power to reproduce our experiments, we shall approach—at a long interval, I admit—the advantageous ground occupied by the chemists and the natural philosophers, and arrive at, at any rate, a prophetic foretaste of the exactitude of their results.

I now proceed to the dose proper for the cure of secondary states; states similar to those produced by large or excessive doses of a drug. I quote from Dr. Hale again. He says: "What is the proper dose to be prescribed for secondary conditions?" The history of the treatment of paralysis with *nux* and *strychnia* is the best answer to this question. I can find no record of cases of paralysis cured by the middle or higher potencies of this medicine. The fact that it is absolutely necessary to use appreciable doses of *strychnia* for the cure of the various forms of paralysis, is ample proof of the law of dose, which assumes that for *secondary* symptoms *appreciable* quantities must be prescribed. A spasm of the sphincter vesicæ may disappear under the use of *nux* 30, but a paralysis of the same sphincter will require at least the 3x to remove it. A paraplegia from congestion of the chord may give way to *strychnia* 12, but a paraplegia from anæmia of the cord will require the 1° or even the 1x. This class of cases may come under the enantiopathic law as far as regards dose; for I suppose it will be conceded that the 1 or 1x of *strychnia* will not paralyse, but will excite. Here, therefore, an excitant dose is given to remove an opposite state of paralysis, and the case is brought under the category of the ex-President's illustration from the action of alcohol. In both sets of cases, however, the homœopathicity of the remedy is the reason of its being given. It will produce both the states for which it is given. In each case it is given in a dose far below that which is sufficient to produce the state for which it is given; as if it were necessary to go up stream to affect the waters below. In the first case, that of excitement, the remedy has to be given in a very small dose, far beneath that which is capable of exciting the state it is meant to remove; yet it seems to be an agent in the direction of producing it, and we are left at a loss to account for its curative action. Now we really know very little about the mode in which nerve action is propagated. We are apt to suppose that an action of excitement is like the course of a smoothly flowing stream; it may, however, be an action of oscillations and alternations, comprehending opposite states; and this state of things may be quite inconsistent with a persistent state of spasm or pain. We must recollect also that the nerve in question is in a state of disease—of excitement, and we do not know what alterations of action the smallest stimulus may set up. However that may be, the fact exists, and is demonstrable, that an exceedingly small dose, quite incapable of producing an appreciable effect in health, is capable of moderating or removing morbid excitement which a larger dose of the same medicine is capable of setting up. I shall never forget a case of this kind which occurred to me many years ago.

A young lady, a teacher at a school, when walking out with the scholars on a cold frosty day, when a sharp north-east wind was blowing, was seized with sharp, violent pleuritic stitches. I found her in bed; a hard pulse of 120; in great agony; every breath caused acute stabs; every movement was acutely painful, yet she was so restless she couldn't keep quiet. One dose of *aconite* 30 was the only medicine I gave her. In a short time after taking it—five minutes, she said—a most violent perspiration broke out, the excessiveness of which she wanted terms to describe, and all her pains left her. The next morning I found her free of pain and fever, but weak.

The second case, where the cure is apparently enantiopathic, may not really be so. The fact is, though we know that the action in the dose given would produce an opposite action in health, we dont know what it actually does in disease, more than to diminish or remove the actually existing state of torpidity. In general this is done gradually, and takes say weeks or months, and repeated doses; so that the result looks more like the effect of a slow process of nutrition than of a change of action— as is the case, I believe, in galvanic cures.

But little seems to be known about the way in which the nervous activity is produced or regulated. Some physiologists attribute it to chemical action; somewhat in the way that a train of gunpowder is fired. One is tempted to speculate on the quantity of combustibles that Captain Webb must have had in his body when he swam across the Channel; but the wholesome reflection that one knows nothing about the matter, makes one feel that ridicule is out of place. We of all men know that the *reductio ad absurdum*, as used against ourselves, has been much oftener the mirror in which the ignorance of our assailants has been revealed, than the magnifying glass which made manifest the minuteness of their knowledge. The theory of molecular movement in consentaneous arrangement, as soft iron takes on magnetic action when subjected to a galvanic current, is yet unproven, and does not seem to help us much in our speculations on curative action.

There is a class of cases in which apparently we do not have to do with opposite effects; I mean, where the sympathetic system of nerves is affected. Here we meet with every variety of symptom, both in kind and degree, so that the scene reminds us, as regards its variety, more of the solar spectrum, or the chromatic scale, or the movements of a spider's web, than of the simple antagonisms of the spinal nerves.

In such a state of things, opposition is lost in variety, and the negation of a positive symptom is to be found in a state of health, and not apparently in an opposite state of disease. I do not wonder that our valued colleague, *nulli similis aut secundus*, Dr. Dudgeon, should be at a loss to find an opposite to waterbrash. He is as acute as any of us in finding opposites—witness his most felicitous and delicious illustration of feline opposition; but it is clear that, with his usual sagacity, he sees that there is more in a homœopathic cure than is dreamt of in the doctrine of opposites merely.

Still it is possible that behind this scene of apparently infinite variety and complexity, there may be a set, I do not say of wire-pullers, but of wires pulled, whose states may range between extremes through the finest gradations, expanding as they affect nutrition, secretion, motion, or sensation, into the endless variety of phenomena we have to observe. This would be a beautiful instance, among the multitude of others by which we are surrounded, of simplicity arising out of complexity, of general laws evolved from particular instances, of radii pointing from immeasurable circumferences to narrower circles, and through them to the great Centre of all, who merely condescends to space to evolve order,—the origin of all law,—being himself eternal and essential harmony. Microscopic anatomy, and careful, systematic experimentation will some day do much to unravel for us these mysteries. Dr. Drysdale's learned and laborious work has done much for us in collecting what has been ascertained and is known on this recondite subject, to say nothing of the value which the work derives from his logical and judicious treatment of the subject. Nerve-cells, disposed over the system in immense numbers, seem fitted to be impressed, each in its way, by every possible variety and mode of impression. Innumerable nervous fibrillæ, invisible to the naked eye; seemingly inextricably interwoven, but never confounded; apparently without beginning and without end, but looping themselves as they lie applied to the manifold organs they influence; sometimes in spirals, sometimes in plexuses, and what not, combine and regulate, if they do not produce all the complex operations of the organism. How they do this, who can tell? Whether they form a circuit or circulation, or both, is yet unknown. Dr. Drysdale, with much to support his views, " is compelled to conclude the force must be a distinct force, not like heat, light, or sound, but a current force analogous to electricity, galvanism, or magnetism, but distinct from these," which he aptly and prudently terms " vis nervosa." Swedenborg saw, underlying these phenomena, a circulation analogous to that of the blood—indeed, a fluid prepared by it, and its very essence and continuation; a circulation corresponding to it in a higher series. Should this view ultimately be adopted, there is nothing in it to preclude the possibility of the analogy to the galvanic circuit which Dr. Drysdale thinks likely. The fluid may be endowed with qualities analogous to those of the galvanic fluid, and act by induction on muscular fibres and otherwise. What a noble field of inquiry lies before us? Not a single fibril of this marvellous web but can be touched by some medicinal agent in a suitable dose, and its action revealed by the symptoms excited. Microscopical anatomy will go hand in hand with microscopical physiology, and pathological disturbance render manifest to our consciousness what is continually going on unfelt and unperceived: itself affording a new application of an instrument of immense power. I mean medicinal action scientifically used. Even to this power a knowledge of the homœopathic law will greatly add, by giving us the means of controlling or checking the phenomena.

There is a question I will briefly touch upon, to show that it has not escaped my notice. I mean the dyscrasias, consisting, as they seem to do, in an abnormal chemical composition of the fluids. Produced as these often are by improper diet, it is rational, I think, to exclude such as come under this category from the domain of medicinal agency, and to treat them with reference to their cause—

I mean, dietetically. I am aware of the complexity of the subject, and the various causes to which these states may be referred; but I think it right to notice cases which fall without the limits of the homœopathic law, though they belong to a class which includes others, upon which that law may be brought to bear.

Now, Gentlemen, a curious subject of speculation arises. How is it that a mode of procedure in medicine, such as ours, should have drawn upon itself the repudiation—even the anathema—of men of liberal education, who profess to be in search of the best mode of healing disease? A system such as ours, founded on a larger induction from facts than any that has been made in the whole history of medicine; put forth in no partisan spirit (though it is true that some of our number had homœopathy on the brain during the earlier years of its existence); bolstered up by no attempts to conceal weak points, but honest and straightforward. What is it that has made the great bulk of the profession—honest, plain men; men certainly not of deep thought, but good common sense, practical men—set us down as either fools or knaves?

I do not deny that the idea of a law of healing, which should be of universal application, is *primâ facie* improbable. The fact of a complex organism, liable to derangement in an infinitude of modes by an infinity of agents!—Is it possible that this variety of disorder can be rectified in one and the same way? This question can easily be answered; but I am putting it as it would appear to superficial thinkers. To those who dont think —that is, to the great bulk of the profession—it would present no difficulty. The medical world has never been remarkable for its repudiation of sweeping generalities founded on insufficient data. Humoralism, solidism, vitalism; the speculations of Brown, Cullen, and Broussais are the most familiar, but by no means the only instances of the truth of this assertion. When, at the very time that homœopathy was beginning to assert its claims, a man of celebrity, Dr. Armstrong, was crying out, " The lancet is the right hand of medicine and calomel is its left," and was being applauded to the echo by a very large portion of the medical world, we may be sure that hasty generalization was not the ground on which the claims of our system were so discourteously rejected. Its want of plausibility it was that damned it. If a new theory accords with the prevailing notions of the time, it has every chance of being accepted with open arms. But antagonism or antipathy, narçotism, and counter-irritation were the received modes of treating disease; homœopathy, however, was the expression of a fact, especially as explained at the time, utterly irreconcilable with these notions. That like should cure like; that medicines acting in the same direction as the disease, and on the same parts, should arrest disease, was Beelzebub casting out devils—and just as likely. But to crown the whole, the doctrine of infinitesimals shocked at once the experience which men thought they had of the immunity of the body from the minute noxious influences which surround us, and their ideas of the very possibilities of action. Such a monstrous absurdity seemed to render exaggeration impossible, and every statement fair which put the absurdity in the strongest light. Thus to give to " airy nothings a local habitation and a name," and to pretend to cure disease with them, was a mode of statement which satisfied every one who didn't care about truth, and gave to every witling the means of laughing to scorn the greatest discovery, perhaps, in the annals of medicine. The mirror was held up to the public, to be sure ; but it was the mirror of the intellectual state of the men who held it, not of the facts of the case ; and thus, as Pope once said on a similar occasion, according to my friend, Mr. Proctor,

" Did coxcombs vanquish Berkely with a grin."

Since that time, however, the prism in spectroscopic arrangement has demonstrated the inconceivable minuteness of matter ; and physiological research, aided by the microscope, has revealed the fact that animal organisms are composed of an infinitude of most complex molecules, in a constant state of change ; so that the form is the only thing that appears to remain fixed, but the substance is in constant flux : as the rainbow that in the sunshine constantly spans the waterfall, apparently unchanged, while the particles that are the material element of its existence are in a constant state of flux. Thus the scorn of yesterday bids fair to become the glory of to-day—at any rate, of to-morrow ; and the doctrine of infinitesimals, which a generation ago could not be conceived as possible—a doctrine which that generation could not bear, on account of the limited extent of their information—is likely in the next generation to become a necessity of belief; the only doctrine that will square with the then present state of knowledge.

This delay in progress would not have occurred, had men acted on scientific principles, and had tested experimentally the state of the case. Whenever, like an emperor of Germany who was "*super grammaticam*" in virtue of his kingship, they venture to judge the possible by the limits of their knowledge, they play fantastic tricks before high heaven, and excite in more enlightened intelligences pity or ridicule, according to the moral state of the beholders, and merely fret their hour on the stage, instead of having taken their place in the real business of life.

The lesson has its value: there are other things which are quite as improbable as small doses—quite as much opposed to prevailing ideas ; things which a rational and modest man will carefully test before he denounces.

I have alluded before, in speaking of the reaction in the medical world which is taking place, to the endeavour to test the action of drugs on animal organisms. I regret, however, that animals are preferred for these experiments to the human organism. Results thus obtained must frequently mislead. Hahnemann, speaking just eighty years ago of such experiments, says : " How greatly do their bodies differ from ours ? A pig can swallow a large quantity of *nux vomica* without injury, and yet men have been killed with fifteen grains. A dog bore an ounce of the fresh leaves, flowers, and seeds of monkshood ; what man would not have died of such a dose ? Horses eat it when dried without injury. Yew leaves, though so fatal to men, fatten some of our domestic animals."* And after other examples, he adds : " This much at least is certain, that the fine internal changes and sensations which a man can express by words, must be totally wanting in the lower animals. In order to try if a substance can develope very violent or dangerous effects, this may in general be readily ascertained by experiments on several animals at once ; as likewise any general manifest action on the motions of the limbs, variations of temperature, evacua-

---

* I have reason to doubt the accuracy of some of these statements, but believe, however, that experiments on animals are not safe guides in therapeutics.

tions upwards and downwards and the like, but never anything connected or decisive that may influence our conclusions with regard to the proper curative virtues of the agent on the human subject. For this such experiments are too obscure, too rude, and if I may be allowed the expression, too awkward." Had Hahnemann read the Report of the Committee of the British Medical Association, published in the *British Medical Journal* last year, I think he would hardly have asked permission to use the term " awkward." All the powers of his sarcastic wit would have been exercised to show the folly of expecting normal results from proceedings so abnormal, in a sphere so different. Research cannot, however, long remain in this uncertain state. There is too much industry and too much ingenuity at work to be long satisfied with fruitless labour. One has only to cast his eyes over the *Handbook of the Physiological Laboratory*, prepared by Messrs. Klein, Burdon Sanderson, Brunton, and Foster, to have evidence of the minuteness of research and of the wealth of instrumental ingenuity which is being applied by these sappers and miners of the army of progress in the investigation of the phenomena of life. Among these self-denying workers I must not omit the name of Gamgee, who would rather pass a night in his laboratory than spoil an observation or lose an idea. Such industry and such ingenuity must ultimately be applied to drug-disease, and we shall have provings marked by an exactitude in observation, a minuteness of detail, and a precision in characterization and definition, of which we have all sorely felt the need in the selection of our remedies. Every advance in experimental accuracy, every discovery in science must work in our favour; for we stand on the solid rock of fact—on a law of nature—empirical, if you like, but founded on a larger induction from facts than any in the realm of therapeutics. Such a law may be explained by further scientific investigations; that is, resolved into a larger law, including it; but can never be shaken, and must at last be universally accepted. In the mean time we can bear with the lets and hindrances to our course which we experience; with the loss of the countenance of men who stand high in public opinion, but who dare not meet us for fear of losing that eminence; with the weakness of noble men, who would be nobler if they were less timid, and didn't care so much about hornet's nests; with the misrepresentations in the journals of the profession, which we are not allowed an opportunity to contradict or to rectify; with exclusion from access to the general medical public by our publications, unless we will sink the mention of homœopathy altogether; and lastly, with exclusion from the public offices of honour and emolument, and the high places of the profession.

All this is but the outward show and seeming of a monster—

" Monstrum, horrendum, informe, ingens, cui lumen ademptum "—

whose vitality is at a very low ebb, and who begins to be ashamed of his existence; but beside him we see advancing toward us a charming young creature, enlightened by our principles, animated by our feelings, and so like us that we would fain claim her as a daughter; but strange to say, she doesn't know her own mother, though I would fain hope that her blushes indicate a consciousness that she is ashamed of the disclaimer. To have called such a rare creature into existence is enough for us; and we are content to await the coming of ripe reason, for the disappearance of some foolish, but not, everything considered, unnatural feelings.

To drop the language of metaphor, it is a matter of notoriety that the literature of the profession has for some years been largely imbued with our principles, and its practice enriched with our medicines; and that these acquisitions have been treated as treasure-trove—that is, as treasures, the owners of which cannot be found, though they are well known. It is known as a fact, that if one of our members, of average abilities, should disown our name, repudiate our language but not our principles, and leave our ranks, he will be received with acclamation; should he write a book, rich in the spoils of our literature, it will be honoured and reviewed with praise, and its writer be exalted to the lecturer's chair, to teach the very truths, with some change of language, which we for nearly half a century have been outlawed for proclaiming. Valuables appropriated without acknowledgment are, however, dangerous property; they breed disunion in the camp; and our hard-headed brethren of the north are already beginning to cry out that they know where the spoons came from, though the crests have been effaced. There are occasions when honest men come by their own. But,

Gentlemen, it is not the appropriation I grudge; I deplore that want of a free and generous and candid and just spirit which is manifest in men who still ostracise those through whom they are enriched. Most welcome are they to all truths that can enlighten humanity; most welcome are they to every medicine which can alleviate suffering; above all and peculiarly, most welcome are they to all men who think they can best serve truth *incognito*. For ourselves, let ours be the spirit of the noble Paul: " They put us in; nay, verily, let them come and fetch us out." We wait the time when a more enlightened generation will· honour the memory of those whom their fathers denounced. We wait the hour when the Hahnemannian oration shall take its place beside the Harveian, and be pronounced by the same man from the same chair, with equal or superior honours. We shall be there in spirit, if not in body.

ADDITIONAL FACTS AND REMARKS IN ILLUSTRATION OF ANTIPRAXY.

By WILLIAM SHARP, M.D., F.R.S.

" He should be humble-minded, and a diligent searcher after truth ; . . . . and in proportion as the veil becomes thinner, through which he sees the causes of things, he will admire more the brightness of the divine light, by which they are rendered visible."—SIR HUMPHREY DAVY.

" There is in the world no kind of knowledge, whereby any part of truth is seen, but we justly account it precious."—RICHARD HOOKER.

THE Address given at Leamington in 1873 (Essay XXII.), contains experimental proofs of the contrary action of larger and smaller doses of the same drug in health, from provings of the following well-known substances :—

> Aconite.
> Digitalis.
> Spigelia.
> Veratrum.
> Opium.
> Mercury.
> Phosphorus.
> Tartar emetic.

In Essay XXVI. some further provings and cases were recorded with reference to

> Oxalic acid, and
> Chamomilla.

Your attention is now invited to some experiments in health with larger and smaller doses, and to the curative action of the smaller doses of

> Castor oil.
> Wild chamomile, and
> Bayberry.

Castor oil (*Ricinus communis*).

On the 31st of March, 1876, I had some conversation with a gentleman well-known for his scientific acquirements, on the subject of Antipraxy. With a warmth of expression perhaps not free from contempt, he exclaimed:— " You do not mean to say that small doses of *castor oil* will produce constipation?" I had not tried the experiment, but I have confidence in the uniformity of natural laws, and answered:—" I do not doubt that they will." On returning home I immediately procured some *castor oil*, and made a trituration of two small drops in ninety-nine grains of sugar of milk. Of this trituration twelve powders were weighed out, containing one grain each. These powders were taken to another scientific gentlemen, unacquainted with homœopathy, who had previously offered to me his services as a prover, and were given to him without any hint either as to what they contained, or as to what effect they were expected to produce. He was requested to take one powder night and morning for six days, and report to me the result.

On the 18th of April he called, and told me that the only effect which he had noticed was *the complete confinement of the bowels for five days ;* and as this had made him uncomfortable, and was causing headache, after taking six powders in three days, he discontinued them.

I then showed him the *castor oil,* and the trituration made of it. He was at first much surprised, and then after a pause deliberately said :—" There can be no doubt at all of the effect which followed the taking of the powders." He added that he was not easily acted upon by medicines, and that he had never taken *castor oil* before. He is in robust health at present.

This, then, is the action of the smaller doses of *castor oil* in health. If anyone doubts the contrary action of the larger doses, he can prove them upon himself.

CASE—*Diarrhœa.*

Castor oil may now be used as a remedy for some kinds of diarrhœa; and I have had an opportunity of testing its powers, as was most fitting, upon myself.

On September 7th of this year I was well in the morning, but felt cold all day, and as a consequence found in the evening that my dinner was not being comfortably digested. A dose of *pulsatilla*, the medicine which commonly suits me best, was taken. On going to bed diarrhœa came on and disturbed me through the night; the pulse became rapid; a nasal catarrh which obstructed breathing was added; and I became greatly exhausted. At first *veratrum* was taken; then brandy and water was given me, and afterwards *camphor*. All this was fruitless, and about four o'clock I began taking the *castor-oil* powders (a grain of the first trituration in each). After the first came the sure sign of relief: a little quiet sleep; after the second in an hour, more sleep; after the third, in another hour, a longer sleep. After the first powder no more disturbance of the bowels.

The seat of the action of *castor oil* is in the bowels; and this alike in health and in disease; and also in the larger and the smaller doses. This is its local action; and in this it is an illustration of *Organopathy*.

The action of the larger doses is to cause diarrhœa; the action of the smaller doses is to cause constipation; and this alike in health and in disease. This is the contrary action of the larger and the smaller doses; and in this it is an illustration of *Antipraxy*.

If the curative effect of the small dose is viewed with reference to the effect in health of the larger doses, the cure is wrought by a *Homœopathic* action. If it is viewed with reference to the effect in health of the smaller doses, the cure has been brought about by an *Antipathic* action.

Wild Chamomile (*Matricaria chamomilla*).

" I have proved the first dilution (one hundredth of a drop of the sap of the plant) sufficiently to learn its action on the liver. On a healthy person its effect is to produce motions like those of a healthy baby; it increases the secretion of healthy bile." *

To learn the action on the liver of larger doses, two provings have since been made for me by a gentleman in good health. These are his notes:—

" April 28th. Five drops of the mother tincture (half sap and half spirit) taken at night. Half an hour afterwards, rumbling in the stomach. Next morning less free

Essays on Medicine, 10th Edition. Essay XXVI., page 790.

evacuation than usual; and this continued the same for four days afterwards ; the colour *darker* than usual.

" May 14th. Ten drops taken at night. Half an hour afterwards rumbling in the stomach.

" 15th. Morning evacuations as usual in quantity, but rather *darker*.

" 16th. No evacuation.

" 17th. Evacuation very small in quantity; slight indigestion during the day.

" 18th. Everything as usual."

It is, I think, evident from these provings, that the actions of the hundredth part of a drop of *chamomilla*, and and of five or ten drops are, so far as the liver is concerned, in contrary directions.

In Essay XXVI. two remarkable cases, showing the curative action of the first dilution of *chamomilla* in jaundice and in diabetes are given. The following case of diabetes certainly springing from liver disease, is another equally remarkable :—

CASE.—*Diabetes*.

1871. Mr.——, after a residence of several years in India, had fever, and was sent home, some years ago; he was suffering from his liver and from great debility. He recovered, but was generally conscious that he had a liver. May 26th, 1871, when he was 47, he came to me complaining of an "angry thirst;" of losing flesh; and of feeling very weak. The water had a specific gravity of 1043 ; an ounce contained sixty grains of solid matter, the greatest part of this being sugar. The quantity of water in twenty-four hours was between nine and ten imperial pints. The pulse about 90, weak.

The remedy given was tincture of *chamomilla* 1st centesimal dilution, a dose three times a day.

June 5th. Very much better in all ways; very little thirst now; pulse 80, less weak; quantity of water reduced to four imperial pints; the sp. gr. 1033. The medicine continued.

14th. Better, but feels to need more food than when in health. His diet has not been restricted to animal food; with a good deal of strong beef-tea and meat, he takes green vegetables, eggs, brown bread and butter, tea and claret. The urine is now in about the natural quantity, this varies but does not exceed four pints; sp. gr. 1028, clear. The medicine continued.

20th. A little better in all ways. Sp. gr. 1025. To take no medicine.

24th. After four days without medicine, the " angry thirst" returned a little yesterday, a great deal to-day; pulse 80. The medicine resumed.

28th. After four days of medicine the thirst is again gone; but the same amount of strength has not yet returned. Pulse 76; sp. gr. 1030, thick. The medicine continued.

July 5th. Feels better but not stronger; has a little thirst; quantity of water natural; sp. gr. 1026. The medicine continued.

12th. Pulse 82; sp. gr. 1015. The medicine continued.

25th. Pulse 88; sp. gr. 1026. The medicine to be taken now only night and morning.

After this he went to the sea, and continued better.

Sept. 6th. Very little, if any, of the diabetic complaint left; but on returning from the sea he fatigued himself, and he now speaks of the old condition of the liver, and of debility. Tincture of *cinchona* 1, a dose three times a day.

Soon afterwards he took cold, and had a feverish illness with pain in the liver. This was treated with *aconite* and *belladonna*, and was removed.

Oct. 5th. He is fairly well now; liver feels right; bowels regular; urine thick. The *cinchona* repeated.

18th. Says he has no ailment left but debility. *Titanium* 2, a dose twice a day.

Nov. 22nd. He tells me to-day that he has not had so good a liver for twenty years.

1876. August 31st. This gentleman had a dangerous illness from inflammation of the veins of the leg, two years ago, brought on by over-walking in Switzerland, from which he recovered with difficulty. He is now, I believe, well, though he continues the diet he has become accustomed to.

Bayberry (*Merica cerifera*).

In the year 1862 my attention was attracted to the *herbalists*, as they have long been called, and to their practice at the present day. It appears that they use remedies from the vegetable kingdom only, and among

these many which are not " officinal," or which have no
place in our Pharmacopœias ; that they use them on the
old principles recognised by the medical profession ; that
they gain their knowledge of the medicinal action of the
plants by experiments on the sick; and that this knowledge, like that of their " regular" contemporaries, is kept
indistinct by several remedies being given in combination
with each other.

The plant which is most in favour with them is the
bayberry (Myrica cerifera).   It is a shrub found in most
parts of North America.   Its berries by boiling yield a
wax similar to bees' wax, from which the plant derives its
names of wax-myrtle, or candle-berry, or Myrica cerifera.
The bark of the root is the part used in medicine.   It is
said that the best substitute at present known in this
country is the bark of the blackberry root.

There are valuable provings of the larger doses in Dr.
Hale's "New Remedies," made by Dr. Walker.   From
these it is seen to have a powerful action on the liver ; so
that " complete jaundice, with bronze-yellow skin ; scanty,
yellow, frothy urine ; loose, clay-coloured stools, destitute
of bile; was produced by it." *

The following is a proving of the first dilution of
bayberry, made by a friend, with reference to this action
of the liver :—

" I have taken one drop of the tincture night and
morning for the last seven or eight days; during which
time my bowels have been rather more active than usual,
and the colour of the excreta much lighter, *i.e.* of a
lighter and brighter yellow than usual.   I have noticed
no other effects which might not have been accidental."

CASE.—*Disease of the Liver.*

For several years I have prescribed *bayberry* in certain
affections of the liver, and generally with satisfaction.
The following is a recent case :—

1875.—Nov. 6th.   Mr.——, about 79 years old ; has
had an excellent constitution, and has led a very active
life, until about fifteen years ago.   During this latter
period he has been ill several times.   He is now quite
prostrated, so that his end seems near.   He is quite

* *New Remedies*, by EDWIN M. HALE, M.D.   3rd Ed., page 327.

helpless in both mind and body; his *right* leg is extensively dropsical; the sphincters have lost their power; he is in a deplorable condition. He refuses all medicine, so that whatever is to be given him must be given under disadvantages. He is in the habit of taking a glass of brandy and water after an early dinner; and into this brandy and water was put a dessert spoonful of a solution of three or four drops of the mother tincture of *bayberry* in a tumbler of water. This was repeated every day till the middle of January.

By this time he is much improved in every way. For the sake of making some change, *taraxacum* is now given instead of *bayberry*, and in a similar manner, and one dose daily.

By the middle of February all swelling of the leg is gone; a good deal of muscular power, particularly that of the sphincters, is regained; the mind can exercise itself; he takes daily drives. Medicine is discontinued for a fortnight; he is not so well, and it is resumed.

He improves daily; in the beginning of June he goes to the sea; and now (August) is reported as " pretty well."

It may be thought that this recovery, remarkable as it is, might have been made more rapid, had the medicine been given more frequently. A second dose was at first given him in his evening tea, for two or three days; but this made him sick, and therefore was discontinued.

REMARKS.

1. *The action of drugs in health in all doses.—Primitive Homœopathy.*

Hahnemann has given us very little information as to the *doses* taken in his numerous provings. But we understand that small as well as large doses were tested; and that whatever symptoms were produced in healthy persons, by small doses as well as by large ones, were noted down in his " Materia Medica" and " Chronic Diseases;" and that *all these symptoms* are to be taken as guides in prescribing the drug for similar symptoms in disease.

It is only since the discovery of *Antipraxy, i.e.,* the contrary action of the larger and the smaller doses in health, that any reason can be given why this should not be so. We know, now, but we did not know before, and

Hahnemann did not know, that the effects of only the larger doses in health are those which are to be followed in prescribing on the principle of *similia similibus curantur*.

We know now, but we did not know before, that the effects produced in health by the smaller doses, are precisely those which are available as remedies in disease; and drugs in these doses are efficacious, when we prescribe them on the principle of *contraria contrariis curantur*.

As regards the action of the larger doses of drugs, our use of these drugs in small doses as medicines is *Homœopathy*. As regards the action of the smaller doses, our use of them is *Antipathy*. Hahnemann and the earlier homœopathists were not acquainted with this distinction.

2. *Change in the Definition of Homœopathy.*

The discovery of the contrary action of the larger and smaller doses of drugs, necessitates a change in the definition of homœopathy, and in the meaning of *similia similibus curantur*. All who are familiar with the writings of Hahnemann and his successors, know well that, until now, the meaning of these words has been this:—

Drugs are remedies for those symptoms of disease which are similar to the symptoms produced by them in health.

Provings in health have been made for this purpose in all doses great and small. The opposition, hitherto, has been the drug in health, and the drug in disease.

So distinctly has this been the case, that we are seldom informed by what doses the symptoms were occasioned in the remedies of the Materia Medica most extensively proved. Whatever effects have followed the taking of a drug in health in any dose great or small, these effects have been looked upon as the similars by which its use as a medicine is to be governed.

It is true that Hahnemann was gradually led to reduce the doses he prescribed, but the reason he gives for this is to avoid aggravations. That he had no notion of the contrary action of the smaller doses to that of the larger ones is further proved by this, that in his later works he wishes all drugs to be tested in the 30th dilution; and the effects which follow are to be used on the principle of *similia similibus curantur*.

That this is the view hitherto taken by homœopathists is so plainly true, that it admits of no contradiction. And it will not have been without surprise that the following sentence was lately read from the pen of the Editors of the *Monthly Homœopathic Review*:—

"There is no difference of opinion among homœopaths, *so far as we ever heard*, as to the meaning of *similia similibus curantur*, viz., that a drug given in small doses will cure a case of disease which presents symptoms similar to those produced by a large dose of the same drug when given to a healthy person." *

It is to be hoped that this will in future be the definition of homœopathy; but certainly it was never Hahnemann's teaching; and it is so far from being the "opinion of homœopaths," even at the present day, that I fear there is yet among us only a very small minority which is prepared to receive it.

3. *The Doctrine of Primary and Secondary Actions of Drugs.*

Hahnemann tells us that "most medicines have more than one action;" and he is at great pains to discover and explain to us their different kinds of action. In his earlier writings he thinks that they may be described as *direct* or *primary*, and *indirect* or *secondary*. "The first," he says, "gradually changes into the second; and the latter is generally a state exactly opposite the former." He thinks, however, that this character belongs chiefly to the vegetable medicines, and he gives *opium* as an example; while "the metallic (and other mineral?) medicines," he believes, "are exceptions, as *arsenic, mercury, lead*." †

In Hahnemann's later writings these changes are spoken of as *alternating actions ;* and in his latest, the distinctions he has previously made seem to be given up.

The opinions of his successors upon this subject have been very various and contradictory. So that a common experience in mental effort has been our experience in this; perhaps every possible conjecture has been put forward, and at length nearly all have been abandoned.

It must be remembered that all these views of drug-action, whether of Hahnemann, or of those who have

* *Monthly Homœopathic Review*, for August 1876, page 526.
† *Hahnemann's Lesser Writings*, page 312.

succeeded him, are views of the action of drugs *in any and all doses;* they describe differences or contraries in the effects produced by the drug; not those which result from the action of different doses of the drug.

It follows that the contrary action of larger and smaller doses of the same drug—to which the name of Antipraxy has been given—is a more recent discovery; and one which is independent of all the discussions which had previously been carried on respecting primary and secondary actions.

4. *Experiments on Animals.*

Some medical men are now becoming acquainted with contrary action of the larger and smaller doses of drugs by painful experiments upon the lower animals. Against such experiments as these I have protested for many years, as unnecessary and cruel. Satisfactory individual facts, sufficient to establish the collective or general fact of Antipraxy, can be obtained by safe experiments upon ourselves; and it is upon these experiments that I have exclusively relied. It is apparent that all the provings given in the Address at Leamington are of this character; the induction was made from them; and it needs no support from the dissection of living animals.

Experiments on the lower animals, with very rare exceptions, should cease, not only by reason of their cruelty, but also by reason of the superiority in accuracy and value, of experiments upon ourselves. It may safely be contended that very nearly all the useful knowledge we can have of the action of a drug may be obtained by experiments upon ourselves; while that which is sought for by cruel dissections of living animals is so uncertain and contradictory as to be really useless. In confirmation of this we have just now had the testimony of a writer who is favourable to such dissections. He says :—

" On reading over the summary of these experiments in the younger Wood's treatise on Therapeutics, one is surprised to find that every possible view of it has been taken by various observers, many of them quite contradictory, and yet all the result of careful experiment and deductions therefrom." *

* *Monthly Homœopathic Review,* July 1876, page 442.

5. *Experiments on ourselves.—Hahnemann's merit.*

It cannot be too often repeated that Hahnemann's claim to respect rests upon the example he set us of seeking to learn the properties of drugs by experiments upon himself and his friends when in a state of health. The superiority of this method, alike over experiments on the sick, and over those on the lower animals, must be firmly maintained, until both these inferior modes of experiment are abandoned.

That experiments upon sick persons which are injurious to them are still largely continued is painfully evident, even to those who are only partially acquainted with the current medical periodicals. It makes the heart sick to read the "fatal results" of wrong medicines and over-doses which, from time to time, are put on record; and still more sick to think how many of such must occur which are not recorded. Sad examples might easily be given, but they would be too personal. It is sufficient to say that they give the keenest point to the exclamation of a gentleman who, while on a tour in a remote part of Wales, was suddenly taken ill, and on asking for a medical man to be sent for, was told that there was not one within thirty miles; "then," said he, " I shall die a natural death ! "

6. *Theories and Hypotheses.*

Theories and hypotheses, that is, so far as these are imaginary *explanations* of natural phenomena, have often been protested against in these Essays. It is necessary to repeat this protest again.

For there are writers who have accepted the fact of the contrary action of the larger and smaller doses of drugs, but they are not content to express it as a fact; they must express it in words conveying a theoretical explanation of the fact. For example, it is asserted that drugs paralyse in large doses, and stimulate in small ones. This is an assertion of more than we know, and of more than can be proved. The contrary might be said also, that drugs stimulate in large doses, and paralyse in small ones; and examples might be adduced which seem to prove both assertions.

Theoretical explanations are the bane of science. The only explanation of any fact in nature is the discovery of another fact which is its cause; and until this cause is discovered, true wisdom directs us to own frankly that we do not know what the cause of the fact in question is. To invent an imaginary cause is to deceive ourselves and others, and to set up a barrier against the progress of knowledge.

It is right to ask questions, and it is useful to make guesses; but the only legitimate use of such questions and guesses is to suggest new experiments. This is the true sphere of hypotheses, and in this sphere they are often of the highest practical value. If suffered to range beyond this distinctly defined sphere, they are obstructive deceits.

Why the water in rivers and lakes freezes at the surface and not at the bottom, is a question which may be pertinently asked by a student of natural science. No one has any doubt of the fact, nor does it need much thought to determine that the fact is important; for it is by this method of freezing that the life of the inhabitants of the waters is preserved.

The fact which explains this is now well known. Substances contract or diminish in size as they lose heat. Water does this from its boiling temperature at 212° Fahr. till it is cooled down to about 40°; then its density is greatest; and on losing more heat, instead of contracting further, it gradually expands until its temperature has fallen to 32°, when it becomes solid. Now it is evident that while the surface of a river or lake is being cooled down to 40° no vertical motion will take place among the particles of the water. When this temperature has been reached, the upper layers of water, being heavier than the layers below, will begin to sink; and this process of sinking will continue till the surface freezes at 32°, when as a solid, it expands still more, and remains at the top, while the water at 40° has fallen to the bottom.

The student's question is satisfactorily answered; but if he asks further for an explanation of the contrary effect of heat in different quantities, we do not know any fact which explains it, and cannot answer his question.

The contrary action of different doses of drugs on man's health is a parallel case. In certain larger doses the action is in one direction; in certain smaller doses the action is in the contrary direction. We do not yet know any fact which explains this contrary action.

7. *Facts explained by Antipraxy.*

The contrary action of the larger and smaller doses of drugs is yet an unexplained fact; but, as it seems to me, it is itself the explanation of some other facts which are highly interesting to us. For example :—

Taken in connection with Organopathy—the local action of drugs—it is a reasonable explanation of homœopathic cures. The larger doses of drugs produce effects similar to the diseases for which the smaller doses are given as remedies; these smaller doses act in the opposite direction to that of the larger ones; and this contrary action is contrary to the disease, and becomes a remedy for it.

There is another question which is still more earnestly put—Why are small doses to be given at all? How can they do good? This also is answered. These small doses are *direct remedies*, acting in the direction contrary to the disease. When the right drug is selected, to give it in the smaller doses is the best possible treatment.

Again, another question also receives an answer, though, perhaps, not the only answer. The contrary effects so often mentioned among the symptoms of the same drug in Hahnemann's provings are perplexing. We are not told by what doses these contrary symptoms have been produced; but if one series of them has been caused by the larger, and the contrary series by the smaller doses, which is probable, then this perplexity is removed.

Here are three important questions receiving their answer from a fact. This fact, then, is of much value.

We are, now-a-days, forbidden to think of final causes; but in reality the final cause of this law of the action of drugs is manifest—it makes them remedies for disease. We do not yet know the physical cause of this law, any more than we know that of the contrary effects of different quantities of heat upon the density of water. We are not thereby hindered from appreciating their usefulness, nor from admiring the skill by which they were designed.

8. *Constant and minute observation.*

As the light of the sun is the beauty and the glory of the earth, so the light of truth, when it shines within us, is the beauty and the glory of our minds. The mind sees it with delight, and rejoices in the possession of it. Especially is this so when a long struggle with darkness, and an earnest looking for the light, have preceded its appearance.

It seems to me that the knowledge of the *local* action of drugs, and the *contrary* action of larger and smaller doses, is the shining of the light of truth into our minds, on the difficult, perplexed, and dark subject of the action of medicines.

You cannot wonder, therefore, that I continue, in spite of the feebleness of age, to recommend such bright views to your attention. And these efforts do not spring from selfishness, but from a strong desire to impart this knowledge, and the pleasure which accompanies it, as freely and as widely as possible.

As the best means of satisfying yourselves of its truth, let me press upon you the necessity of constant and minute observation. " Whoever *intends* to observe shall always find something worthy of his observation." Let me give an instance to explain my meaning.

On May 20th (1876), I had a laryngeal catarrh, and took for it *spong.* 1, a drop for a dose ; benefit quickly followed ; the medicine was continued three times a day ; on the third morning, when nearly if not quite well, a rather larger dose brought on immediately a violent reproduction of all the symptoms, sneezing, coughing, &c , which lasted for about an hour, and then gradually passed away. Here, I think, may be observed the two contrary actions of *spongia*. But it would have been very possible for both of them to have taken place without being observed.

As another illustration, I remember its being said that Dr. Wollaston had discovered a new metal in a specimen of a mineral given him which weighed only a few grains.

Let me, then, recommend to you careful and minute observation of whatever is passing before you. There is still a great deal of interesting and important work to be done, in order to learn with greater accuracy the action of drugs. Who will try to teach us exactly what is the action of *nux vomica* 1, *pulsatilla* 1, *belladonna* 1, and so on—the first dilution of each of the polychrests? Whatever these doses do in a healthy organ, they will attempt to do in the same organ when it is not healthy ;—the action in both cases will be similar.

Until the contrary action of the larger and smaller doses of each drug has been ascertained by actual experiments in health, the dose cannot be fixed by any rule but that of the judgment or fancy of each practitioner.

9. *Limits of the human mind.*

It is of unspeakable moment to be acquainted with, and to remember the limitation of the human mind. At the last meeting of the section of Physics in the Scientific Exhibition Conferences held in Kensington on the 24th of May, 1876, the President (Mr. W. Spottiswoode, LL.D., F.R.S.) concluded some eloquent remarks by saying :—

"They had evidence in that building that science was not the exclusive possession of any age or country, but *knew no limits save those of time and space.*"

We are not going to break a lance with the *metaphysicians*, but in *physics* it is of necessity that words have precise meanings; and Mr. Spottiswoode is to be thanked for speaking so plainly of the limits of time and space. Creation had a beginning, and time began with it; its duration is the limit of time; its boundaries are the limits of space. God only is eternal and infinite. But Mr. Spottiswoode must not say that science, by which we understand him to mean human knowledge of creation, has no other limits save those of time and space. Science has another limit, and one of much narrower dimensions —the limit of the human senses and intellect. There is no science, that is, no human knowledge of God's works, outside the powers of our bodily senses and our mental faculties, perception, memory, and judgment.

It is of practical importance to us to understand and remember this limitation. We shall not observe with sufficient care, nor reason with sufficient precision, if we lose sight of this narrow boundary. We may be very certain that the works of God extend *far beyond this boundary;* and we should pursue our investigations with a continual consciousness of this fact, and with a continual reference to it.

10. *Some criticisms replied to.*

Before concluding, I am tempted to notice a few friendly criticisms, which I hope to do in the same friendly spirit. Here is one :—

"The bare facts are just so many 'bricks' or 'rough stones'—it is the part of science to build these into structures. The theorist who constructs facts into theories, is an architect. The man who only collects bricks and stones, and insists on their lying there unutilized, has only a brick or stone yard."

I could have been content, and not only content but thankful, had I been only a gatherer of stones and a maker of bricks, with which others might lay the foundation and build the temple of therapeutics ; but have I not done something more than this? Are not *Organopathy* and *Antipraxy* true inductions, or collective facts? and are they not firm foundations upon which the therapeutics of the future must rest? It is true that they are not theories but facts; facts, however, which are far more useful and durable than any theories. Carrying on observations is gathering stones, and instituting experiments is making bricks, and this is useful employment; but when these stones and bricks have been carefully laid side by side and one upon another, something like a foundation and a building begin to appear; and this is a substantial and lasting building on a solid foundation ; while I venture to say that explanatory speculations are castles in the air, baseless and transitory.

As in every chamber of God's temple of the universe, so in the physician's chamber, nothing happens by chance; all is governed by law. It is our high privilege, not to be imagining or inventing theories, but to be trying to discover these laws. How noble the employment! How useful the labour! Not building castles in the air, but gathering stones and making bricks, and placing them one upon another, so that a day may come when the temple of medicine shall be finished.

Dr. Richard Hughes closes the subject in which we are at present interested, with these words :—

" It is to me *inconceivable* that a substance which in moderate quantity excites any function should in a somewhat larger one depress it. . . . . *I* cannot *think* it."*

I should be sorry to say anything unkind, but, really, all that we learn from this very strong declaration of Dr. Hughes, is the limit of his own power of thinking. Natural phenomena, not being confined within the same limit, continue ; and it may be hoped that others will be able both to observe and to conceive them.

* *A Manual of Pharmacodynamics*, 3rd Ed., article " Opium."

Dr. Edward Madden offers this remark :—

" Only one series of experiments have been made on the human subject with the object of testing the direct effects of small doses in health. I refer, of course, to those of Dr. Sharp on himself. . . . . Until his experiments are repeated and confirmed, they cannot, by themselves, be regarded as conclusive."*

May I suggest to Dr. Madden that the best thing he can do, is to set himself diligently to work in the repetition of these experiments. I hope he will do so ; and if he can devote the necessary amount of time, patience, and minute observation to the provings of different doses of some of the most important drugs, he will render good service to his profession.

Another friend finds fault with me for introducing two new words—*Organopathy* and *Antipraxy*—into medicine. But a new fact discovered, as well as a new theory invented, must have either a new name given to it, or an old name must be used for it in a new sense. It may sometimes be difficult to decide which is best, as there are objections to both. Whichever renders most easy the understanding and the adoption of the new truth is to be preferred. In the present cases I think the new names were not only best but necessary.

Again, I have been blamed for not being simple and intelligible ; and have been told that " it is always safer to explain as if teaching a beginner, and not to conclude that because readers ought to understand this or that, that they do so. . . . . Plainly stated facts are valuable, but the deductions from them must be simple, if you mean them to be telling."

Assuredly, next to the search for truth, nothing has been aimed at in these Essays so earnestly, as that they should be distinguished for simplicity, clearness, and the absence of hard words and technical expressions. This has brought upon me from others the censure of writing more for the public than for the profession. So that in the eyes of critics, an event which might have been thought an impossible feat has been accomplished—the shipwreck of my barque on both sides of the Sicilian

* *Monthly Homœopathic Review*, Sept. 1876, p. 591.

straits. I have not time to set sail upon a second voyage.
Nor do I think it necessary. I have written plainly, and
I have written professionally. Perchance, it may be your
duty, and for the good of your patients, to try to understand what has been written.

Dr. NANKIVELL said it seemed very plain that the action of a
small dose of castor oil in health, was the opposite to that of a
large dose; and also that they had a similar action from the small
dose of castor oil when given in disease:—so that the same small
dose that produced constipation in health, produced also constipation in diarrhœa. Dr. Sharp said the primary action of
castor oil was to be no guide to them in prescribing at all; that
they were to be guided only by its secondary action. But they
had here a plain experiment of castor oil in infinitesimal doses
producing constipation. If they individualised that constipation, might not a trituration of castor oil, say No. 6, cure
constipation according to the homœopathic method? Was not
the antipraxy of which Dr. Sharp spoke, a limited antipraxy?
Might they not get from No. 6 trituration of castor oil a curative
action in constipation, and from No. 2 trituration a curative
action in diarrhœa, the curative action in each case being thus
produced by a distinctly less dose than that which produced the
similar symptoms in health? Dr. Sharp said "No;" but in
our President's Address the instance has been given of *nux* in
small doses curing spasm dependent on an excited action of the
cord, and of *nux* in larger doses curing where spinal paralysis
existed: the smaller dose curing just the opposite condition of
things to what the larger dose cures, and the indications for
prescribing being drawn from the primary as well as from the
secondary action of the drug. He threw it out as a suggestion
to Dr. Sharp, to try in the next case of constipation that he got,
whether a No. 6 dilution of castor oil were as successful as a
tablespoonful and much more effectual.

Dr. DRYSDALE said they had had the subject before them very
often, but not too often. The opposite action of small and large
doses had a certain amount of virtual truth, but only in the fact
that it required to be merged into a higher and larger law. It
was true as a matter of fact in many instances, but was not to
be perceived in all physiologically. That was the point. If
true at all, as an explanation of homœopathic action, it would
only be proved universal by taking into account the therapeutic
action, and then of course it was quite correct to say that a
small dose in curing, produced the opposite effect of a large one
which produced the disease. But this was nothing but a mere
reassertion of the homœopathic principle, and was in no sense
an explanation of it. To make it an explanation, as was

attempted by Dr. Sharp in the word "antipraxy," it was necessary to prove that all homœopathic medicines had this action on the healthy body, and also that it was by virtue of this primary pathogenetic action—still acting as such—that disease was cured. It was therefore by the primary antagonistic action that cure was obtained This theory—for it was a theory, whether the facts were true or not—was opposed as follows: First, it took no account of the numerous exceptions where no such opposite action had been demonstrated, even in affections of mere plus and minus. Secondly, it took no account of qualitative disease, such as gout, rheumatism, syphilis, scurvy, &c., of which no opposite producible by small doses was intelligible. Thirdly, a definite quantity of the antagonistic medicine would always be as necessary for the cure as for the production of disease ; and that quantity would be the same and even greater than what was necessary to produce the effect in health, *e.g.*, if two drops of aconite (pure tincture) quickened the pulse, and $1/_{20}$th of a drop slowed the pulse in health, it would always require at least $1/_{20}$th if not more to antagonise a quick pulse of disease. This, however, was contradicted by experience of the wide range of homœopathic dose ; the rule for which was, that it must not exceed the dose requisite to produce the full physiological effect, while it might vary to a wide extent below that. Fourthly, if the antagonistic theory were true, it would still be primary, and therefore liable to be merely palliative, requiring to be constantly kept up and in increased doses, being liable to the exhaustion and secondary opposite state of all primary actions. Fifthly, it took no account of the double and opposite action of all agents in one and the same dose, if sufficient to exert any vital action beyond the line of health. For it was a universal law that every function and every vital action if unduly stimulated and exalted, fell for a time into a corresponding opposite state of diminished action. This was a universal law to which all exceptions were only apparent. It gave, therefore, a firm basis of fact for a law of double and opposite action of all poisons and medicines in which might be sought an explanation of homœopathic cures ; for it was plain that in as far as disease was an exhausted or lowered action, any poison that could produce such disease carried within itself one aspect of its power, which would tend to counteract the opposite stage of a similar exciting cause. The dose here must be small ; and here we had an example of a small dose having an action just the opposite of a large one ; and in this sense "antipraxy" was true, but in this sense only. The supposed example where small and large doses produced physiological primary opposites were not very numerous, and each was explicable on its own merits. It was a fact that the susceptibility of different parts and nerve centres to different agents varied widely; and one organ or part would be affected by a dose which would not affect another, although a higher dose would. For example, a moderate light would produce contraction of the pupils; a stronger one would cause involuntary closure of the eyelids. A small dose of *aconite* would stimulate the inhibitory nerves of the heart and slow the pulse, while a larger one stimulated the accelerating nerves and overpowered the former, and a still larger one might bring on secondary exhaustion and paralyse them all. All similar actions required analysis each for itself. Dr. Sharp had always overlooked this, that one and the same dose produced two opposite actions. There were always two actions from one and the same dose, and there were a great many actions from different doses; but as regarded particular functions there was always a double action. They must unravel each case, and separate the double and opposite action of the same dose from antagonistic actions which were both primary, and depended on the different susceptibility of different organs or parts. When this was done, he believed the opposite physiological action of large and small doses would be found to occupy a subordinate place, and would be incapable of explaining the general law of homœopathic cure.

Dr. R. HUGHES wished to explain that what he said was to him "unthinkable," was not that large and small doses of drugs occasionally produced opposite phenomena. This was a fact about which there was no question. Where he diverged from Dr. Sharp, was in the explanation of this fact. He could not agree with him that it implied an opposite action of the drug within the system. Such an opposite action was to him inconceivable. He thought that a better explanation should be sought, and that it might often be found in a disentanglement of the complex phenomena. He considered that Dr. Sharp's "organopathy," by its narrowness of view, had much to do with his "antipraxy." If they thought of organs and functions as single, they might account for their variations under drug action by a mere *plus* and *minus*. But when they realised the complexity of the life of every part, and the number of channels through which drugs might act upon them, they began to think of the possibility of other explanations. He concluded by illustrating his remarks by the influence of *opium* on the brain, and *morphia* on the bowels.

EXPERIMENTS TO SHOW THE ACTION OF DRUGS ON THE PULSE.

By T. D. Nicholson, M.D.

Since Dr. Sharp's paper, read at the Congress three years ago, I have looked in vain for more facts confirming or refuting his views as to the action of drugs; and though considerable discussion has been evoked at each Congress since, it is to experiment and not to hypothesis we must look to tell us whether Dr. Sharp is right in his belief of the antagonism of large and small medicinal doses. A few months ago, therefore, I began to experiment on my own person in the same way as Dr. Sharp; and though there are comparatively few observations to record, I have thought them worth bringing before this Congress.

My task seemed very simple, viz., to test the action of large and small medicinal doses of drugs on the circulation. To attain this, I have used the sphygmograph and the thermometer, as well as counted the rapidity of the pulse. Nearly all my observations here recorded were made in the early morning and in bed, when few or no disturbing causes could exist; and in every case, from the beginning of the experiment to the end, I did not move from the reclining position I had assumed, except sufficiently to take the medicine. I may further add that no two experiments were made in one day.

Firstly, I had to discover to what extent my pulse varies during an hour's observation, without any drug whatever. I tried this on several occasions. The first time the lowest number counted was 50 and the highest 53, and the pulse fell two beats in the half hour. The second time it rose from 47 to 49. The third time it fell two beats. The fourth time it varied between 48 and 50, but once I counted 54. In the fifth observation it rose from 49 to 52, and finally jumped up to 55 in eighteen minutes. I give the details of this observation, where I found the greatest variation in the pulse rate.

1st minute	...	...	...	49
2nd ,,	...	...	...	49
3rd ,,	...	...	...	49
4th ,,	...	...	...	51
5th ,,	...	...	...	52
8th ,,	...	...	...	50
9th ,,	...	...	...	52
10th ,,	...	...	...	52
11th ,,	...	...	...	50
15th ,,	...	...	...	50
16th ,,	...	...	...	50
17th ,,	...	...	...	52
18th ,,	...	...	...	55

This shows the great difficulty in drawing reliable conclusions from experiments where the rise and fall is within narrow limits. But in each case when the pulse thus rose suddenly three or four beats, it was but momentarily, and it immediately resumed its former rate. In my experiments, therefore, I have generally counted the pulse two or three times, so as not to record a mere momentary rise. I may add, that I tried both with the sphygmograph on the arm and without, and the pressure of the instrument seemed not to affect the pulse at all.

Remembering, then, that I must assume a variation of at least three beats per minute during my hour's experiment, I began to try *aconite* in doses of φ tinct.

In my first experiment, the pulse fell three beats after six doses of one drop each every ten minutes. In my next, the pulse varied but one beat during the hour, and the thermometer rose 0.2 F. Then I tried two-drop doses, and found a fall of two beats, and 0.6 F. Then increasing doses of from two to five drops every few minutes showed no marked variation in either rapidity of pulse or temperature; and lastly, a longer experiment of an hour and a half was made, during which the pulse fell four beats in the first quarter hour, and then gradually recovered it, and stood at the end of the experiment at the original number, after twenty-two drops *acon.* φ had been taken, and the observation continued half an hour after the last dose.

Following Dr. Sharp, I then tried *acon*. 1 dil. The
first experiment showed a fall of two beats with doses of
two drops every fifteen minutes; the second experiment
presented no change from the normal pulse, and the
third showed some irregularity, but no definite variation;
whereas the fourth marked an increase of two beats.
There was no variation of temperature.

Since then I have made two observations with *acon*. 1x
dil. In one there was a rise of five beats, and in the other
a fall of three beats, and in neither a fall of temperature.
When the pulse rose I took drop doses, and when it fell
two-drop doses, every ten minutes.

I confess that it is with some disappointment that I find
I cannot draw similar conclusions to Dr. Sharp's from my
experiments. In no case was there a definite rise in the
pulse rate after the exhibition of *acon*. φ, nor was there
any fall after the 1st decimal or 1st centesimal doses.

Dr. Sharp says: "One or two drops, 1st dil., first
" quickens the heart's action for a short time (one, two,
" or three minutes), and then retards it;" and that " one
" or two drops of the sap of the plant (two or four drops
" φ tr.) quickens the heart's action, and no retardation
" follows.

The rate of my pulse thus affording no indication of the
action of the drug, I will examine the sphygmographic
tracings. And first, I must premise that I made several
observations with the sphygmograph when uninfluenced
by any drug, and found no noticeable variation within the
hour. I may mention also that Dr. Burdon Sanderson
says in his *Handbook** (p. 66): " Notwithstanding the
" infinite variety of forms observed in different persons,
" the tracing of the pulse of the same person is the same
" at all times, so long as he is in health."

The changes manifested by *acon*. φ are constant in four
observations, and agree in telling the same story. The
results of 1x dil. are similar, but less in degree, whilst 1st
cent. dil. shows no noticeable variation.

My pulse, to commence with, in each experiment shows
a short rise with the primary expansion of the artery, then
a curve with the concavity downwards corresponding to
the systolic distension, afterwards a very slight fall and
rise, just sufficient to mark the diastolic collapse and subsequent brief expansion followed by the normal descent
during the heart's pause.

° *Handbook of the Sphygmograph*, 1867.

The following are the details of the third experiment, in which the effect of the drug was most marked.

1st min....Pulse 53...Temp. 97.8   1st tracing.
15th ,, ... ,, 53...   *Acon.* Ø gtt. ii. taken.
30th ,, ... ,, 51...   {   ,,   gtt. ii. ,,
                            { 2nd tracing.
40th ,, ... ,, 51... ,, 97.7 *Acon.* gtt. ii.   ,,
50th ,, ... ,, 50...   ,, gtt. ii.   ,,
60th ,, ...   {   ,, gtt. ii.   ,,
                            { 3rd tracing.
80th ,, ... ,, 51...   *Acon.* gtt. ii.   ,,
86th ,, ... ,, 51... ,, 97.2 4th tracing.

Tr. *Aconite* Ø.

Fig. 1.—Normal pulse at commencement.

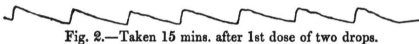

Fig. 2.—Taken 15 mins. after 1st dose of two drops.

Fig. 3.—Taken 10 mins. after 4th dose of two drops.

Fig. 4.—Taken 15 mins. after 6th dose of two drops.

Tr. *Aconite* 1x.

Fig. 5.—Normal pulse at commencement.

Fig. 6.—Taken 10 mins. after 3rd dose of two drops.

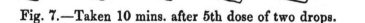

Fig. 7.—Taken 10 mins. after 5th dose of two drops.

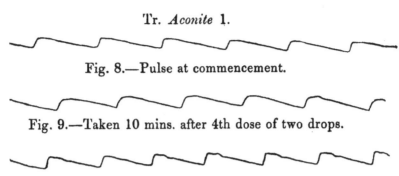

Tr. *Aconite* 1.

Fig. 8.—Pulse at commencement.

Fig. 9.—Taken 10 mins. after 4th dose of two drops.

Fig. 10.—Taken 10 mins. after 6th dose of two drops.

The effect of *acon.* φ in every case is a more vertical primary rise, then a quick and slight descent and rise again, forming a double curve instead of the single downward curve; and the remainder of the line is unaltered. The pulse hence becomes softer, with a fulness yielding to the finger, and shows a tendency to dicrotism. There is a more sudden expansion of the artery, but a diminution or unevenness of arterial tension. This may be caused by a more powerful contraction of the left ventricle, or a loss of elasticity in the vessel, allowing it to yield more to the ventricular action. I infer the latter to be the true explanation, because the total length of curve or curves showing the systolic distension remains unaltered. But this change of arterial elasticity may be due to change of capillary pressure, or at anyrate probably indicates capillary dilatation.

To quote again from Dr. Sanderson's *Handbook* (p. 64), he says:—" The states of the circulation which produce " true dicrotism, are just the opposite of those which " favour the development of the second event (systolic " distension). The one implies fulness of the pulse, the " other the contrary. The one expresses the continuance " of the arterial expansion, the other its abnormal ab- " breviation. Both alike depend on the proportion which " the quantity of blood projected by the heart at each " strike bears to the capillary resistance. The smaller the " quantity thrown into the aorta by the ventricle, the " sooner it is got rid of by the capillaries, and the more " dicrotous does the pulse become. If, on the other hand, " the capillaries are diluted, the effect is the same; for in

E

" either case, the collapse of the artery is accelerated, and
" the period of its expansion abbreviated."

I do not think that capillary dilatation is positively
proved as the effect of *aconite* in these experiments; but
the changes present, viz., the rapid distension and alteration of systolic curve, show a tendency to the pulse of
pyrexia, not the hard pulse characteristic of the rigor, but
rather that of reaction when the patient's condition improves.

My conclusion, therefore, is that whilst *aconite* in small
material doses has no marked action on the frequency of
the pulse or the temperature of the body, the sphygmograph shows it to be antipathic to the first stage of
fever or inflammation.

Digitalis.

In two experiments with *dig.* φ, I have observed the
pulse slightly retarded, but it fell three beats in an hour
after taking six drops in drop doses every ten minutes,
and only two beats after twenty drops in three drop doses.
In two other experiments the pulse had not varied more
than one beat per minute during the hour. The temperature remained stationary. The pulse varied so much
after taking 1st dil., that no conclusion can be drawn as
to its action. The sphygmographic tracings show but
little change.

I have experimented also with *belladonna, cactus,*
spigelia, and *lycopus,* but have no satisfactory results to
communicate. *Cactus* shows the most definite change by
the sphygmograph—a change similar to that produced by
aconite.

Dr. Sharp congratulated Dr. Nicholson on having begun the
series of provings of small doses. He hoped he would continue
them, and he felt convinced that the longer he studied them the
more interested would he become in the experiments.

Dr. Cooper thought the paper showed them how interesting
it was to have a large number of experiments from which
draw deductions. They had two learned men finding out the
action of *aconite* upon the heart, and they found them diame-
rically opposed. Dr. Sharp had on a former occasion asked
Dr. Nicholson to set to work and try experiments upon himself
That gentleman had now done so with scientific instrument
that could not err, and he had used every effort not to make

mistake, and they found that he had arrived at a different conclusion to that of Dr. Sharp; and with regard to the primary and secondary action of drugs, it did not to his mind at all remove the difficulties that beclouded homœopathy upon the dose question. From time to time it was found they had to take into account the varying susceptibility of patients, and some of the higher dilutions would produce quite as great effects sometimes upon patients as comparatively small doses of medicine. He would instance cases of several drugs. He remembered giving the 200th dilution of *arsenic* and producing apparent symptoms, where 3rd dec. produced no symptom whatever. Such instances as that they were meeting every day, and it seemed to him that with regard to the dose question they must separate altogether the effects they obtained from *palpable* quantities from the effects they obtained from the higher dilutions. One was to a certain and only limited extent governable by law, and for the other they had no law at all, for they were completely in the dark as to the action of the higher dilutions. They were not able to say that a dose of the higher dilutions would produce certain effects, though that was not the case so much with *palpable* doses of medicine.

Mr. CLIFTON thanked Dr. Nicholson for making "a few more bricks," (laughter). Many of the objections raised against Dr. Sharp's paper had been hypothetical. They wanted new facts. They wanted more provings of those confirmations which went to constitute facts. They were facts as far as they went, but they required more provings if they were to rely upon them so as to be able to draw any deductions from them.

Dr. WILDE said it was evident that they wanted to know more of this subject. These experiments of Dr. Nicholson's were facts equally with Dr. Sharp's, and if they had nothing more to satisfy them, he thought they must really withhold their opinion as to what was the true explanation of homœopathy. The things which had struck him more forcibly than Dr. Sharp's experiments, were those experiments of Dr. Anstie and others upon *aconite* and *digitalis*. These had been performed with great care, and went to show the reverse action of large and small doses. He thought those experiments of which they had heard that day remained to be proved by yet further experiments.

Dr. PEARCE observed that it would have been much more satisfactory if Dr. Nicholson's experiments had been made upon some person who was not aware of what he was taking. They knew the influence of the mind over the pulse, and they were aware that a man could control his pulse by mere thought; and however accurate Dr. Nicholson might have been in observing upon his own circulation, he did not think the results were so satisfactory as they would be in one ignorant of the character of the medicine, or of the alteration in the dose he was taking.

After some remarks by Dr. MOORE and Dr. HOLLAND on the action of *digitalis*, a vote of thanks was proposed by Dr. POWELL to Dr. HAYLE for his able address, and carried by acclamation, and the business of the Congress terminated.

TRANSACTIONS

OF THE

BRITISH HOMŒOPATHIC

CONGRESS,

HELD AT LIVERPOOL,

On THURSDAY, SEPTEMBER 13TH, 1877.

ALFRED C. POPE, M.D.,

PRESIDENT.

𝔓𝔲𝔟𝔩𝔦𝔰𝔥𝔢𝔡 𝔟𝔶 𝔄𝔲𝔱𝔥𝔬𝔯𝔦𝔱𝔶.

LONDON:

E GOULD & SON, 59, MOORGATE STREET, E.C.

1877.

Price Two Shillings.

PREFACE.

The Eighth of the new series of Congresses was held this year at Liverpool, with Dr. Pope as President, whose eloquent address was received with enthusiasm.

The papers are reprinted from the *Monthly Homœopathic Review.*

The discussions on the papers were very much curtailed, and Dr. Skinner was unable to read his essay in consequence of want of time. He, however, exhibited and explained his Fluxion Potentiser for making centesimal potencies.

By the general consent of the assembly ample time was allowed for the discussion of the name of the London School of Homœopathy, and it was decided by a large majority that the name should remain unchanged.

The next Congress is to be held at Leicester, on the fourth Thursday in September, 1878.

J. GIBBS BLAKE, *Hon. Sec.*

November, 1877.

1878—LEICESTER. *President—Dr. J. Gibbs Blake.*

Vice-President—A. C. Clifton, Esq. *Treasurer—Dr. E. M. Madden.*

General Secretary—Dr. J. C. Huxley, 24, Bennett's Hill, Birmingham.

Local Secretary—Dr. George Clifton, 53, London Road, Leicester.

The Executive Committee consists of the Officers for the year, together with the Presidents of former years.

1870—BIRMINGHAM. *President—Dr. Drysdale.*

1871—OXFORD. *President—Dr. Madden.*

1872—YORK. *President—Dr. Black.*

1873—LEAMINGTON. *President—Dr. Sharp.*

1874—LONDON. *President—Dr. Dudgeon.*

1875—MANCHESTER. *President—Dr. Bayes.*

1876—BRISTOL. *President—Dr. Hayle.*

1877—LIVERPOOL. *President—Dr. Pope.*

Members.

Dr. Anderson, Croydon.
Dr. Bayes, London.
Dr. Gibbs Blake, Birmingham.
Mr. Joseph Blake, Sheffield.
Dr. Edward Blake, Reigate.
Mr. Hans Blake, Wolverhampton.
Dr. Bryce, Edinburgh.
Dr. Burwood, Ealing.
Dr. Dyce Brown, London.
Dr. Black, London.
Dr. J. G. Blackley, London.
Dr. Bryce, Edinburgh.
Dr. Butcher, Reading.
Dr. Burnett, Liverpool.
Dr. Butcher, Liverpool.
Dr. Brown, Liverpool.
Mr. A. Clifton, Northampton.
Dr. G. Clifton, Leicester.
Dr. Fenton Cameron, London.
Dr. Dudgeon, London.
Dr. Drysdale, Liverpool.
Dr. Drummond, Manchester.
Dr. Drury, London.
Dr. Engall, London.
Dr. E. Flint, Canterbury.
Dr. Geogegan, Liverpool.
Dr. Hawkes, Liverpool.
Dr. Hayward, Liverpool.
Dr. Hughes, London.
Dr. Hewan, London.

Dr. Hudson, Liverpool.
Dr. Harris, London.
Dr. Hitchman, Liverpool.
Dr. Hale, London.
Dr. Harvey, Southport.
Dr. Mackechnie, London.
Dr. Mahony, Liverpool.
Dr. E. Madden, Birmingham.
Dr. Moore, Liverpool.
Dr. Moorhouse, Bowdon.
Dr. Moir, Manchester.
Dr. Nicholson, Clifton.
Dr. H. Nankivell, Bournemouth.
Dr. Procter, Liverpool.
Dr. Pope, London.
Dr. Perkins, Manchester.
Dr. Powell, London.
Dr. E. Roche, Norwich.
Dr. Russen, Manchester.
Dr. Ricketts, Wigan.
Dr. Rowan, Barnsley.
Dr. Roth, London.
Dr. Gordon Smith, Liverpool.
Dr. Simmons, Cheltenham.
Dr. Skinner, Liverpool.
Dr. Wyld, London.
Dr. Eubulus Williams, Clifton.
Dr. C. Wolston, Croydon.
Dr. W. Wolston, Edinburgh.
Dr. Christopher Williams, Belfast.

ON THE CAUSES OF PROFESSIONAL OPPO-SITION TO HOMŒOPATHY.

By Alfred C. Pope, M.D.

Gentlemen,—The circumstances under which we meet together to-day are both unusually interesting and unusually important. This year—1877—is the jubilee year of homœopathy in England. Fifty years have elapsed since the first notice of homœopathy appeared in a British medical periodical. Fifty years have passed away since the first physician who practised homœopathically in this country settled in the metropolis. And now after fifty years of bitter hostility on the part of the majority of the medical profession towards the therapeutic doctrine, upon the truth of which we have insisted, and towards those who have adopted it as the chief basis of their drug-prescription, we have, during this year, heard, for the first time, the public expression of a desire that our exclusion from consultation and discussion with the majority should no longer be demanded. A fitting utterance this for a year of jubilee!

While heartily sympathising with the desire that the obstructions which have been presented to the scientific culture and professional advancement of those physicians who have investigated and adopted the doctrine of homœopathy should be removed, that every encouragement should be given to *all* members of our profession to engage in scientific research; while admitting that what has been termed the "reunion" of the profession is a matter of deep importance to every member of it; I nevertheless feel that if this so-called "reunion" is attempted to be purchased by attenuating or obscuring any of those principles for which we have contended—principles of the truth of which we have daily experience—or if the language in which our overtures are couched is susceptible of justifying the insinuation that we are ready to acknowledge that we have overrated their importance—the effort will and ought to prove abortive; while if, in order to conciliate opponents, we cast ungenerous reflections upon those who, during these fifty years have devoted their time and energy to develop and promulgate homœopathy, we shall be exposed, and rightfully exposed, to the contempt, the well-earned contempt, both of the profession and the public. Tactics such as these will never lead to "an honourable peace founded on mutual respect."

The feeling that the breach should be closed which for half a century has existed between physicians who practise homœopathically and those who do not admit that they do so, has been growing, and that somewhat rapidly, of late years. It is a feeling that all well-wishers of medicine, all who would that our profession should be worthy of the honour it expects to receive, will anxiously encourage. Most sincerely do we all desire the "reunion" which has been suggested, most gladly shall we welcome the "peace" which has been "asked" for. But just in proportion as this reunion is desirable, and this peace is something to be welcomed, do I esteem it as of the highest importance that no misunderstanding should anywhere exist either as to the therapeutic views we entertain, or as to what we regard as the cause of the estrangement we have always deplored.

This question of reunion is one which, in my opinion, ought to be, and, if it is to result in any good, must be treated as one independent of any opinions we or others may hold upon scientific subjects. Professor GAIRDNER, of Glasgow, never uttered a greater truth in medical ethics than he did when he said, "No one has a title to say to anyone else, I insist that you believe so and so, or I will disown you as a professional brother." The British Medical Association has said to the members of the profession, We insist that you do not believe in homœopathy or consort with those who do—if you do, we shall disown you as professional brethren; and this threat has been carried out.

As in therapeutics the removal of the cause of a disease is the first step to its cure, and as for the removal of the cause its recognition is a necessary preliminary, so here in dealing with the *homœophobia*—as it has been termed—which characterises so large a proportion of our medical brethren, I shall avail myself of the opportunity I have of addressing you to-day in an endeavour to point out what I conceive to be its *cause*.

First of all, I will ask your attention to the conclusions others have arrived at on the same point.

Dr. WYLD has told us that "the adverse and intolerant treatment we had hitherto met with from the profession arose in a great measure from the bad example shown by HAHNEMANN and his early disciples of an extreme and intolerant sectarianism on their part towards that medicine which, however powerless for good it might have become, was yet the result of 4,000 years' experience and thought." Again, he says that HAHNEMANN was "the first to give offence." "That the views of HAHNEMANN were extreme and intolerant." That for the measures of injustice which have been meted out to us by our non-homœopathic brethren, we "have, to no inconsiderable extent, had" ourselves "to blame." That it was the conduct of homœopathically practising physicians that "naturally led to those reprisals on the part of orthodox medicine which culminated in the resolutions of the British Medical Association in 1851." Pretty broadly has Dr. WYLD intimated that in openly acknowledging that we believed in homœopathy we had "traded on a name;" that by the use of the word homœopathic in our literature, our societies, and our dispensaries, we had, in an *ad captandum* manner, repulsive to all right thinking members of our profession, succeeded in drawing to our "consulting rooms the patients of other men." By others we have, in various terms, beer told that we have wilfully separated ourselves from the profession.

Now, Gentlemen, I maintain, and I hope to be able to prove to you to-day, that the opposition which has beer persistently levelled against homœopathy in this country during the last fifty years has had nothing whatever to de with the alleged intolerance either of HAHNEMANN or his early disciples; that, in the professional conduct of those medical men who have been the means of making homœopathy known throughout the length and breadth of the land, and its influence felt throughout the entire practice of medicine, there has been nothing to justify the ostracism which has existed; that in admitting our faith in homœopathy, in taking the only means at our disposal to make its advantages known, we have not been justly chargeable with personal advertising; and that, until a few years ago, it never occurred to anyone so to regard the designation of our journals, societies and dispensaries; neither has the separation which has occurred been wilful on our part

On the contrary, the exceptional position we have beer

placed in has been due wholly and solely to the ignorance
of the profession regarding well nigh all concerning homœopathy, to the persistency with which by the publication of
palpable caricatures of it, as though they were genuine
representations, the medical press has sustained, and
indeed almost compelled this ignorance. The history of
homœopathy in this country from 1827 to 1877 is full of
evidence that an almost entire absence of knowledge
respecting homœopathy, combined with many utterly
erroneous and not a few equally absurd notions concerning
it, lies at the bottom of all the opposition it has met with.
Hence, Gentlemen, it is to the removal of this ignorance,
to the substitution of facts regarding homœopathy for the
assumptions which have been entertained respecting it,
that we must look for the reunion which has been sought,
for the peace which is to bear fruit in mutual respect, in a
mutual anxiety to discover and follow truth. Therefore it
is that I look upon the excellent lecture* recently delivered
at Birmingham, at a meeting of the medical profession in
that town, by our Secretary, Dr. GIBBS BLAKE, as being
far more conducive to the restoration of good feeling, to the
renewal of professional intercourse, to the establishment
of professional association in scientific research between
homœopath and anti-homœopath, than I can the letter of
Dr. WYLD to Dr. RICHARDSON, offering "terms of peace."

In 1827 in the *Edinburgh Medical and Surgical Journal*
appears the earliest reference made to homœopathy in this
country. In the July number of that journal, Mr. JOHN
EDWARD SPRY published a paper entitled, *An Outline of
the Homœopathic Doctrine, or the Medical Theory of
Hahnemann.* It presents a brief, but tolerably accurate
definition of homœopathy. It is a simple statement. No
evidence is brought forward in favour of it, no argument
is offered against it. Mr. SPRY contents himself with
declaring the doctrine to be visionary, and consoles his
readers with the assurance, that "however ingenious the
theory may sound, it appears too ridiculous, in its application, ever to obtain supporters on this side of the Channel."

In the October following, the *Medico-Chirurgical Review*,
edited at that time by Dr. JAMES JOHNSON, in noticing

---

* *A Lecture Addressed to the Medical Profession on "The Place of
the Law of Similars in the Practice of Medicine."* By J. GIBBS BLAKE,
M.D., &c. Birmingham: Cornish Brothers, New Street. London:
H. Turner and Co., 77, Fleet Street. 1877.

Mr. SPRY's ESSAY, expressed a very decided opinion respecting homœopathy. It is denounced, *in limine,* as the " GERMAN FARCE "—this definition being emphacised by being printed in capital letters ! " The gist of the homœopathic system," says the writer, " may be easily and briefly stated. Hippocrates broached the fanciful doctrine that a disease should be cured by things that induce a state opposite to that of the disease, *contraria contrariis curantur.* The German professor strikes out on a path diametrically opposite, and maintains, that disordered actions in the human body are to be cured by inducing action of the *same kind,* but only slighter in degree, *similia similibus curantur.* The doctrine of antipathy had much foundation, both in reason and fact. Thus the burning heat of fever naturally suggests cooling drinks and cool air; constipation calling for purgatives ; diarrhœa for astringents ; soporose diseases demand irritation ; irritation calls for sedatives, &c. But what shall we say to homœopathy? Do venesection and purgatives induce diseases resembling pneumonia, ophthalmia, hepatitis, and other inflammations, when these are cured by the above means ? The idea is preposterous."

In connection with this extract from Dr. JOHNSON's *Review,* it is interesting to know, what I have reason to believe is perfectly true, that Dr. QUIN, who in 1827 commenced the practice of his profession in London, had, three years previously, mentioned the subject of homœopathy to Dr. JOHNSON, and by him had been urged to continue his inquiries into its merits, and having completed them, to write an article for the *Review* upon it. Dr. QUIN, as we all know, did pursue the investigations he had commenced ; and on his return in 1827 he informed Dr. JOHNSON of the conclusions at which he had arrived. The request for an article was not renewed ; but on the contrary, the brief, hasty, and ignorant denunciation of homœopathy, from which I have quoted, formed the only reference to it that Dr. JOHNSON allowed to appear in his *Review.*

I cannot but regret that Dr. QUIN made no attempt to correct the erroneous impression Dr. JOHNSON's article was calculated to produce. Had he succeeded in doing so an *impetus* to the spread of homœopathy among members of the profession could not fail to have resulted ; while, had he been refused a hearing, the determination to keep the profession in the dark upon all concerning this important therapeutic doctrine, which has ever marked the periodical literature of our profession, would have been even more conspicuous than it is now.

During the next few years, homœopathy appears to have attracted but little attention from the medical profession. Dr. QUIN was frequently absent from England, and, when at home, was actively engaged with the duties of a large, fashionable, and successful practice; while little or nothing was done to introduce the subject to the notice of the profession. During 1838, or somewhat later, Dr. UWINS, a physician in good repute at that time, was induced by his brother, the well-known artist, to make the acquaintance of Dr. QUIN, and from him to learn something of the new therapeutic method. About the same time, Mr. KINGDON, a surgeon in extensive consulting practice, had his attention drawn to homœopathy by gentlemen engaged in business in the city, who had heard that they could be cured more rapidly, and certainly more pleasantly, by homœopathy than by the measures ordinarily employed. An introduction to Dr. QUIN was followed by enquiry, and enquiry by clinical experiment. Dr. UWINS and Mr. KINGDON, being convinced of the value of homœopathy, desired to make it known to their professional brethren. They endeavoured to do so, the latter in a paper read by him at the *London Medical Society* in November, 1836, and the former, in one he presented a few days later, to the *Westminster Medical Society*. The discussions reported in the *Lancet* of that date are extremely interesting. Mr. KINGDON's paper, while showing some knowledge of homœopathy, evinced a serious desire to understand it more thoroughly. In concluding, Mr. KINGDON said, "after what I have seen, or, if you please, what I fancied I have seen, I feel that it is the duty of every medical man to look into it (*i.e.*, into homœopathy), for it is certain, either that a number of cases do better without medicine than with, or that these unimaginable doses of carefully prepared medicine do impress the nerves so as to influence the actions of life." In the discussion, which followed its reading, Mr. DENDY, Mr. HEADLAND, and Dr. LEONARD STEWART, said that they thought the subject to be one which it was the duty of the Society to investigate carefully. Dr. UWINS, with his larger experience, was more pronounced, and expressed his belief, that one day homœo-

pathy would be a universal creed. On the other hand,
Dr. JAMES JOHNSON ridiculed the whole subject; and
Dr. WHITING, the President, following in the same strain,
asked if any member had ever seen a case of peritonitis,
pleuritis, or pneumonia, treated with infinitesimal doses of
aconite—a query to which there was no response. Dr.
UWINS, in the course of his remarks, had stated that he
felt sure the day would come when lancets would be super-
seded by *aconite*, and when they would consequently
" rust in their cases." A prophecy—in twenty years later
literally fulfilled—which drew from Dr. CLUTTERBUCK, the
eminent physician of the London Fever Hospital, the
observation that " there was something shocking in an old
and respected member of their Society anticipating a time
when lancets would rust in their cases!" At the conclusion of the discussion, a resolution was proposed
by Dr. CLUTTERBUCK, and seconded by Dr. JOHNSON, to
the effect that homœopathy was unworthy of consideration. It was, however, withdrawn on the understanding
that the subject should never again be mooted in the
Society.

During the same month a Dr. BUREAU RIOFFREY read a
paper on *Hahnemannism* at the *Westminster Medical Society.*
He entered into no examination of HAHNEMANN's views,
but occupied his time in denouncing them as a tissue
of absurdities, offensive to common sense and contrary
to observation. Dr. ANTHONY TODD THOMPSON, when
speaking on this occasion, regarded the whole subject as so
visionary that it could only be treated with ridicule.
Mr. COSTELLO said that in his opinion all practitioners
who adopted homœopathy were actuated in so doing by
sordid motives, and sordid motives only. A fortnight later
and Dr. UWINS read, at the same society, a paper on the
Modus Agendi of Medicines. In it he supported the homœopathic principle, within certain limits, and in a tentative
manner. He referred to " a thing called an editorial
article, in a bungling medical journal, written by some one
who considered homœopathy and small doses to be one and
the same thing. Small doses," Dr. UWINS argued, " were
important, nay glorious incidents, arising out of homœopathic research, but they were no more homœopathy
itself than might was always right." Dr. ADDISON was
the chief speaker at the close of Dr. UWINS' paper, and
he asserted that the followers of HAHNEMANN were either

persons only fit for lunatic asylums, or such as were influenced merely by sordid motives.

The next incident, which points to the mode in which homœopathy was received by the profession, occurred two or three years subsequently, when the late Dr. EPPS sent to the *Lancet* reports of a few cases in which he had used *arnica* with advantage. These were inserted; but on Dr. EPPS, who was a personal friend and political partisan of Mr. WAKLEY'S, sending other illustrations of disease cured by homœopathically selected medicines—they were returned with a note from the sub-editor, stating that the publication of such cases was, owing to the avalanche of letters they had received protesting against those that had already appeared, impossible

In 1846, the late Sir JOHN—then Dr.—FORBES published in the *British and Foreign Medical Review* that well-known article, "Homœopathy, Allopathy, and Young Physic." This was the first, and even now it is, with, I believe, but two exceptions, the last occasion on which homœopathy was adversely reviewed by one possessing some degree of theoretical and literary acquaintance with it.

With the tone of this article, with the manner in which the character and labours of HAHNEMANN were reviewed, no homœopathist could do otherwise than feel satisfied. Nay more, the appearance of a critique, evidently written in a spirit of fairness, gave us hope that at last we were likely to be met in a manner which would compel honest enquiry —an enquiry which would ensure the triumph of truth over error. But what was the result? Sir JOHN FORBES was driven from his editorial chair; he had ventured to criticise homœopathy with a degree of fairness and honesty which the medical profession of that day refused to endure.

Finally we arrive at 1851, when the *British Medical Association*, in a series of resolutions, denounced homœopathy, all who practised homœopathically, and all who co-operated professionally with those who did so.

Such, Gentlemen, has been the manner in which the medical profession has received the doctrine of homœopathy. The discussion of the subject was burked from the outset; all enquiry into it was not only discouraged, but any enquirer rendered himself liable to be represented by his medical neighbours as a person who was either partially demented, or a mere seeker after filthy lucre, as one regardless of the lives and interests of those who confided in him. It was impossible to bring the *rationale* of homœopathy before any medical society; any public examination of the results accruing from the practice of homœopathy on a large scale was out of the question; the medical journals were closed to any mention of it, save in terms of ridicule or of misrepresentation.

Every professional avenue through which enquiry might have been instituted, and some definite conclusion have been arrived at, was barred. To impress a knowledge of homœopathy upon the profession through the profession, had been, by the profession, rendered impossible.

Had all this arisen through any unprofessional conduct on the part of the representatives of homœopathy in this country? For several years Dr. QUIN was the only physician practising homœopathically in England. No physician was ever more scrupulous in deferring to the susceptibilities of his medical brethren than was Dr. QUIN. So much so was he, that he has incurred the charge of not having been sufficiently active in making known the important truths of which he had the honour and the responsibility of being the British pioneer. Dr. UWINS and Mr. KINGDON both resorted to medical societies to expound homœopathy; Dr. EPPS sent the reports of his cases to the leading medical journal of the day; a wealthy banker offered, through Dr. WILSON, to bear the expense of filling a number of empty beds—beds empty for want of funds—in St. George's Hospital, that homœopathy might be publicly tested; but all was to no purpose.

Gentlemen, there was no intolerance among the representatives of homœopathy. None was charged against them; they took no unprofessional methods for making known those therapeutic principles of which they were, in proportion as they felt their value, bound to disseminate the knowledge. They had no secrets; they professed no mystery; they desired above all things to communicate every information regarding the mode of practice they had learned the value of. The great body of the profession refused to afford them any opportunity for doing so. Was then homœopathy to be excluded from all discussion because the profession would not listen? Was Dr. EPPS to be silenced because the *Lancet* would not permit him, through its pages, to communicate to his professional brethren the results of his clinical observations? Were the sick poor to be denied the advantages of homœopathy, because a physician who practised homœopathically was prevented from holding office in a hospital? I trow not! If homœopathy could not be examined before the usual tribunals in matters medical; if it could not be made known through 'the ordinary professional channels; if it could not be illustrated in established charities—other *media* must be found. Hence arose the pamphlet setting forth what homœopathy was; hence came the handbook of domestic medicine; hence came the homœopathic periodicals; hence came the Homœopathic Dispensary; hence came the Homœopathic Society; and hence has come—and that none too soon—the London School of Homœopathy. Had homœopathy been enquired into in the same way as other topics of professional interest were examined, no institutions of this kind would have arisen. It is, indeed, very doubtful whether the word " homœopathist "—from the continued use of which some, who owe a large proportion of their power to do good from homœopathy, would seem now to shrink—would ever have come into general use. Assuredly it would not have done so to anything like the extent it has done.

When in 1851 the British Medical Association prohibited its members from practising homœopathy, and from associating with those who did so, we were in possession of what study and experience had convinced us was a therapeutic truth of the highest importance; a truth, the importance of which was rendered all the more conspicuous by the scepticism, which prevailed among nearly all the more experienced physicians of the day respecting the value of drugs in the treatment of disease; a truth, the importance of which was rendered yet greater still, by the fact that it provided a means for the discovery of specifics—the very kind of discovery in which Professor ALISON and others had declared the hope of therapeutics to lie.

By acting upon this great therapeutic truth, the practice of medicine, from being exclusively traditional and empirical, became one based upon a strictly scientific foundation. Our drug remedies were chosen upon a principle the validity of which the records of the past, and the experiments of recent times had proved to have so wide a range as to have been, not without reason, regarded as universal. The mode of studying the properties of drugs was one that was independent of tradition, was exact in its method, and fruitful of information to an extent no plan previously proposed could boast of. We were also convinced that, in order to cure, the necessity for disturbing the organism by inducing the physiological action of drugs, injurious in proportion as they were powerful, did not exist. That, when prescribed homœopathically, medicines were best exhibited in a form, and in a quantity, which precluded the possibility of any injury being done to the patient.

These, Gentlemen, are the principles, of the truth of which we were convinced, of the immense importance of which we were well assured. These were the principles that the *British Medical Association* ordered us to abandon; for entertaining which the Association threatened us with every species of annoyance. We were not, indeed, excommunicated from the profession—though efforts were made to bring influence to bear upon the College of Surgeons in London, and the College of Physicians in Edinburgh, to remove the names of such of their members as were known to practise homœopathy. Thus to separate us from the profession to which we had been admitted, thus to cut us off from it was found, however, not to be within the power of any man, or any body of men.

In the presence of these facts, what was the duty of those who had seen reason to believe that homœopathy was true? Were they, in meek submission to an intolerant majority (a majority utterly uninformed on the doctrines they denounced), were they, haunted by the fear of being regarded as quacks, and represented as impostors, to abandon principles they knew to be scientifically sound, principles they had found to enable them to control disease, so much more completely than any they had been wont to rely upon, principles that were known and felt by all who trusted them, in their professional capacity, to be of the highest advantage to them? NO!—a thousand times, NO! The duty of all who believed in homœopathy then was perfectly clear. In proportion as they believed in these principles; in proportion as they valued them; in proportion as efforts were made to prevent their being testified to; in proportion as obstacles were placed in the way of their development and elaboration, was it their duty to extend the knowledge of them; to cultivate them; to place their advantages within the reach of the sick among the poor. Prevented, as I have shown we were, from performing these obligations through the ordinary channels of professional literature, professional societies, and established hospitals, we were compelled to issue periodicals, which should direct special attention to the great therapeutic question, for the due setting forth of which we had, by virtue of our knowledge of its importance, become responsible; to institute societies in which these principles might be discussed, their range of operation gauged, the best method of putting them in practice ascertained; and to open hospitals and dispensaries in which their application might be illustrated. And I thank God, Gentlemen, that those upon whom lay the responsibility of doing all that could be done to advance the interests of therapeutics in the direction of homœopathy, were equal to this their responsibility, that they did not allow the fear of the taunt, the unjust taunt, of proceeding in an unprofessional manner, to prevent them from substantiating the accuracy and worth of these principles. They did make known, by book and pamphlet, what homœopathy was, and how homœopathy might be practised; they did meet together, and, by discussing questions of pathological, therapeutic and clinical interest, endeavour to add to the knowledge already acquired, and correct the observations they had made; they did establish hospitals and dispensaries where homœopathy might be studied, and the poor might receive the advantages to be derived from this therapeutic method.

In so working, in thus developing homœopathy, no intolerance was shown, no unprofessional conduct exhibited. Nothing was done which a true sense of duty did not compel to be done—nothing, that the obligations we undertook on admission to the profession, did not render it incumbent upon us to do. To have done less would have been to hide our talent in the earth, at the bidding of an intolerant, and, so far as homœopathy is concerned, an ignorant majority. Had we done less, we should have been unworthy of the profession to which we belonged, should richly have deserved all the hard things that were said of us, all the ignominious epithets which were so unceasingly hurled at us.

Further, the propriety of the course taken has been abundantly justified by its fruits. The practice of homœopathy, though in a scientific manner limited to a comparatively small body of medical men, empirically pervades the whole practice of medicine. Compare the treatment of disease to-day, with that which prevailed five-and-twenty years ago; compare the text-book of Materia Medica of 1877 with that in use in 1850; compare the method of studying the action of drugs pursued a quarter of a century since, with that which is taught to-day; compare the amount of medicine prescribed a few years back, with that which is ordered now! In each direction the principles we have contended for, which we have taught and exemplified in practice, are seen to be operating. And recollect, gentlemen, all this has been accomplished by those very means which are now represented as "Trading on a name," as accounting, more or less, for the antagonism we have met with, as having "naturally led" to the "reprisals" to which we have been exposed.

I have said enough, and more than enough, to prove that those members of our profession who have investigated and adopted the homœopathic method of drug selection, are not in any way responsible for the exclusion from professional privileges with which we have been visited. That here and there individuals practising homœopathy may have offended against the *lex non scripta* of professional ethics I do not doubt; but that as a body we have done so I utterly deny. To use the words of the late Sir John Forbes—" that there are charlatans and impostors among the practitioners of homœopathy cannot be doubted; but, alas, can it be doubted any more that there are such, and many such, among the professors of orthodox physic?" I assert, without fear of contradiction, that medical men practising homœopathy have conducted themselves with the fullest regard to professional decorum, and they have done so in spite of much provocation and many temptations to the contrary.

From the sketch I have now given of the manner in which homœopathy was received by the profession, from the determination which has been evinced to admit of no enquiry into the doctrines expressed by that word, we must conclude, that the efforts which were made to stamp it out were made, not on account of any intolerance, any sectarianism on the part of those who expressed their belief in it, but solely because the profession were unaware of what was understood by homœopathy, because of the misrepresentations—misrepresentations never allowed to be corrected—which the medical press has never wearied of circulating regarding it, and all who practised it.

And thus, notwithstanding that the principles regulating drug selection, the study of drug action, and of dosage, upon which we have so strongly insisted as true, are daily

observable in the general practice of medicine, the same
impediments to professional association as those in force
five-and-twenty years ago are present to-day. Notwithstanding that the most popular works on therapeutics
bear testimony—silent testimony—to the truth of homœopathy, this method of prescribing is still denounced in very
much the same terms as those which have been employed
since first it was introduced into this country. Why this
is so, is an enquiry worthy of some consideration.

True it is, that those practitioners who have adopted the
suggestions of RINGER and PHILLIPS are, to all intents and
purposes, daily practising homœopathy in a large number
of cases. But it is unfortunately also true, that they are
unaware of the relation subsisting between the physiological
action of the drug they use, and the pathological condition
they prescribe it to remedy. They know nothing of the
source whence Dr. RINGER and Dr. CHARLES PHILLIPS derived
the therapeutic hints they have communicated to them.
They know nothing of the principle which first pointed to
them as remedies in the very conditions in which they use
them. The statements made known to them through
these channels they accept without enquiry, just as they
have ever been in the habit of accepting similar statements
regarding the remedial properties of drugs, viz., on the
ipse dixit of some favourably reviewed author.

Hence, I conclude, that the continued opposition to those
members of the profession who openly admit that they
derive their drug-therapeutic knowledge from homœopathic
research is due now, as it was fifty years ago, to ignorance
of what homœopathy means.

Of late years we have been assured that the opposition we
now encounter from our medical brethren is owing to the
fact that we are known by a distinctive name. We are
called "homœopathists," and we admit that we are
"homœopathists." Yes, we admit that we are homœopathists. In so doing we acknowledge that we regard the
law of *similars* as that therapeutic principle which is best
adapted for the selection of drugs to cure disease. We do
not, however, assert that it is the only principle on which
it is necessary for the physician to act in the treatment of
every case that comes before him, or in every part of every
case ; neither do we deny that disease is ever cured by
remedies prescribed on other principles.

Within the last month the *Lancet* has told us that when we "give up a profession of the homœopathic system," that is, when we are prepared to allow that homœopathy is not true,—we shall no longer be homœopathists: and, *à fortiori*, so long as we do acknowledge the truth of homœopathy are we homœopathists—and that I admit is correct enough. We are also told that when we cease all connection with homœopathic societies, hospitals, and journals, we shall cease to be homœopathists. That I deny. Whatever may be our connection with societies, hospitals, and journals, if we select our drug remedies on the homœopathic principle we are homœopathists. But, did we discontinue our connection with such institutions, we should cease to have any opportunities of making homœopathy known. And that it is, and not professional reunion, which the *Lancet* so earnestly desires.

As I have already stated, the frequent and general use of the word "homœopathist" is traceable to the fact that homœopathy has never been allowed to be a fitting subject of enquiry through the ordinary channels for the investigation of professional questions. Had the practitioners of homœopathy not been excluded from medical societies, journals, and hospitals, the principles they have striven to promulgate, and as I have shown, have so considerably succeeded in forcing upon the practice of medicine generally, would never have come so prominently under the notice of the public as they have done. Doubtless, some physicians would have rejected the homœopathic theory, while others would have adopted it; and probably enough the latter would have been known as homœopathists, just as the followers of BROWN and BROUSSAIS were known as Brunonians and Broussaisists; but this distinction would have been restricted to professional circles; no ostracism would have ensued in the case of the homœopathist, any more than it did in that of the Brunonian or the Broussaissist of the past. Dr. WYLD, on a recent occasion, said "it has been argued that the followers of BROWN and BROUSSAIS were not ostracised because they enrolled themselves as Brunonians and Broussaisists. This reply," continued Dr. WYLD, "is ingenious, but not logical; because they never attempted to open Brunonian dispensaries, and self-supporting Broussaisistic medical institutes. They never traded on their name, and never by their name drew to their consulting-rooms the patients of other men." The reply to this, not very generous, rejoinder is, that the followers of Brown and Broussais were never on account of their therapeutic views excluded from filling posts at hospitals and dispensaries. Had they been so, doubtless institutions, where they could have put their views to the test of public practice, would have arisen, and having arisen, would have been known by some designation more or less indicative of their *raison d'être*.

It is, then, because of the opposition the profession has ever shown to the investigation of homœopathy, because of the hindrances to enquiry it has ever placed in the way of the enquirer, because of the determination with which all who practice homœopathically have been prevented from filling public appointments in existing medical charities, that such as are now known as homœopathic have been so called.

It is the professional opposition to homœopathy which is responsible for the word homœopathist, not the word homœopathist which is responsible for professional opposition to homœopathy.

Now, however, we are told that if we can get rid of the words homœopathist and homœopathic, the chief obstacle in the way of our being eligible for posts of professional honour, as well as for admission to professional societies, will be done away with.

' So far as a certain number of medical men are concerned, I believe that this proposition is true. But, as regards the great majority, we have no evidence that our abandonment of these terms would in any way influence them in doing us justice. How, I would ask, are we to speak and write of the doctrine signified by the word homœopathy without using that word? The word homœo-therapeutics has been proposed as a substitute; well, Gentlemen, "a rose by another name would smell as sweet," and possibly the word homœo-therapeutics might come into general use in a few years. But it lacks the historical significance of that we now employ. And yet more, this discussion about a word, a name, this dispute as to whether we shall express our meaning in seventeen letters instead of in ten, strikes me as somewhat puerile, as worthy only of the schoolmen four or five hundred years ago—and not of the medical profession of our time.

Then, again, with reference to the word homœopathist, we find that throughout all time the advocates of certain doctrines in science, certain principles in politics have ever been known, and I expect ever will be known, by a name derived from the word used to define such doctrine or principles. Such a consequence seems to me both natural and inevitable. If, then, we are determined to maintain the thesis that homœopathy is true, we cannot avoid being regarded as homœopathists, any more than the devotees of spiritualism can escape being termed spiritualists. Hence, Gentlemen, I do not see how the disuse of the words homœopathy and its derivatives is to be accomplished, so long as the opposition to homœopathy continues in the shape it has assumed during the last half century.

As I said just now, it is the opposition to this method of drug selection which has led to the very general use of the word, and it can only be by the cessation of this form of opposition that the word can ever cease to be so generally employed as it has been.

Another excuse for the ostracism we have had to endure is found in the hypothesis that we are "sectarian," that homœopathy is "sectarianism." This word sectarian— what is it but a term of reciprocal reproach bandied to and fro between opposing parties.

Originally, the word " sect " signified a following, taking its derivation from the verb *sequor*. It is first met with among the Grecian schools of philosophy. THALES, for example, was the founder of the Ionic sect of philosophers ; that is to say, the pupils he taught at Miletus in Ionia adopted his method of philosophising in preference to that of PYTHAGORAS, the founder of the Pythagorean school or sect. Again, among theologians the word sect is used to denote a "separation," a "cutting off" being derived in this instance from *seco*. Upon certain more or less understood principles, one body of Christians takes the title of "Church." Others, whose enquiries have led them to regard as erroneous some of the doctrines taught by the "Church," have united themselves together for the public worship of God. They have separated themselves from, have cut themselves off from what is called the "Church," and formed themselves into what is regarded as a sect.

Is this word sectarian applicable to us as homœopathists ?

1st. Are we followers of HAHNEMANN ? In the sense in which Dr. MATTHEWS DUNCAN is a follower of HIPPO- CRATES, or Dr. WILKS of SYDENHAM, so are we followers of HAHNEMANN. HAHNEMANN enlarged our knowledge of therapeutics, precisioned our method of drug selection, defined the best, the only really satisfactory plan of ascertaining the action of drugs. We have gladly availed ourselves of his researches; and, yet more, have warmly acknowledged our obligations to him. But, on the other hand, we have neither done, written, nor said anything implying that blind faith in all that HAHNEMANN ever wrote or taught, which the disciple of THALES or PYTHAGORAS would have deemed it his duty to have exhibited as a member of his sect. By none have the doctrines HAHNEMANN taught been so rigidly scrutinised, as by those who have most earnestly contended for the truth of homœopathy! While it is undeniable that some of his earliest followers, under the influence of that immense force of character which HAHNEMANN ever exhibited, did, in obedience to the stern demands he made upon them for unhesitating confidence in every theory he broached, accept as true much that investigation has since shown to be untenable hypothesis; it is equally true that it has been by other of his disciples that the fallacies into which he was betrayed were most completely exposed.

We accept so much of HAHNEMANN's teaching as experience has proved to us to be sound, unhesitatingly rejecting whatever in it we have found to be erroneous.

In the sense, then, in which the word was anciently used, we cannot be said to be sectarian.

2nd. Again, have we cut ourselves off from the profession, have we separated ourselves from it as the Church of England is said to have done from that of Rome, or the Baptist from the Church of England? Certainly not. A proportion of the members of the profession, having formed themselves into societies, have resolved not to associate with us. It is not we who have refused to have any intercourse with them. We are ready and willing to co-operate with them in their efforts to promote the science and art of medicine, are anxious to learn from them, and discuss with them, the results of their observations; to communicate to them, and carefully examine the criticisms they have to offer upon such conclusions as our experience may have led us to form.

The sectarianism which prompted the exclamation "Stand by, for I am holier than thou," is confined to that portion of the profession which rejects, without examination, all that HAHNEMANN ever taught, and rejects it main-

because he taught it. The sectarian position, I conclude, is therefore inappropriately assigned to homœopathists. We are not the blind, unreflecting followers of any man. We are within, not without the pale of the profession of medicine.

Though the form which characterises the opposition to homœopathy to-day, varies little, if at all, from that which it has taken during the last fifty years, the tone in which homœopathists are spoken and written of is far less acrimonious and abusive than it was. Ere the influence of homœopathy had been felt in this country, those who had adopted it were described as "lunatics"; when it had grown to be a power, they were set down as "knaves or fools;" now that the teachings of HAHNEMANN have become more or less generally absorbed into the practice of medicine, we are pushed aside as "sectarians."

The causes of the opposition are the same now as they ever have been—an almost total absence of any information of what is meant by homœopathy; an absolute refusal to ascertain what is understood by it; an unrelenting determination to suppress, by every possible means, every opportunity presented of learning what it really is, and how it can be practically tested.

All the many and various means which have been used to "stamp out" homœopathy, have not prevented this great principle from gaining an ascendancy in practical medicine, it will now be impossible to suppress. Silently, secretly, and amid many apparent denials, homœopathy is, for all practical purposes, largely taught in the medical schools of this country. True, it is taught after an empirical manner only; this, however, is but the prelude to its being taught scientifically. Gentlemen, it is to the work we, and others who have preceded us during the last fifty years, have done, that it is owing that homœopathy is taught empirically—it depends upon those of us who are now actively engaged in making daily use of the truths that have been handed down to us, that homœopathy shall be taught scientifically. Having obtained so much, shall we now remove our hands from the plough? Shall we rest satisfied with the empiricism of SIDNEY RINGER—or shall we press onward until that empiricism receives the thoroughly scientific interpretation, of which we know it to be susceptible? If we believe that in homœopathy are contained those advantages we in the past have asserted that it pos-

sesses; if we are mindful of the reputations of those who
have preceded us in originating, sustaining, and developing
homœopathy; if we are conscious of the elevating, and
intellectually satisfying character of a scientific therapeutics,
and of the uncertainty and disappointing features of a
therapeutic method that is merely empirical; if, in a word,
we feel that in promoting the progress of homœopathy, we
are performing our duty to science, to our profession, and
to the public—we shall never cease to maintain, to illustrate,
and to enforce by every means in our power, those medical
doctrines, of the truth of which the public avowal has
brought upon us so much unmerited obloquy.

Gentlemen, there is no room for compromise; there is
no cause for compromise; nay more, I feel perfectly
assured that, were we ready to sacrifice, in however small
a degree, any principles, of the verity of which we are
assured, for the purpose of conciliating those who differ
from us, with the view of acquiring certain professional
advantages from which we are now excluded, to the end
that we may pursue our several professional careers with
greater ease and comfort to ourselves—we should in so
doing draw down upon us the contempt of those who have
arrayed themselves against us—and, what is worse, we
should most thoroughly deserve to be despised by them.

If homœopathy is not true; if it can be shown that the
doctrine of similars is a false doctrine; that the study of
the physiological action of drugs on the healthy, is not the
best way of ascertaining the properties of such substances;
if it can be proved that a small dose of a homœopathically
selected medicine is not adequate to the end for which it is
prescribed—let no one, who has hitherto believed that these
principles are true, shrink from demonstrating and admitting what he now feels to be his error. But, so long as we
do believe that evidence in abundance has demonstrated
the reality of these principles, so long as we have reason to
believe that they are not only true in themselves, but
collectively present us with a therapeutic method of far
higher value to physicians than any that is taught at the
present day—so long, I trust, shall we persevere in declaring their truth, persevere in teaching their practical application, persevere in pressing them upon the attention of the
profession.

While earnestly, constantly, and courteously contending
for and propagating the doctrine we have professed to

believe, we must also insist upon the restoration of those rights and privileges of which, by the arbitrary vote of a tumultuous meeting, we were six and twenty years ago unjustly deprived.

While I freely admit that there is no professional obligation imposed upon one physician to assist another in the way of consultation, I deny that any body of men has a right to say to its fellows, You shall not meet in consultation, on any plea whatever, those who believe in such or such a doctrine or theory of medicine; still less has such a body the right to enforce its mandates by threats of deprivation of professional status in the event of their not being complied with.

Again, I acknowledge that it is perfectly within the scope of any society to decline to receive any member of the profession it may regard as objectionable; but no society can justify the refusal of its membership to any one on the ground that his therapeutic views differ, however considerably, from those of the majority of its members.

Equally unjust, and still more detrimental to the interests of science is it, that the avowal of a belief in therapeutic doctrines, which have not been enquired into by the majority of the profession, should suffice to prevent a physician from holding a public medical appointment.

On the removal of the disabilities which exist in these directions we must continue to insist, until the good sense, right feeling, and increased information of a majority are sufficiently in the ascendant to do us justice. From all that has recently come to my knowledge I am glad to be able to believe that this period is far less distant than the past history of homœopathy might lead us to suppose. We look for their removal on the ground that every member of the profession is bound to act according to *his* experience and knowledge, and not according to the experience and knowledge of his neighbour. Medicine is not a completed science, is not a perfected art—very far is it from being either. There is no finality in homœopathy. One of the most thorough-going homœopathists, and one of the best instructed physicians who ever practised homœopathically, has said : " The law itself may be but a stepping stone to a wider generalisation, which shall one day embrace both it and something beside, and which shall make clear some things which we now see darkly."—*Homœopathy the Science of Therapeutics*, p. 27. Much have we corrected in the teachings of HAHNEMANN, and doubtless, as observations multiply, as the various avenues by which research is made increase in number and become more thoroughly explored, will the doctrines we at present hold be more accurately formulated, what of error attaches to them be removed, and principles of a yet higher and more far-reaching character be discovered.

In accomplishing this great work every member of the profession must take a part. Homœopathist and the opponent of homœopathy must work together, each animated with but one purpose, each rising superior to the views his previous investigations have led him to confide in, each prepared to regard impartially the new lights evolved by deeper and yet deeper research, both together striving with energy and zeal for the development of truth, for the fixing yet more securely still the foundations of that science on which is built the most beneficent of all the arts—the Art of Medicine.

At the close of the address Dr. HUGHES, of London, moved that a vote of thanks be accorded to Dr. Pope. In doing so he said, I have much pleasure in proposing that a very cordial vote of thanks be passed to Dr. Pope for the able address he has just read to us. (Applause.) Evidently from the applause he has received throughout, he expresses the sentiments of this body, and it is most important at this crisis of our history that an eloquent, forcible and frank expression of opinion should go forth to our medical brethren. Such an address has been read to-day, one which is well fitted to take rank with the series of able addresses we have from time to time heard from the chair at our Congress, and I am sure we shall all join heartily in this vote of thanks. (Applause.)

Dr. GEORGE WYLD, London, seconded the motion. He said, I beg leave to second the vote of thanks to Dr. Pope for his able address. I think Dr. Pope's address has been a manly exposition of homœopathy, and as a *resume* of the historical view of homœopathy—it is a very interesting and valuable paper. While thanking Dr. Pope for his excellent paper, as he has made my letter—so to speak—the text of it, perhaps you will allow me to say a few words. Dr. Pope has said that in my recent efforts for peace in the profession, I have used expressions which seem ungenerous. Gentlemen, I should be very sorry, indeed, to have used such expressions, and I trust a want of generosity is not my characteristic. (Applause.) Dr. Pope has also quoted one of my expressions, where I said that the intolerance of Hahnemann naturally led to the intolerance of the allopathists. I maintain that proposition. I say that Hahnemann was intolerant in his old age. He enunciated the theory that all diseases could only be treated by similars ; and I say that that proposition of Hahnemann was sectarian and intolerant, and naturally led to intolerance on the other side. Now I want to explain the definition of "naturally." I have corresponded with Dr. Pope in reference to that word, so that he knows what my view of it is, but I should like you, gentlemen, to know it also. When I say naturally I don't mean justifiably. Take the illustration of two children playing together ; they quarrel, and one pulls the other's hair, and the latter having a stick in his hand knocks the former down. (Laughter.) I say that is a "natural" exhibition of temper on the part of an ill-tempered child, but I don't justify that exhibition of temper. (Laughter.) And so it is with the opponents of homœopathy. I would have liked, while Dr. Pope was generous, that he had given me credit for a little more generosity. These efforts to produce peace in the profession I believe have produced very great results. (Dr. Clifton —"Disasters.") Mr. Bradley, of Manchester, assures me that my letter has been the cause of bringing about, in Manchester, a very kind feeling on the part of the allopathic practitioners towards the homœopathic. I have not another word to say, but I beg of you to believe that in anything I have done in this matter I have had the good of homœopathy in view. (Loud applause.)

The motion according a vote of thanks to Dr. Pope, for the address he had delivered, was then carried unanimously.

The PRESIDENT, in acknowledging the compliment, said, Gentlemen, I thank you very much for the kind manner in which you have received my paper, and for the attention with which you have listened to it. With regard to the remarks of Dr. Wyld, it is perhaps better for me to say nothing about them, because discussion does not take place on this paper, but I may say that I took Dr. Wyld as I found him in print, and I put the interpretation on the words to which they " naturally led," one which everybody, I think, has put upon them except Dr. Wyld himself.

The PRESIDENT : Before I call upon Dr. Drysdale to read the paper of which he has given notice, I will read one or two letters which I think it may interest you to hear. One is from a gentleman who formerly occupied the chair I now fill, namely, from Dr. Sharp. He writes as follows :—

" Rugby, *September 12th*, 1877.
" My dear Mr. President,

"Many thanks for your invitation to meet you at the Congress once more, and many regrets that it is not in my power to do so.

"Of the seven Congresses which have been held since their revival, I have attended six, and have read a paper at five; so that it is to be hoped that in this as well as in other ways I have done "what I could" to fulfil my duty to the sick while I was able.

"Give me leave, however, to salute you, and all who meet you at Liverpool, and to express the wish that you will have a friendly and happy meeting, and also to express an earnest hope that the differences which seem at present to exist among you will be discussed with mutual consideration and forbearance, and be brought to a successful issue.

"It is certain that there is something in homœopathy worth contending for, and not only worth contending for, but also worth bearing shame and reproach for. (Applause). And this shame and reproach will assuredly be wiped away. (Applause.)

"What that something is I have given all diligence to discover, and, with all respect to others, to explain. Part of it is expressed in three general facts or laws, namely—

"The local action of all drugs. The contrary action of certain ranges of larger and smaller doses. The existence of an intermediate range of doses possessing the action both of the larger and the smaller doses, or which have primary or secondary actions opposite to each other.

"These three general facts have been discovered by following the example, first set us on a large scale by Hahnemann, of experimenting with drugs in health.

"In the use of drugs as remedies these laws are more or less interfered with by *predisposition*, and by *disease*. To the investigation of this interference time and thought and experiment would gladly have been devoted, had it pleased God to have continued my life and health one or two years longer. Others will undertake this. A clearer knowledge of this part of the subject will contribute, in the future, to the better relief of our fellow creatures suffering from illness.

"May I conclude by expressing the hope that the members of the Congress will retain an affectionate remembrance of

"Their sincere friend and fellow labourer,

"WILLIAM SHARP."—(Loud cheers.)

The PRESIDENT then said: Then I have also a letter from Mr. Charles Grayson, which I will now read.

"THE HOMŒOPATHIC DISPENSARIES OF LIVERPOOL.

"I regret that, owing to a sharp attack of illness, I am deprived of the pleasure of dining with you this evening, the more so because I had promised to say a few words respecting the Homœopathic Dispensaries (Liverpool), of which I am chairman. The following particulars of their work, however, will probably be interesting to the members of the Congress.

In 1856 the average weekly attendance was 895, and the total for the year, 19,565. In 1866 the figures were 669 and 34,808 respectively ; in 1876, 1,251 and 65,085. These numbers are still on the increase, giving, I think, a conclusive reply, so far at least as Liverpool is concerned, to the recent mendacious statement in the *Lancet*, that homœopathy was dying out of sheer inanition. (Hear, hear.) Perhaps few laymen have had the same opportunities as myself of comparing the relative results of allopathic and homœopathic treatment. During a period of nearly thirty years I have been a member of committee of one or other of our largest medical charities, and am so still, as well as a regular visitor, the result of my experience being a firm and solemn conviction that the homœopathic system is as much superior to the allopathic as the latter is to no treatment at all. In proof of this assertion I may add that the average number of times patients require to attend our dispensaries is only about half that at the general medical institutions."

Dr. MOORE, the Vice-President (in the chair), expressed his regret that the time for the morning meeting having expired, it was impossible to discuss the very interesting paper for reading which they felt so much obliged to Dr. Hughes. In the name of the Liverpool Homœopathic Medico-Chirurgical Society he then invited the members to luncheon in an adjoining room. At the conclusion a vote of thanks to the Society was proposed by the President, carried by acclamation, and acknowledged by Dr. Skinner.

ON THE DOUBLE AND OPPOSITE ACTION
OF DRUGS.

By J. J. DRYSDALE, M.D.

I PROPOSE to confine myself to some remarks on the bearing of the double and opposite action of drugs on the attempted explanations of the homœopathic principle by Dr. Sharp and Dr. Hughes.

Our first difficulty in dealing with Dr. Sharp's thesis is to define what it is he can with propriety claim as his thesis. He states, " That the action of small doses of drugs is in an opposite direction to that of large doses was first suggested as a general fact or law at the Congress at Leamington in 1873." ¦This is not sufficiently definite, for the fact that large and small doses have an opposite effect has been known from time immemorial, and it is a necessary part of the Brunonian theory, and of Hahnemann's theory, and has been specially dwelt on and carried out in its completeness in explanation of the homœopathic mode of cure by Fletcher and his followers. What Sharp must claim if he claims anything at all in this field is that the double and opposite actions already known are in fact absolutely different actions with no causal connection : and that the homœopathic cure is to be accounted for by the simple antipathic or antagonistic action of one absolute effect on a diseased state, resembling the other or opposite effect. It was added by Dr. Sharp that it is only the effect of small doses which can thus be used. Now as this does not follow from any admitted causal relation between the two opposite effects, it is a mere dictum or dogma, for why should not either of these absolute effects antagonise the other ? Here at once we have a serious objection to the whole theory, and one which places it in theoretical consistency far below either the Hahnemannian one of reaction of the organism, or the Bruno-Fletcherian one of exhaustion of irritability : for both of these imply a causal relation between the double and opposite actions, and the small dose is a necessary corollary from them : and a plain and palpable explanation both of their double and opposite nature, and their power of cure is found in the changed state of the organism, induced by the operation of the drug. The established fact that a moderate dose of a stimulus, whether general or specific, is an excitant, and an excessive or too long continued action of the same is followed by depression and exhaustion, and in fact a state just the opposite of the former, is a reasonable mode of accounting for the fact of the apparently double and opposite action. And the equally well-known fact that when the dose was from the first excessive the depressant effect will practically be represented alone, gives us in addition a clue to the apparently different absolute actions of different classes of medicines without the hypothesis that either the same drug may possess two absolutely different and opposite actions as asserted by Dr. Sharp, or that all drugs have only one absolute action, although this may be either primarily excitant or depressant as maintained by Dr. Hughes. It must be admitted that there is a specific difference between excitants and depressants, but it cannot be admitted that that is such as to contradict the fact that all positive agents have an excitant action liable to be followed by a depressant one, and therefore the absolute action is primarily excitant alone, although from the change it induces in the organism, that may be practically so managed as to manifest a double and opposite action. Now it has always been known that as the small dose is excitant, that action may be exhibited most prominently, and even maintained for a time without much perceptible appearance of the secondary or opposite effect if small doses are given, while if an excessive one is given at once, we have hardly anything but the secondary exhaustion. But there is an intermediate single dose, by which both the double and opposite effects may be seen, *i.e.*, first the one and then the other in succession, without any fresh dose. Hence when Dr. Sharp's assertion of the double and opposite absolute effects were brought forward, he was reminded of the double and opposite actions of one and the same dose, thus plainly showing that there did not exist any such double absolute power in the drug, but the apparent effect depended on the change induced in the organism itself; for even if different sizes of dose had such opposite action, it was simply impossible that the same dose could display at the same time such power. In his essay of March, 1877, Dr. Sharp tells us that on the principle of studying one thing at a time, the time had then come for his studying experimentally that point. The principle of studying one thing at a time is certainly unexceptionable, but one is tempted to wonder why the previous essays were published before this essential point was studied. At any rate we are glad he has at last studied the subject in its completeness. But we were hardly prepared for this statement of the result :—

" In 1873 it was shown that small doses, having action in certain fixed directions, occupied a chamber of their own, and that large doses, having actions in directions opposite to those of the small doses, occupied another chamber. I have now the pleasure of showing that the same key which opened those chambers, opens the door of the vestibule which connects those two chambers together. The middle doses have two actions— the first action is that of the small doses, the second action is that of the large doses. These are the doses about which so much has been said as having primary and secondary or alterna- ting actions. The nearer this middle dose is to the small on- which produces but one action, the more will its action partak- of the action of the small dose, and the less of the action of th- large dose, and in like manner the nearer it approaches to th- large dose, the less will there be of the action of the small dos- and the more of that of the large; finally the action of the sma- dose will disappear, and there will be but one action, which *i* that of the large doses.''

This is a very surprising mode of stating matters. We had been under the impression that we had all been in the middle chamber all along, and had handed out the key to Dr. Sharp, who was wandering outside in the dark and cold! It really is quite superfluous to go into detail to show how in this sentence the whole theory of absolute action is abandoned, as every one will see at once who has not a pre-conceived idea to support.

With respect to some of the objections to the so-called antipraxy of Dr. Sharp, which he assumes to have refuted in his essay of March, 1877, he asks, Where are the numerous exceptions where no opposite has been demonstrated? Well! do tea or coffee produce sleepiness and mental hebetude in small doses, or in any way except as the secondary effect of the over-stimulation caused by full doses? With respect to specific irritants of seat, what is the opposite action of small doses of *belladonna*, whereby it cures erythema, erysipelas, eczema, and other skin diseases? What is the opposite small dose action of irritants of the stomach, which in full dose cause nausea, &c.? Or, take the whole Materia Medica of Hahnemann and choose almost any of those admirable groups of a few signs, which, in a single sentence, give us the clue to the true homœopathic cure of morbid states, and tell us what the opposite states would read like if produced by a smaller dose, and above all show as experimentally that such have been produced. This brings us to the few experiments made by Dr. Sharp, and on which, no doubt, he founds the statement that the opposite action in small doses has been shown with every drug which has been tried. These have been analysed by Dr. Hughes in the April number of the *Monthly Homœopathic Review*, and I fully concur in the conclusion that they are quite insufficient to establish the statement founded on them. And I will add, that besides the insufficiency of them in number to establish the individual fact in each case, and the false inference drawn from a few even correctly stated facts in such complicated functions as are dealt with, Dr. Sharp overlooks the fact that it requires different amounts of the same stimulus, or drug, in order to act at all on different organs, and, therefore, different and apparently opposite effects have, in many instances, nothing to do with double and opposite action on a particular part : e.g., a moderate light stimulates the retina and reflexly the filaments of the third pair, causing contraction of the pupil, while a stronger light produces contraction of the orbicularis, and even, in some cases, the whole complicated operation of sneezing. So with drugs, a small dose of aconite or of atropin, and many others, will increase the action of the inhibitory fibres of the par vagum and slow the heart, while a larger one will stimulate the accelerators, or the cardiac muscles themselves, and quicken the heart's action. A small dose of tart. emet. will act on the bronchial membrane, while a larger one will be an emetic, and so on. Now, all these things complicate the matter excessively, and deprive the few isolated results given by Dr. Sharp of their whole value as decisive of the question. Furthermore, each of these separate stages of action must have its double and opposite action. For instance, the natural contraction of the pupil in reading, or looking at small objects, will cease to be brought about if the stimulus is too long continued, and dilatation will ensue, even though the same amount of light falls still on the retina. In the inhibitory stimulation the slowing will be followed by a quickening of the pulse, by the fatigue of the regulating action constantly required, and which had been over pressed, &c., &c.

Before, therefore, we can demonstrate an absolute two-fold effect of any drug, all these things which depend on merely relative circumstances in which the organism itself plays a part, must be taken into account and probed to the bottom in every case.

We see thus the futility of the attempt to explain cure by a merely two-fold apparent action, without regarding the inner processes in which this result is brought about. We have, first, the different degrees of susceptibility to drugs, like other stimuli, possessed by different organs and parts of our most complicated organism. By this means an ascending scale of effects may be produced by different doses of the same drug, and these differing widely in accordance with the specific function of the organ affected. Many of these effects may be quite opposite in the resulting phenomena, and thus double and opposite effects may apparently lie in the absolute nature of the action of the same drug. There is, then, the necessary exhaustion which follows over excitement of the same organ or part, producing an exactly opposite apparent result of the action of large and small doses, as well as these two stages exhibited in the action of single doses. On these two principles can be explained all the known double and opposite actions of large and small doses, without the hypothesis of Dr. Sharp that drugs have two absolute and opposite actions in large and small doses.

At the same time, I admit that the bare principle of a primary excitation, followed by a secondary collapse or exhaustion, is insufficient, *per se*, to explain numerous and important *qualitative* changes in the living matter produced by the exciting causes of disease, and by drugs, and which are met by the homœopathic law of cure. Here, I think, we had better still rest that law on an inductive basis, viz., that it simply expresses a general fact, established by a sufficient number of experiments, which cannot be said of the professed explanation, that in all cases the remedy has the power of producing an exactly opposite action in some dose on the healthy body, as Dr. Sharp maintains. In diseases of mere *plus* and *minus* of vital action, on the other hand, the Brunonian theory of excitement and exhaustion gives an *a priori* explanation of the double and opposite action of drugs, and of the homœopathic law of cure.

My third objection to Dr. Sharp's theory was as follows:

"A definite quantity of the antagonistic medicine will always be as necessary for the cure as for the production of the disease, and that quantity will be the same, and even greater, than what is necessary to produce the effect in health, *e.g.*, if two drops of *aconite* (pure tincture) quicken the pulse, and $^{1}/_{26}$ of a drop slow the pulse in health, it will always require at least $^{1}/_{26}$, if not more, to antagonise a quick pulse of disease."

To this Dr. Sharp replies:

"The contrary action of the small dose applies, not to a single dose, but to a series of doses, *e.g.*, from a small quantity of the pure tincture or crude drug to the third dilution or trituration, the millionth part of a drop or grain, thus leaving scope for the different susceptibility of the patient, and the varying cases of disease."

This means, I presume, that all doses below $^1/_{20}$ of a drop in the illustration *tend* to show the pulse, although only that dose has been found to do so in the healthy body. This is an assumption to begin with, but besides that we must have some definite point fixed if there is to be any meaning in the expression small and large doses. I maintain, therefore, that if the theory of antagonism is true, you must give the dose known by experiment to be capable of producing that antagonism. The same objection does not apply to the *relatively* antipathic action of the homœopathic medicine on the Fletcherian theory. Here you have to fill up a want, and you do not know how small a quantity may be required to fill that want, and restore vital action to health, whereas you do know that a very small excess of excitation will still further depress the lowered action in which disease consists. This also enforces my fourth objection, which Dr. Sharp professes not to understand, and characterises as muddying the waters like a cuttle fish :

" Fourthly, if the antagonistic theory were true, it would still be primary, and therefore liable to be merely palliative, requiring to be constantly kept up and in increased doses, being liable to the exhaustion and secondary opposite state of all primary actions."

It seems, however, plain enough that if all preternatural excitations are followed by a corresponding exhaustion or depression, the slowing of the heart from excitation of the inhibitory nerves by $^1/_{20}$ drop must be followed by exhaustion as above seen, just as much as the more palpable action of a purgative is by an opposite state, and so on. The same must also be the tendency of all primary actions, whether the opposite actions of small and large doses depend on their affecting different organs or not.

Thus we see generally that all attempts to *explain* the action of medicines require knowledge of the intimate pathology of disease and drug action ; and, in fact, all attempts to explain on an empirical principle are vain. This applies also to Dr. Hughes's objection to Fletcher's explanation, viz., that even supposing it applied to inflammatory diseases, still that is only a part of diseases, and, therefore, it fails as a universal explanation. This is granted, and for my part I would look for no explanation until the pathology of the disease is understood. Nevertheless, I think Dr. Hughes has underrated the extent of the application of the principle of secondary exhaustion of irritability as used by Fletcher in respect to inflammation and diseases dependent on it or allied to it. In the first place Dr. Hughes says, that on this theory the same objection applies as to Sharp's theory, viz., that the antagonistic action of the small dose during the cure is liable to the exhaustion which follows all over-stimulation, and it will consequently soon be followed by the said opposite stage of exhaustion, so that any amendment will only be temporary, and will be similar to that of opiates in sleeplessness, purgatives in constipation, &c. Now this shows a misapprehension of Fletcher's theory altogether. In that, mere vascular *plus* and *minus* of action is not the whole case, but the vascular or parenchymatous tissue is understood as the seat of nutritive and vital activity in general, and the qualitative change produced by the exciting cause of disease is always held to be of importance equal to the seat in determining the specific nature of the remedy. An inflamed part is looked upon as one in which the total vital process is in a state of secondary depression of a special character, even though the product of secretion or nutrition is increased in quantity. What then is the best remedy? It is a stimulus such as corresponds to the quality required, and just enough in quantity to bring the vital action up to the line of health. If such is given there is no secondary depression after it, for two reasons—first, because the stimulation was not raised *beyond* the line of health ; and, secondly, which is the most important, because cure itself depends on restoration of the living matter ; and that is like all vital processes, an irritation or a process to which an appropriate *stimulus* is essential. The homœopathic remedy therefore is presumed to be the efficient agent of the *regeneration* of the living matter of the part, and thus, so far from exhausting, as all excessive stimuli do, it actually restores the nutrition and finally the functional irritability of the diseased part. This is a very different view of Fletcher's theory from that given by Dr. Hughes, and it is one which I have followed out and endeavoured to adapt to the newer pathology opened up by the protoplasmic theory of life in my lectures at the London Homœopathic Hospital, in 1876, and which were listened to by Dr. Hughes. The subject is, however, far too complicated for the views of anyone to be fully appreciated by once hearing a lecture, so I must defer entering on it fully till I have the opportunity of completing the subject treated of summarily in these two lectures. In the meantime, I may say that Dr. Hughes and I agree much more nearly than he seems to think, and that he follows my views very closely. I have fully admitted the merely *secondary* character in importance of the vascular disturbance, and even that of the vaso-motor nerves, while the *primary rôle* in the action of stimuli and the exciting causes of disease is played by the protoplasm of the tissue itself; and also laid stress on the fact that the qualitative change in the protoplasm is to be regarded as probably more important than any merely functional quantitative disturbance. But at the same time I still uphold the opinion that there must be a primary stimulant stage in the action of all positive agents, however complicated with the more important qualitative change; otherwise it is impossible to explain the homœopathic cure with depressants. This in fact Dr. Hughes is compelled to admit—

"There are no opposites to many concrete diseases, or even to many symptoms, such as pains. But there are, or must be, opposites to the morbid state or states which lie at the bottom of these surface indications; there must be some reverse direction to that which the abnormal change has travelled, and along which the part may be conducted back to health. This thought seems as true as it is subtle."

I am still inclined to think that in those qualitative disturbances which have no opposites, and which are among the most important indications for homœopathic cures, there is some anterior subtle process in the vital activity taking place in the latent stage; and which may be one of exaltation of the germinal faculty incapable of displaying itself before the secondary stage comes on. This latter is the first we become cognisant of through symptoms, but it is still a secondary stage, and in reality one of germinal depression and degradation. If the truth of the process be not somewhat of this nature, what is the latent stage in such diseases? And how otherwise can we imagine a homœopathic cure possible, seeing that all vital processes are far too complicated to be represented by mere physical vibrations which might extinguish each other as in the instance of light waves, and which theory I am glad to see Dr. Hughes has at last abandoned.

Discussion on the foregoing paper having been invited,

Dr. HUGHES spoke as follows :—As Dr. Drysdale has referred in his interesting paper to some remarks I made on the subject in the lectures I delivered at the hospital last January, I venture to say a few words in reply to his observations. I gladly accept Dr. Drysdale's statement that he does not feel that I differ much from him. Indeed, I should feel unhappy, and that I was wrong, if I differed very much from him, and I am very glad to find that I am more on his side than otherwise. (Hear, hear.) At the same time, the point on which I do feel I differ from Dr. Drysdale is this, that I cannot see my way to regarding the symptoms of depression so often manifest in the action of drugs as always resulting from previous over-stimulation. When I see a drug like *gelseminum* administered in quite moderate doses produce immediate depression, first of the muscles of the eyeball and then of the other muscles throughout the body, I cannot suppose that there has been any primary latent stage of stimulation upon which this depression is a secondary exhaustion. There must be long continued stimulation to produce this. Finding no such condition, I venture to submit the hypothesis that depression is primarily present, and until more evidence is brought to show that this depression is a secondary exhaustion, I must continue to think so. I was aware that Dr. Drysdale in the lectures he delivered last year made some modifications in his previous putting of Fletcher's views, but not having had the pleasure of reading them in print afterwards, I derived but a general impression to that effect. When I read them I shall derive a great deal more information, and I have said in one of my lectures that Dr. Drysdale would now probably not put it in that way. I think we shall all derive instruction from reading Dr. Drysdale's paper which he has just read to us. We have got something by hearing it read ; we shall learn still more when we come to read it for ourselves. (Applause.)

Dr. DYCE BROWN (London): I was extremely glad to have had the pleasure of hearing the interesting paper of Dr. Drysdale. I had not the opportunity of hearing his lectures in London, a circumstance I much regretted, but from Dr. Hughes's lectures I gathered that Dr. Drysdale had a good deal modified his views on the action of drugs, and I am very glad to hear, from the paper read to-day, that Dr. Drysdale essentially agrees with those who believe in the opposite action of drugs in large and small doses. Dr. Hughes speaks, in his lectures, of the double action of drugs being one explanation of homœopathy, and then afterwards gives as a really different theory the reverse action of large and small doses. It strikes me that is a pity, because they are essentially the same. Those who speak of drugs having opposite actions, mean as a rule, that those two opposite actions are developed by large and small doses respectively, and it is only because the particular fact of large and small doses having this reverse action has been brought out more prominently of late, that it would have the appearance of being a separate explanation from the former. If we suppose that one action is developed by the small dose and the opposite action by the large dose, there must be a point between the two where the one passes over into the other. Now, it is quite possible that the medium dose Dr. Sharp speaks of may in the first place produce the stimulant or primary action, but being rather too near the point of balance, may be immediately followed by the secondary or large dose action; so that on this explanation we see, I think, the truth, the correctness, of Dr. Sharp's view. This point that Dr. Sharp brings out—viz., that the medium dose may produce both actions—is in fact only a corollary from the fact that a drug produces two reverse actions, and that these two reverse actions are produced by small and large doses respectively. You come to a point where the balance is easily over-topped, and you thus have, first the primary action and then the secondary action from this *one* dose. Of course, I agree entirely with what Dr. Drysdale points out—and it is very important to consider in discussing these theories of the action of homœopathic remedies—that some organs as well as some persons respond more quickly to one dose of a medicine than other organs or persons do to the same dose: consequently it is impossible to make a mathematical statement of what is a large dose and what a small dose, or what dose will infallibly produce the primary and what the secondary action. You can only approximately name the dose which, in the majority of cases will produce the primary or the secondary action. Everyone knows that there are some persons so susceptible to the action of certain medicines, that an extremely minute dose will produce an effect which could be produced in other persons only by a very large dose, so that it would be impossible to state accurately what is for every person or for every organ a large dose and what a small dose. And this consideration, I think, does away with one of Dr. Hughes's objections to the double action theory, namely, the impossibility of stating what is a small dose, or what given dose would invariably produce the same action in every individual. Dr. Hughes, in his lecture, falls (if I may say so) into a misunderstanding in reference to exhaustion following upon stimulation. He says that this exhaustion is simply an exhaustion of the system after the stimulus of the medicine—a want of power of vital reaction. That may be, but the exhaustion is not a want of power to respond to all stimuli, but—and this is important to keep in mind—only to the one stimulus which has produced the reactive exhaustion; and it is when we use *another* drug which has a similar action that the organisation re-acts, and is stimulated again to health by a small dose. Then, as to the important point mentioned by Dr. Drysdale, and also by Dr. Hughes in his lectures, that there is no opposite of pain, &c. I think the view which Dr. Drysdale brought forward to-day, and which he quoted from Dr. Hughes, is really the true explanation of the difficulty. In stating the theory of the double and reverse action of remedies in large and small doses, we only state it generally. We must make a number of sub-divisions, as it were, which may require a more minute explanation, but which are not exceptions, and all we can do is to offer a general theory which will, in a comprehensive way, explain the action of drugs. (Applause).

Dr. EDWARD BLAKE (Reigate) said: May I be permitted to remind members that although it may be a convenient form of expression to speak of "The action of drugs on the body" there is, apart from mechanical and chemical processes, no such thing in reality. It is therefore quite erroneous to speak of the action of a drug upon the body; it is the body which acts upon the drug, and to Dr. Sharp is due the credit of first clearly bringing this fact before us. To approach the subject from the other point is to look through the large end of the telescope, and then to wonder that we do not see the stars. Were it true that drugs really act on the tissues, we might, by a stimulant strong enough, haply raise the dead. This is an obvious corollary. There is no vital nor physiological force in such an inert mass of matter as a drug. If you put a drug into the body it is the vital tissues that re-act upon the drug. Thus, when we introduce five grains of tartar emetic into the human stomach, what takes place? The stomach takes immediate steps to rid itself of the irritating visitor. If it succeed through vomiting, there is no further result: if it fail, and absorption take place, then the various emunctories do their best to expel the unwelcome intruder. These efforts we call secondary actions. But on account of physiological relationships these efforts set up other disturbances known to us as tertiary symptoms. But in each case it is plainly the tissues acting on the poison, not the poison on the tissues. If I understand that Dr. Drysdale looks upon all drugs as primarily excitant, I cannot agree with him. It is no more true than that all diseases are primarily examples of depression. Take a drug with a very simple well-known action, the nitrite of amyl. Inhale a few drops, and the immediate effect is to cause vaso-motor paresis of the head and neck, with suspension of cardiac inhibition. The enormous accumulation of epithelial cells in the cases of a foul tongue, and of carcinoma, are examples of physiological activity in disease.

Dr. H. NANKIVELL (Bournemouth): I thought at first that I

was going to agree with what Dr. Edward Blake has just said, viz.: that we ought to discuss, not the action of the drug on the body, but the action of the body on the drug. But as a matter of fact his antithesis is a false one, for what we have really to consider is the action of the body under the influence of the drug. The instance adduced, that of the emetic action of tartar emetic is also unsuitable, as we cannot really look upon this as belonging to the primary, but to the secondary class of action, *i.e.* of re-action. The whole system is utterly depressed even before vomiting occurs. The same is true, though perhaps less markedly, of ipecacuanha. There must be some action of ipecacuanha on the stomach, which precedes nausea and emesis, and which therefore constitutes its primary stimulant action. I quite agree with what has fallen from Dr. Drysdale and Dr. Hughes, on the difficulty of conceiving an opposite to certain symptoms, pain and so on; but this difficulty is of course removed when we consider that there must be an opposite condition to that in which the nerve substance is when pain is felt. The difficulty is so far a verbal and not a real one. The reaction which we find the system to undergo in the presence of large doses of a drug, indicates to us the tract of tissue along which the same drug in small doses will act in a health-giving manner.

After a few remarks from Dr. MOORE (Vice-President)—

Dr. HUGHES was called upon to read the paper, of which notice had been given.

THE TWO HOMŒOPATHIES.

By Dr. RICHARD HUGHES.

IN the year of our Lord 1790, when the eyes of all Europe were fixed upon the rapidly evolving drama of which France was the theatre, there was a man in Germany intent upon far different matters. This man was a physician, in the prime of his life; his name was Samuel Hahnemann. An accomplished scholar, both in medical and general letters; a profound chemist; the friend of the illustrious Hufeland—he was utterly dissatisfied with the state of therapeutics in his day. One of its few bright spots seemed to him to be the treatment of ague by bark. He pondered much over the *rationale* of this curative action —so simple, so direct, so effectual. How could other medicines be so used? How could other diseases be so treated? It occurred to him to try the effect of this bark in health : he experimented on his own person. He found that it set up a fever very like that which it cured : the relation between its disease-producing and disease-curing properties was that of similarity. Its operation, therefore, was an instance of that " similia similibus " which Hippocrates had recognised as occasionally holding good, and whose claims to notice and possibilities of fruitfulness as a therapeutic principle had been noticed by more than one writer. If it obtained in the present notable instance, the inference was obvious. Was it not possible that other cure-work like that of bark in ague might rest upon such relationship between drug and disease—might have been got from it occasionally in the past, might be got from it continuously in the future ?

The question was a reasonable one ; but it was only a question. It had to be answered by observation and experiment—by reviewing the cures on record, and endeavouring to obtain new ones. Both were fully carried out. Hahnemann's *Organon* contains a copious list, drawn up from medical literature, of cures of disease effected by drugs which on no less satisfactory testimony were declared capable of causing similar conditions in the healthy. And his own experience, which was published from time to time, showed him that the power of similarly acting medicines was most undoubted, and their manner of curing greatly preferable. He now considered that the question had been answered affirmatively, the induction deductively verified; and, after suggesting it as a new method in 1796,* in 1806† he confidently put forth *similia similibus,* ὁμοιοπάθεια, as the cardinal principle of therapeutics.

He had not gone far, however, in working out the method, when he found that to do so properly required a much fuller knowledge of pathogenetics than that possessed at the time. Records of poisoning and over-dosing were not scanty; but they referred only to a small number of very active substances, and to the large and crude effects of these. A few typical and severe diseases were here pictured, and served for the early application of the method. But if it was to be carried out systematically, if the great variety

* In his "Essay on a new principle for ascertaining the curative power of drugs " (*Hufeland's Journal,* vol. II. See Dudgeon's translation of his Lesser Writings, p. 295).

† " The Medicine of Experience " (*Hufeland's Journal* for 1806. See translation, p. 497).

of morbid conditions which come before the physician were to be "covered" by corresponding drug effects, his knowledge of the latter must be indefinitely increased. With Hahnemann, to perceive this need was to feel the obligation of supplying it; and to feel the obligation was to fulfil it. He at once set to work to "prove" medicines on his own body and that of other healthy persons. In 1805 he had collected sufficient material of the kind for publication; and it appeared in his treatise *Fragmenta de viribus medicamentorum positivis*, which contains pathogenetic effects of twenty-seven drugs, obtained from the ingestion of single full doses.

But yet another step had been taken before this time. In prescribing medicines according to the rule *similia similibus*, Hahnemann of course gave them singly, and without the complex admixtures so common in his day. He administered them, however, in the usual doses. It is not surprising that his patient's symptoms, even though ultimately removed, were often in the first instance severely aggravated. It needs no argument to show that the ordinary doses of *arsenic*, against which even a healthy stomach needs to be shielded, would increase the irritation of one already inflamed—for which, nevertheless, the homœopathic principle would direct its being given. So Hahnemann found, and he reduced his doses accordingly. He did so by mixing his solutions or tinctures with definite proportions of some menstruum, as water or alcohol. The now well-known advantages of dilution came out in this process; and he found that attenuation could be carried to an extent hitherto undreamt of without the remedial power of the drug being lost. Accordingly, in his treatise on the *Cure and Prevention of Scarlet Fever*, published in 1801, we find him recommending *belladonna*, *opium*, and *chamomilla* in fractional quantities about equivalent to our third centesimal dilution, and defending his practice in *Hufeland's Journal* of the same year.

His complete method, constituted as now described, is set forth in the luminous essay entitled "The Medicine of Experience," published by him in the same journal for 1806. He there expresses his conviction that "as the wise and beneficent Creator has permitted those innumerable states of the human body differing from health, which we call diseases, He must at the same time have revealed to us a *distinct* mode whereby we may obtain a knowledge of diseases that shall enable us to employ the remedies capable of subduing them; He must also have shown to us an equally distinct mode, whereby we may discover in medicines those properties that render them suitable for the cure of diseases." To obtain this practically useful knowledge of disease, he maintains, we must abandon all speculation as to its essence, and content ourselves with a faithful and detailed picture of its manifestations, with their predisposing and exciting causes when these can be discovered. To ascertain the properties of medicines we must experiment with them on the healthy human body, noting the symptoms which result in their order and connection. We must then, if we wish a permanent and curative effect, administer in disease that drug whose effect most nearly resembles the morbid condition before us. To give, as is ordinarily done, remedies whose primary action is opposed to the diseased state we have to treat (as opium for sleeplessness), is mere palliation, and useful and necessary in but few cases. Finally, curative—because similarly acting—remedies must be given in comparatively small doses, lest excessive aggravation or undue reaction should occur; and so sensitive is the diseased body to their influence, and so purely dynamic their mode of operation, that doses of extreme minuteness—even to a millionth part of those ordinarily given—will often suffice for the end proposed. Such medicines, also, should be given singly; and the doses should not be needlessly repeated—each being left to work within its ascertained term of action. "If," he sums up, "as is not unfrequently the case when there is a sufficient supply of well known medicines, a positive remedy perfectly appropriate to the accurately investigated case of disease be selected, administered in a suitably small dose, and repeated after the expiry of its special duration of action, should no great obstacles come in the way (such as unavoidable evolutions of nature, violent passions, or enormous violations of regiminal rules), and should there be no serious disorganisation of important viscera, the cure of acute and chronic diseases, be they ever so threatening, ever so serious, and of ever so long continuance, takes place so rapidly, so perfectly, and so imperceptibly, that the patient seems to be transformed almost immediately into the state of true health, as if by a new creation."

I have brought these facts, dates, and quotations before

you as the best mode of exhibiting the first of the " Two Homœopathies " I am proposing to discuss to-day. The therapeutic method they describe presents several aspects for consideration.

I. It would, I think, be impossible for any unprejudiced person at the present day, standing in the light of the medical knowledge now enjoyed, and having some acquaintance with the doctrine and practice current in Hahnemann's time, to doubt that the reform thus proposed by him was a real and most beneficent one. Pathology, at the end of the eighteenth and the beginning of the nineteenth century, was a tissue of the most baseless hypotheses ; the therapeutics associated with it were a mixture of violence and confusion. Men were treating, as Hahnemann says, " unknown morbid states with unknown medicines," opposing fancies about the one to fancies about the other. In the stead of this most unsatisfactory system he proposed a method alike simple, intelligible, and innocuous. It consisted, as we have seen, in the following elements :—

1. The apprehension of disease by its symptoms, *i.e.*, as we say, by its clinical characters and history.

2. The ascertainment of the powers of drugs by experimentation on the healthy human body.

3. The application of drugs to disease by a principle which at least insured directness of aim.

4. The administration of remedies singly, instead of in complex admixture.

5. Their prescription in doses too small to aggravate existing troubles or cause extraneous ones.

Who can doubt the blessing it would have been to mankind had such a method been adopted when Hahnemann promulgated it ? Who can reckon the thousands that would have been saved from the murderous and poisonous doings universally prevalent in the days when bleeding and mercurialisation reigned supreme in therapeutics ? If the profession can go no farther with Hahnemann ; if even they feel his system imperfect for fully dealing with disease in all its forms, let them at least admit the vast advance it made upon the practice of its day, and its anticipation of much that is now regarded of unquestionable importance.

2. If this is the aspect which Hahnemann's original homœopathy has for the practitioners of medicine in general, it has no less important bearings for those whom adherence to his doctrines has formed into a distinct body.

The great majority of these, at least in the old world, have been converts from the recognised modes of practice. The expositions of homœopathy which have satisfied their reason, the cures which have established their faith, have been of the kind we have seen in the earlier writings and practice of its founder. They have accepted his method as he himself then conceived it—with its law of similarity, its provings of medicines on the healthy, its single medicine, and its small dose. But they do not think they need follow him in the rejection of the pathology of their day, as he in that of his. They find him allowing the existence of certain specific diseases, always essentially identical, for which fixed remedies can be ascertained; and they think that the advance of knowledge has identified many more of the same kind. They prefer to work the rule *similia similibus* with pathological similarities, where these are attainable; though in their default they thankfully use the comparison of symptoms. Accepting his statement that attenuation within the millionth degree hardly weakens the power of a drug for good, while it robs it of power to harm, they freely use such fractional quantities; but they rarely go beyond this limit, and as a rule steer closer to the other end of the scale. They do not mix medicines, but they often alternate them; and they supplement them more or less freely with such agents as—lying outside the range of pure homœopathic medication—are commonly called auxiliaries.

On the other hand, there are many—especially in America —whose views of homœopathy have been formed upon the later teachings of the master, of which I shall subsequently speak; and some of these have become more Hahnemannian than was Hahnemann himself. Among these colleagues of ours there has often displayed itself an intolerant spirit towards such as occupy the more independent position I have described above. My good friend Dr. Lippe, of Philadelphia, is a leading spokesman of this party; and he is at present breathing out threats of exclusion and excommunication against all who cannot subscribe to the full homœopathic creed, as he conceives it. Hard words are used of these, of which " mongrel " seems the favourite; and they are bidden to depart from the associations of the true followers of Hahnemann, and to profane the name of homœopathy no more.

Now I must protest with all my might against such narrowing proceedings. If men have, *in bonâ fide*, cast in their lot with us; if they have sought membership in homœopathic societies, have written in homœopathic journals, and worked in homœopathic hospitals and dispensaries; if they are content, out of devotion to the common cause, to co-operate with their stricter colleagues in spite of what they must consider their extravagances, surely the latter may be content to co-operate with them. All recognise the method of Hahnemann as their rule of practice; but some stop short at a certain stage of his elaboration of it, and think that beyond this limit it is unverified. Why should they not do so, if such is their deliberate judgment? And why should those who go farther vilify them and refuse their fellowship? Their practice is surely good practice as far as it goes—far superior to that of one who rejects the master's teachings altogether. Pathological similarity must be better than no similarity at all. It may be a pity to alternate, but it is less injurious than to mix. Auxiliaries may be used far more than is needful; but that is better than using nothing else.

And there is another important consideration to be submitted. Our best hope of winning converts to our system from the old school, and—which is better still—of obtaining its recognition from the profession as a legitimate therapeutic method, lies in the existence of the less distinctive homœopathy I have described. I believe it is vain to expect that unqualified liberty of opinion and practice which we demand. The day is far distant, to my thinking, when the members of medical societies and the readers of medical journals will take patiently the narratives of cures wrought by medicines selected because of minute symptomatic resemblance, and given in highly attenuated doses. But the occasional similarity of disease to drug, and the use of quantities of some fractional exiguity, are not so unfamiliar to medical men in general but that they may come to admit the possibility of such facts having a wider range than they before supposed. As a bridge over the gulf which divides the pure Hahnemannian school from that of modern medicine, I hail the existence of the more moderate homœopathy; and I have hope that upon it there will ere long be much passing to and fro between brothers too widely separated.

If I may give a word of counsel to those whose position I have now been surveying, it would be that they should follow up their own tendencies to the full by testing the capabilities of the mother tincture. Every now and then our brothers of the old school borrow a bit of practice from us, and (though sometimes the reverse is true) by giving larger doses than we have been accustomed to employ they outdo us with our own weapons. We cry out—this is homœopathy; we have been giving such a remedy for many years past. It is true; and yet we have never got such results from it. Recent communications on the use of *phosphorus, silica,* and the alkaline sulphides illustrate what I mean. It is a pity that we should leave such developments of our principle to those who oppose and reject it, when we are ourselves placed on such vantage ground for instituting them.

Hitherto I have been vindicating the legitimacy of the homœopathy taught by Hahnemann up to 1806 to be called by that name, and to be practised by professed acceptors of the system. But it is another question whether it is wise to pause there; and whether, in declining to follow him farther in the elaboration of his method, there may not be involved the neglect of a more excellent way.

It will be remembered that, when he wrote the *Medicine of Experience,* Hahnemann was only 52 years of age. In the ordinary course of things, supposing health and strength to ,be spared him, there were at least twenty years of work remaining to him ere age should begin to dim his perceptions and enfeeble his faculties. Such work, moreover, if less original than that of earlier life, ought to be more matured ; it should naturally contain the ripest fruits of a man's thought and observation. Now the twenty-two years which followed 1806 were those of Hahnemann's greatest activity as a practitioner and a writer. To this period belong the first four editions of the *Organon,* the first and second of the *Reine Arzneimittellehre,* and the first of the *Chronischen Krankheiten.* He is at Torgau from 1806 to 1810, and at Leipzic from the latter year up to 1821, in both enjoying large opportunities of practice; while from 1821 to 1828, at Cœthen, he has leisure to weigh the results of his experience, and to consider the problems of chronic disease presented by the sufferers of this kind who resorted to him there for treatment. It can hardly be doubted that whatever practical developments his method received during such a series of years are entitled to the most respectful consideration of those who accept that method in its essence.

There are four points, it seems to me, at which we discern a distinct advance and elaboration on Hahnemann's part at this time.

1. The first has regard to the principle on which selection by similarity should be carried out. Of course, wherever all the symptoms of a disease are reproduced in the pathogenesis of a drug, there is no difficulty; and where no drug has them all, *cæteris paribus* the one which possesses the greater number would have the preference. But Hahnemann found after a time that this *cæteris paribus* involved a good deal. A mere quantitative dealing with symptoms proved insufficient: they must, he saw, be weighed as well as counted; they must be treated qualitatively. And now, in seeking to appreciate the relative value of symptoms, he was led to two important conclusions: viz., that peculiar and unusual features, both of drugs and of diseases, should count for more than common ones; and that subjective symptoms—and especially those of the mind and disposition—should preponderate over such as were objective and physical. These views led him to attach less importance than he had formerly done to the disease—as nosologically or pathologically defined—which was before him, and to think more of the special sufferings of each patient. The result was the doctrine expressed in the phrase " individualisation," with the provisoes I have mentioned as regards the relative value of the symptoms present.

2. Up to 1806 Hahnemann had affirmed nothing more about the minute doses he had been led to employ, than that they hardly lost any of the efficacy of the medicines, while they robbed them of power to injure. But as he went on attenuating the more potent drugs employed, and as he applied the same process to substances comparatively or absolutely inert, he seemed to find a real development of power to be brought about. While all physical and chemical qualities disappeared, such as odour and colour, alkalescence or acidity; while all actively poisonous properties were lost,—the medicines gained a penetrating energy as curative agents hitherto unknown to him, and a ten-fold wider range of action. Some of them retained this even up to the 30th or decillionth dilution; others seemed to act

D

best in other potencies of the scale, as from the 2nd to the
24th ; very few were the better for no attenuation at all.
Hahnemann's second point, as made at this period, was the
positive efficacy of infinitesimal doses, as prepared according to his manner ; and their general superiority for the
homœopathic treatment of disease.

3. Hahnemann had already warned against the needless
repetition of doses. In the *Medicine of Experience* he
had advised the duration of each drug's action to be ascertained, and the dose to be repeated accordingly. In the
first edition of the *Organon* (1810) he substitutes for this
rule, as based on an uncertain quantity, another which
directed that the effects of a first dose should be allowed to
subside ere another (if necessary) was given. But, whether
by one plan or the other, treatment by single doses became
increasingly Hahnemann's ideal throughout this period. It
shows itself in every piece of practice he mentions, and in
every case he records.

4. It may be thought strange that I should name, as a
fourth step of advance on Hahnemann's part, his doctrine
of chronic diseases. It would be so, did I mean by so
doing to endorse the psora-theory, in its definite depend-
ence on the entity itch. Hahnemann was indubitably in
error about the pathological significance of this disease, as
was Autenrieth and many another before him and after
him. But, stripping his doctrine of all reference to this
particular disease, it remains, in its essential substance, a
most valuable induction from observation and guide to
practice. It is the affirmation that when disease becomes
chronic it is because of some morbid diathesis, some constitutional taint ; that the manifestations of this condition
must not be treated as if they were mere local affections ;
that even the ordinary internal specifics of homœopathy are
mostly insufficient for their cure, and must be supple-
mented by new medicines, of a profound reach and long
duration of action. It was this thought which led Hahnemann to introduce the so-called " anti-psorics " into
medicine—which enriched the Materia Medica with *alumina,
baryta, calcarea, graphites, kali carbonicum, lycopo-
dium, natrum muriaticum, platina, sepia, silica,* an
zincum.

What I have said about the distinction between the
speculative theory and the practical doctrine of chronic
diseases applies to much else in Hahnemann's work at th

time. His discovery of the efficacy and sufficiency of infinitesimals, for example, was mixed up with hypotheses of all disease being a derangement of the "vital force," and of a "dynamisation" effected in medicines by the processes of trituration and succussion to which he subjected them. All this may be rejected, as it generally has been rejected; but the discovery remains. It is thus with the various explanations he suggested of likes being cured by likes. Few receive these, but that *similia similibus curantur* is acknowledged by all his disciples.

Dismissing, therefore, the theories of the master as of doubtful value and only speculative interest, let us fix our attention upon him in the sphere of his true greatness, and consider his practical rules. I can but very briefly indicate the facts and arguments by which they have been substantiated. In so doing, I shall draw chiefly on the writings of our deeply-lamented colleague, Dr. Carroll Dunham. I feel that I am indebted to him for the conviction of the reasonableness of Hahnemann's fuller doctrine, as I was to Dr. Madden many years ago in respect of homœopathy generally.

1. And first, as regards individualisation. It is pointed out that while a few leading symptoms are sufficient to enable us to diagnose the nature of a case, and for this purpose we may ignore the rest, it cannot be so when we are to treat it by the method of similarity. Every appearance the patient presents, every sensation he experiences, every circumstance of amelioration or aggravation of his sufferings, must have some pathological basis, and must be taken into account in the choice of a remedy. Just in proportion as a drug has been found capable of causing all these concomitants and characteristics, will it be the rapid and certain cure for the case in which they occur. If it is otherwise, then, although the drug may have produced the actual disease, nosologically speaking, by which our patient is attacked, yet it may not be essentially homœopathic to the form of the disease now before us. It may be fever we are treating, and our medicine may be truly pyreto-genetic. But suppose that the pyrexia it causes is accompanied with great restlessness and anxiety, while the febrile sufferer under our care lies dull and listless, there is a lack of true homœopathicity between disease and drug. Adherence to the "totality of symptoms" would set us right, though we could not define or explain the difference between the two

cases. Again, our patient may have rheumatic joints; but
their painfulness may be either increased by continued
motion or the reverse. It is obvious that this distinction
must depend on the presence or absence of an inflammatory
condition of the parts, and must modify accordingly our
whole management of the case. But, even though we
knew not its significance, it would symptomatically guide
us to the choice between *bryonia* and *rhus* as the medicinal remedy.

The individualisation of each case, therefore, by the
totality of its symptoms, is the only certain method of
arriving at the true *simillimum* for it among medicines.
The more we generalise, and refer it to a class, the less
happy we shall be in our drug-selection for it. And,
should there be no drugs which correspond to it as whole
to whole, we should select that one which has caused any
peculiar features it may have, if we have good reason to
believe such remedy suited to the essential malady present.
Correspondence at such special points indicates a very close
relationship between disease and drug—far more so than if
common characters only were in question. Subjective
symptoms outweigh objective ones in such differentiation,
for they present less of the common than of the peculiar
features of a case. They are, moreover, of great value, as
being the earliest signs of disorder, before organic change
has begun. They constitute the main phenomena of a
malady at a stage in which it is still curable. I should
have liked, had time permitted, to have read an extract
from the "Address on Medicine," delivered by Dr. Russell
Reynolds before the British Medical Association in 1874,
enforcing the importance of subjective and mental symptoms. "We are bound to remember," he concludes, "that
there are many affections of which they furnish the earliest
indication, and there are not a few of which they are
throughout the only signs." *

2. And now as to the infinitesimal doses of this period,
by which I mean the dilutions from the 2nd to the 30th.
Evidence as to their positive efficacy, and as to the comparative inertness of many medicines unless thus attenuated, is abundant. The best proof of the latter point is
that in the practice of those who confine themselves to the

* See also Dr. Madden, "On Subjective Symptoms," in *British Journal
of Homœopathy*, xxvii., 458; and Dr. C. Dunham, in *Transactions of
N. Y. State Hom. Med. Society* for 1863, p. 68.

lowest potencies such remedies find little estimation or use. But a good deal of consideration is also due, I think, to the position of those who affirm the relative superiority of infinitesimal over more substantial doses. Besides Hahnemann himself, this class includes Dunham, Hoppe, von Grauvogl, and Chargé ; and—to some extent at least, as evidenced by their practice—Tessier and his foremost disciple Jousset. The first-named has shown, from the comparative statistics of Wurmb and Caspar's Hospital, that in pneumonia the action of the 30th decimal dilution was more certain and more rapid than that of the 15th and the 6th, while of the two last the 15th bore away the palm.† There is, moreover, in the general tone of those who employ highly attenuated medicines, a confidence in their remedies, an habitual sense of power and success, which cannot be disregarded.

3. Regarding the use of single doses, instead of a series of them, allowing the medicine thus given to act undisturbed for a reasonable length of time, I can say little at present. When we find so scientific a physician as Professor Hoppe maintaining the reasonableness of this practice, and a veteran like Jahr saying that his best cures have been achieved in this way, which—he truly says—was that of Hahnemann and all his disciples for the first twenty years of homœopathy, it merits our best consideration.

4. And, lastly, as to the doctrine of chronic diseases. I think there can be no doubt of the immense benefit which has resulted therefrom in the past, in the tendency it has given us to look to the possible constitutional origin of local and superficial affections, and to treat them accordingly. This view, and our possession of the "anti-psoric" medicines, has placed us on the same vantage-ground towards all such affections as, e.g., the knowledge of the syphilitic origin of many examples of nervous disease has afforded in general medicine. There is a tendency in a certain school of homœopathists to think of all disease as local, and to neglect medicines which have not an absolute physiological action dependent on dose. Such, for instance, would be the result of my friend Dr. Sharp's system, if it were allowed to embrace the whole sphere of therapeutics. We need, I think, to be recalled to Hahnemann's sounder standpoint if we are not to lose many of the triumphs over chronic disease which have hitherto waited on the steps of those who have adopted his method.

† See *Amer. Hom. Review*, vol. iv,

The second of our " Two Homœopathies " is now before us. It is that which Hahnemann taught and practised between 1806 and 1828. With the further modifications which took place subsequent to the latter date I have nothing at present to do. The new points which a man makes after seventy-four have no *à priori* recommendation in their favour ; and that the first of them here was the fixing the 30th attenuation as the uniform dose of all medicines, whether for provings or for curative purposes, does not invite us to welcome the rest. To make the Hahnemann of 1830-43 our guide is, I think, to commit ourselves to his senility. But the second homœopathy which I have been expounding to-day is the fruit of his ripest manhood, and I think it ought to be more cultivated than it is in England at this time. I doubt whether it is, at least in all hands, applicable to the exigenciès of every-day practice and the treatment on a large scale of acute disease. But when there is more leisure, and especially when chronic disease comes before us, I think that our best hope of making certain and speedy cures, whose brilliancy shall recall the earlier days of our system, lies in our adherence to that (shall I call it ?) higher homœopathy which the genius and toil of its discoverer have elaborated for us.

And as I spoke of the other form of our practice as having an irenical value, in that there was so little in it to repel our colleagues of the old school, so I must think it a great advantage in the more distinctive homœopathy I have now characterised that it will preserve the method of Hahnemann from absorption. That we individually should lose all we now have of separateness in name and position, and should merge in the general body of the profession, is for me a prospect full of satisfaction. My only dread would be lest our method should suffer in the process of amalgamation—should be shorn of its integrity, and remain only in the specific remedies which it has up to this time discovered. Believing that its loss would be a disaster alike to medical science and to humanity, I plead for this fuller carrying out of its developments, in which its distinctive nature is and will remain unmistakeable. Let the full homœopathy of Hahnemann be criticised and tested to the utmost ; but let it not perish !

[In consequence of the lateness of the hour no discussion of this paper was possible.]

PULMONARY EMPHYSEMA, ITS PATHOLOGY AND TREATMENT.

By Edward T. Blake, M.D.

Mr. President and Gentlemen,—On first glancing at our syllabus, you may have felt inclined to complain that I have not selected a very fascinating subject for consideration on so exceptional an occasion as that of our annual gathering.

Yet you will admit that the least attractive manifestations of disease are frequently the most important in their bearings on our practice.

In a clinic given at Guy's Hospital last May, a distinguished pathologist made the following excellent remarks : " Young practitioners often complain of a want of interesting cases; that is, cases of acute disease, neglecting to observe the clinical aspect of chronic changes in the tissues and organs. Disease is mostly a chronic process, ending in acute changes. Acute changes do not often occur in really healthy people."

These observations merit our most careful attention. It is probable that no other chronic condition with which we are acquainted leads up to such various forms of acute disease as that which we are now considering ; and, as the benefit of our fellow men, rather than the performance of brilliant exploits, is the aim of our lives, this is a subject with which we shall do well to thoroughly familiarise ourselves.

Pulmonary Emphysema is a complaint which we *may* all experience in our own persons, for it is the common *route* by which senile decay conducts to death. It is a disease which we *must* all encounter, for it exists at all ages—in every rank of society.

Were I to seek for further apology for my selection, I might remind you that a monograph upon this disorder is not to be found in our writings; this is the more curious when we reflect how largely our literature treats on chronic affections.

Emphysema, in so far as its recognition goes, is a modern disease. Before the time of Laennec it was classed clinically with asthma. Valsalva, Morgagni, Majendie,

Baillie, Ruysch, Floyer, Storch, Bonetus, and Van Swieten, had already recognised its existence after death, but they failed to associate it with its living phenomena.

To Laennec then is due the credit of accurately describing the *ante-mortem* indications of Emphysema, and of relegating them to their corresponding *post-mortem* appearances.

There are those present who were living when René Théophile Hyacinthe Laennec, at the age of thirty-five, was appointed to the Hôpital Necker, where he first used the instrument that made him famous, the stethoscope, which, in Recamier's hand, was destined in ten short years to predict his own fate, and by the very disease,* whose nature he had done so much to elucidate. In this month of September, exactly fifty-nine years ago, and after only two short years of hospital work, Laennec sent forth to the world two small octavo volumes, whose contents were to revolutionise a great department of medical science, to form the basis of modern physical diagnosis, and to exert an influence impossible fully to estimate. These contained the immortal treatise, "*De L'Auscultation Médiate.*"

In handling our subject we cannot do better than adopt Laennec's division of Emphysema into

1. Vesicular,
2. Interlobular,

and as we rarely encounter the second form unless as an after-effect of advanced vesicular Emphysema,† we shall confine our attention to the intra-lobular or vesicular variety.

Vesicular Emphysema is of three kinds :—

I. Partial, lobular Emphysema.
II. Lobular Emphysema.
III. Lobar Emphysema.

As the first of these divisions is a matter rather of scientific interest than of clinical importance, and as the last (lobar) asserts its presence in a way which would be very difficult to misunderstand, we will devote our chief attention to the second form, *i.e.*, lobular emphysema.‡

---

* It is an odd coincidence, that as Lancisi and Corvisart died of heart disease, so the lives of Bayle and Laennec were terminated by pulmonary phthisis.

† Traumatic cases prove, of course, an exception to this.

‡ There is little doubt that when pleurisy supervened in other acute affections of the lung, Laennec describes it as emphysematous "*frottement.*"

Ætiology—To speak of the causation of Emphysema I must rapidly recall the minute anatomy of the air-cells. These air-sacs are not visible to the unarmed eye.

The mottlings we see on a lung are lobules. Lobules are bunches of " lobulettes " (as Waters, in his well-known Fothergillian Essay, calls them); lobulettes consist of collections of air-sacs, six to twelve in number.

Air-cells are not spherical but cylindrical, some of them bulging gently towards the base. In shape resembling a gall-bladder, or the cæcum of the rodentia. A lobulette looks like a dahlia-root, each tuber answering to an air-sac.

Adjacent sacs are separated by a thin membranous wall; when inflated, they tend to become more spherical, but owing to mutual pressure, the parietes are flattened, and they thus become polygonal. If we slit up lengthwise a single living sac in health, we should find it of a rich rose-pink tint, the surface covered with small cup-shaped depressions, eight to twenty in number. These *alveoli* are most numerous at the fundus. As the base of the superficial air-sacs rests on the pleura, these *alveoli* play a very prominent part in the production of lobular Emphysema. In the deeper portions of lung these are supported either by one another, by the bronchial tubes, or by blood-vessels; here it is not so. At some points the alveoli are supported by the thoracic wall, but this is plainly a defective support, not being equally and generally applied, besides that, it is in a constant state of motion. This extraneous support is most inadequate at the apex, at the junctions of pleura with the anterior mediastinum and with the anterior edges of the diaphragm, hence at these points we find Emphysema of most frequent occurrence.

This affords strong evidence that there is a large physical element in the production of lobular Emphysema.

The only invariable element in lobular Emphysema is cough. More than that, we know clinically that the amount of Emphysema is in proportion with the amount of cough : so here practical fact coincides with theoretically probable views.

Laennec held what is known as the " Inspiration Theory " of Emphysema. The bronchia leading to a group of air-cells is blocked by swelling of mucous membrane, or by a mucous plug. Air is suffered to pass into cells, but cannot escape. The heat of the lung expands the air, and tends thus additionally to dilate the sacs and the bronchia. If the sacs be supported circumferentially, they may escape rupture, if not, owing to the pressure of surrounding cells on their sides, they burst at the base, and extravasation of air takes place.

Now this is a most charming theory, coherent in all its parts. But, alas, utterly fallacious! Were it true, vesicular Emphysema would always and immediately set up the interlobular variety. But this is not so. Collapse and Emphysema are not found associated; if co-existent in the same lung, both are not seen in the same part of it.

Again, physiological chemistry teaches us that the external air when inspired, does not pass immediately into the cells, but at first as far as the fine bronchiæ, mingling with the air, already in the air-sacs in obedience to Graham's "Law of Diffusion of Gases," Hutchinson has shown that, contrary to Laennec's teaching, expiration may be much more powerful than inspiration, even though the former chiefly depend *apparently* on the elasticity of the lung, and seem to possess a less powerful muscular apparatus. To Gairdner is due the credit of demonstrating that the effect of plugging a bronchial tube is to lead to *collapse* of that portion of lung supplied by it with air.* So this truly fascinating hypothesis must be abandoned as wholly untenable.

Gairdner, having demolished the hypothesis of Laennec, naturally produced a theory of his own. Having shown that the blocking of air-approach leads to collapse of the lung behind, he urged that the pressure of such a collapsed portion of lung being taken from the circumferential air-sacs, they having no support at this point, naturally give way, probably during forced expiration. Thus, then, Emphysema is produced. Now, gentlemen, if the theory of Laennec was ingenious, surely this hypothesis is perfect! But, unfortunately, we do not find it at all necessary that Emphysema should be preceded by collapse ; we do not find even that the two conditions affect the same locality. There is not only a want of evidence that the same amount of air enters the lung after collapse as before, but we have good ground for supposing that the reverse is the case, for

* This is the condition which was at one time looked upon as inflammatory, and which is still described in many manuals as "lobular pneumonia."

the parieties fall, and the actual cubic content of the thorax is thus soon accommodated to the new state of things.

This could only be true, were the thorax a firm box, with unyielding walls.

It is not the case, as Gairdner and Aitken take for granted, that a certain volume of air must enter the lung at each inspiration. Exactly as much air enters as is required to fill the patent cells—so much and no more. If, then, some cells be abolished, so much the less air is required, so much the less enters the lung.

Again, air is drawn equally to all parts of the lungs, there is no power to determine air to one part more than to another.

Rainey asserted that fatty degeneration precedes emphysematous destruction, but other observers fail to find the fat.

Sir William Jenner now ventilated the view that "fibroid degeneration" paved the way to this disease, and that the yielding nature of the costal cartilages predetermined the site. This preliminary "fibrosis" undoubtedly obtains in some kinds of Emphysema, notably in the Emphysema of the gouty, and perhaps in that type which is seen to perfection in the parturient woman ; but that this view does not invariably commend itself, is shown by the following considerations.

a. The lung is often most rarefied at the apex, where the cartilages are shortest.

b. The disease is seen most frequently and most highly developed in the aged, in whom the costal cartilages are ossified.

Probably Dr. Waters comes much nearer the mark when he tells us that Emphysema is ordinarily produced during *forced expiration.* That is essentially *the* article of his faith. He shows that air is driven upwards by the contractions of the abdominal muscles and of the diaphragm. Violent contractions of muscles so powerful as the *recti abdominales* cause a strong upward draught, this may be seen by the bulging of the supra-clavicular spaces during severe efforts at expiration.

The air-cells give way where they meet with least resistance. This is especially the case at the apex, less so at the anterior free edges. Hence Emphysema is most frequently seen at the apex, afterwards at the fringes.

This holds good to a much more marked extent in extreme infancy, when the seeds of Emphysema are so frequently sown.

In the cylindrical chest of early childhood, there is scarcely any lateral expansion. The breathing is chiefly diaphragmatic. The direction of expulsion is at that time represented by a vertical line drawn nearly directly upwards.

HISTORY OF A TYPICAL CASE.

In this disease it is probably the exception rather than the rule, that advice is sought on account of symptoms evidently connected with the lung itself, unless indeed some other more prominent pulmonary mischief be co-existent.

The history of a typical member of this class is something as follows :—A male patient, in middle life, comes, impelled by some slight gastric, cardiac, or hepatic disturbance, to seek our aid. On searching into the medical history, we hear that he had whooping-cough, or perhaps severe bronchitis in childhood, or failing those, that later in life he has been addicted to severe and *intermittent* athletics. The disease usually advances *furis furtivo pede*, but not always. The patient is often well-built and not badly nourished. The florid colour, the facial hypertrophy, the protuberant sternum, or barrel-shaped thorax, give the delusive appearance of robust health, and of a vital capacity even beyond the average. Such patients mislead both themselves and their friends by being capable of a really remarkable amount of sustained physical exertion, if not compelled to work "against time." They are, however, obliged to plead guilty to a slight but increasing tendency, especially after a full meal, to walk leisurely up hill; and they no longer ascend the stairs two or three steps at a time. They present usually a cheerful face to society, but they become subject to occasional attacks of inexplicable mental sombreness, quite foreign to their nature.

The complexion may be pale at first, then it becomes sallow, then red, and in the last stages even purple. The sclerotic is a little injected, and faintly tinged with bile. The lower lid is full and puffy in the morning. The tongue coated posteriorly, and there is more or less follicular affection of the pharynx. The uvula is frequently found relaxed, and the patient complains, if the night be at all cold, of a cough, especially noticed about 2 a.m. The cough is dry and irritating in character, and is aggravated by the dorsal decubitus, and relieved by lying with the shoulders raised.

Five chief causes of cough may be enumerated :—

1st. The follicular disease of pharynx, causing dry throat.

2ndly. A long uvula, vibrating with the respiration, may titillate the posterior pharyngeal wall.

3rdly. A mass of the characteristic, white-of-egg emphysematous secretion may have to be detached and removed.

4thly. Cold air impinging on the skin may produce a reflex cutaneous cough.

5thly. In the dorsal posture, the abdominal organs generally, but especially the liver, often enlarged in these cases, may press upwards against the diaphragm, driving it in turn against the lung-substance.

The last cause is aided by the gradual filling of the bladder during the night, and by the increase in volume of the intestinal gases, on account of the heat of bed.

Should the patient have acquired his Emphysema in childhood, we find, on inspecting the chest-walls, a prominent sternum and protruding cartilages.

Otherwise the chest tends to become generally deeper in its antero-posterior measurement ; this, with the bulging of the costal insterspaces, gives the peculiar barrel-like or cylindrical form to the emphysematous thorax ; at the same time the dorsal vertebræ become more arched.

Respiration is more or less confined to the diaphragm (abdominal breathing).

Whilst the inspirations are shortened, the expiratory efforts are abnormally prolonged.

In uncomplicated cases the apices, anterior and inferior pulmonary margins, are hyper-resonant. We should bear in mind that tubercle or hepatisation behind an emphysematous stratum will yield, on deep percussion, a normal resonance.* This may induce the medical attendant to pronounce the chest free from disease, when grave mischief is lurking unsuspected.

HEART.—The *heart* tends to dislocation, usually downwards, inwards, and sometimes backwards. Its area is hyper-resonant, whilst deep percussion reveals more or less enlargement of the right heart. The action of the organ is infrequent and quick.

* This is well seen in Case IV.

General Emphysema never spares the heart. For years the affection may be confined to the right side, and the most frequent condition is dilatation of the right ventricle, with secondary tricuspid insufficiency. As this lesion often yields no murmur, its existence is usually ignored, and *that* just at the time when most may be effected for its arrest.

If deep percussion show enlargement of the right heart, and we find slight general anasarca, not caused by anæmia, nor by renal disease, then we may infer the presence of tricuspid regurgitant.

For years, as we have said, the disease may be confined to the right side, but in time, if the patient live long enough, the left ventricle becomes hypertrophied. But why hypertrophy? On *à priori* grounds we should expect atrophy and dilatation. Probably it is because the displacement of the heart flexes the efferent ventricular vessels on themselves, thus narrowing their calibre, and presenting greater resistance to the exit of blood. This would explain, too, the hypertrophy, superadded to dilatation, of the right ventricle in advanced cases. (*Waters.*)

This thickening of the cardiac wall has an interesting analogue in the hypertrophied uterus, secondary to flexions of the body on the cervix.

If in an emphysematous case, one or both of the auricles be considerably dilated and hypertrophied, a condition not at all uncommon when chronic Bright's Disease exists as a complication, we may get what Sibson called a "reduplicated first sound," the *bruit de galop* of French observers. The new sound really precedes the natural first sound of the heart; it is produced by the contraction of the abnormally powerful auricle.

If the sound blend with the first sound of the heart (ventricular systole) we must remember the warning of Dr. George Johnson [*] not to mistake this reduplication for the murmur of mitral regurgitation.

I think it probable that the heart has more to say to the dyspnœa of emphysematous subjects than is ordinarily supposed.

Witness that the dyspnœa does not usually appear at the commencement of exercise, but it supervenes as the inadequate heart begins to flag; this explains why some

[*] Lumleian Lectures, 1877.

highly emphysematous subjects, having a fairly good heart-action, scarcely complain at all of difficulty of breathing during exertion..

In favour of this view, we may note that the dyspnœa is greatly aggravated by such causes as emotional excitement and sudden temperature-variation, both of which especially perturb the heart-action; and again the dyspnœa is soothed by cardiac sedatives.

The dyspnœa of Emphysema is due not alone to lung, or even heart-changes plus rib-immobility, for as the base of the chest enlarges, the diaphragm, instead of being arched upwards, comes to be stretched across the lowest plane tense and flat like the parchment on a drum. In this condition it cannot, by its contraction, increase the capacity of the chest, but, on the contrary, it will tend rather to diminish the thoracic content. Again, in more advanced cases, the enlarged lungs actually bulge the diaphragm downwards, so that its contraction directly compresses the lungs.*

This depressed condition of the diaphragm indicated by Dr. Wilks is aggravated by the physical effect of the engorged liver, usually present, exerting downward traction on the broad ligament.

BRONCHITIS is one of the commonest causes of Emphysema. But the condition so frequently met with as complicating Emphysema, and usually styled "bronchitis," is more accurately a species of bronchorrhœa.

BRONCHIECTASIS, if the patient live long enough, is nearly always present; it is of two kinds:—

1. General—cylindrical or fusiform.
2. Saccular (ampullary).

The site of the saccular form is determined by an interesting anatomical peculiarity in the larger air-tubes. It is the extreme natural thinness of the internal fibrous layer of the large air-tubes at certain points. This is an example of homology of type, the typical perfect condition being seen in a much more highly organised animal, the

---

* To Dr. Wilks we are indebted for pointing out this perversion of the chief function of the diaphragm. To the same accomplished pathologist we owe the recognition by the main body of the profession, of the anti-pyretic properties of aconite, first pointed out by the illustrious Hahnemann.

This "Nicodemus of Homœopathy" is now striving to restore the neglected antimony to its place in the treatment of Emphysematous Bronchorrhœa.

pig! the plicated folds of whose bronchial mucous membrane form a sort of sieve, admirably adapted to the damp and dusty atmosphere inhaled by a perpetually grubbing animal!

ASTHMA.—Long-standing Emphysema is nearly always associated with more or less asthma * . This complication is probably a result of the hypertrophied condition of the circular bronchial muscles. Obeying the laws which govern the idiopathic form, it demands no especial notice here.

HÆMOPTYSIS.—Three conditions lead to spitting of blood in the disease before us.

First, and probably the most usual, is the mere capillary rupture resulting from the destruction of lung tissue.

2ndly. The follicular affection of the pharynx nearly invariably present, is frequently associated with local varicosis. A pouched vein, enlarged by the reflux caused by thoracic obstruction, is easily burst by the effort of coughing.

3rdly. Blood-spitting may result from pulmonary stasis caused by disease of the right heart.

It is this tendency to hæmoptysis which led men, in former days, to diagnose Emphysema as a form of "consumption." And, indeed, should dilated bronchus, with fœtid, purulent expectoration co-exist, the case even now may, by a careless or ignorant practitioner, be set down as " a decline."

This error of diagnosis is the more likely to occur in that the peculiar absorption of the ungual phalanx, supposed at one time to be a sure diagnostic sign of " consumption, is often present in these cases.

Bronchiectasis is the disease that was known to our fore-fathers as "mucous phthisis of the aged."

SPECIAL SENSES.—*Ear.*—Tinnitus is common in the later stages, as a result of the secondary cerebral congestion. Impaired hearing may occur by extension of the follicular affection from the throat along the eustachian tube.

Eye.—No change has been observed which is typical of Emphysema. If the vision be affected it is viâ the heart. It commences by capillary modification, the choroid and retina becoming affected by exudations, collateral circulation from stasis or embolism.

* The symptoms of arsenical wall-paper poisoning so closely simulate, in some cases, those of Emphysematous Asthma, that the possibility of its existence should always be borne in mind in making a diagnosis.

MOUTH AND THROAT.—One of the most characteristic indications of Emphysema is the condition of the mouth. During the earlier stages it may be closed during rest, but it is instinctively opened during exertion. This becomes more and more marked as the disease advances. In time it leads to a peculiar fulness and dropping of the lower lip. In dry weather this aggravates the irritable condition of the pharynx produced by the follicular disease always present in pulmonary Emphysema. Secondary symptoms, such as this condition of the throat, indicate not only a qualitative but a quantitative deterioration in blood-supply; on this account they are valuable as affording an approximate estimate of the amount of cardiac engorgement.

ABDOMINAL ORGANS.—There is more or less dyspepsia, of which one of the commonest symptoms is flatulence. The bowels are torpid, the liver enlarged, there is portal congestion, with resultant pile.

Through the enforced general muscular inactivity, the lower extremities may be quite attenuated, yet on careful pressure in the evening over the lower portion of the tibia, the characteristic "pitting" may be obtained.

Increasing difficulty of locomotion leads to more and more dwindling of the muscles of the legs; the flaccid abdominal walls relax, the belly growing protruberant. Dyspepsia is aggravated by want of exercise, and badly elaborated blood produces deteriorated tissue.

Hernia in men, prolapsus uteri in women, may now complicate the case. Degeneration of lung-parenchyma sets in with the middle-aged, probably the fatty form, with subjects more advanced in life; the air-cells losing their elasticity are ready to give way with the slightest over-exertion. This state of things is common to both the heart and lungs. The cavities of both continue steadily to enlarge. The ordinary exertion of even sneezing, of straining at stool, the result of the constipation present, is now quite enough to break down lung tissue.

If the patient be resident in a catarrhal country, winter may bring some form of acute pulmonary disease, then the necessary fits of coughing will greatly accelerate these processes.

Systematic indulgence in alcoholic drinks, especially in fortified wines and ardent spirits, serves to give our subject a fresh impetus on the downward road, not only through impaired digestion, by putting extra duty on an already enfeebled heart; but also by still farther engorging the liver, thus assisting to land the patient in the advanced stages of Emphysema.

At this point it is impossible to misunderstand the condition we encounter. The appearance is peculiar and most characteristic, .the head seems shrunk into the shoulders, as if a heavy weight had fallen on it, and telescoped it into the thorax, this is due to the raising of the clavicles and shoulders from constant efforts at extra-ordinary respiration. The face expresses anxiety or distress, it is dusky-red and puffy, the former from badly aërated blood, the latter from œdema, and a peculiar hypertrophy of the facial muscles and cellular tissue; the eyes are bloodshot and prominent, the lids baggy, the nostrils flapping and dilated, the corners of the mouth drawn down, the neck looks tendinous, the *sterno-mastoids* and *scaleni* standing out in bold relief. If we watch the patient breathe, we see on inspiration, which is unnaturally brief, the nostrils expand, the mouth open, the hands resting on the head of a stick, or the arms of the chair, the thorax moves but slightly, the lower abnormally-everted ribs actually falling in instead of rising, and the patient resembling a frog in the way in which he seems to bolt his allowance of air.

Unlike asthma the respiration is infra-abdominal, the upper abdomen often remaining unmoved.

Expiration is prolonged sometimes lasting even longer than inspiration (as in Case III.), the patient makes ineffectual efforts to expel the air from a lung that has lost its elasticity. His inability to do so is the cause of great distress. If we apply the stethoscope, we may hear during inspiration the *râle crépitant sec* of Laennec. Laennec attributed this to air entering and dilating the dry emphysematous arcolæ. This cannot be so, because as the air does not pass out of these areolæ, it cannot very readily re-enter them; besides it is so uncertain in its existence that it must depend upon some fortuitous and temporary condition. We know that when the skin is inactive, the subjects of this disease are prone to a glairy, white-of-egg expectoration, the vibration of this in the smaller bronchiæ is doubtless the cause of this crepitation. It is interesting to observe that as the subject of emphysema imitates the *reptilia* in inspiration, so he approaches them at another point, that of internal temperature. The blood-heat diminishes, *pari passu*, with the pulmonary deterioration.

Before this time there appears in some patients a sign of which I cannot find a recorded description, and to which I desire especially to call your attention, to ask your experience concerning it, and your views with regard to its mechanism. It is by no means of invariable occurrence, but I have not yet seen it where vesicular emphysema is absent, and when I do encounter it, it always serves to draw my attention to this rather neglected condition. I refer to a peculiar fringe of dilated branching cutaneous blood-vessels, pale purple in tint, running downwards and inwards from the lower edge of the anterior thorax in the direction of the insertion of the diaphragm.

We know that the venous blood from the thoracic parieties is returned to the heart, partly viâ the intercostals, chiefly by the internal mammary veins ; the latter pass up behind the sternum, and would suffer compression between it and a highly emphysematous lung. This would throw the blood ascending at a disadvantage back upon the capillaries, the internal mammary arteries, exposed to the same conditions as the veins, unable to receive it, it passes to the vessels of the surface, which are free from pressure, and causes the peculiarly dilated condition of the superficial arterioles which we have been contemplating.

Emphysema *rarely* conducts directly to death. In the great majority of cases, a more acute affection of the undestroyed portions of lung figures as the immediate *causa mortis*. Hypostatic, basic congestion is not uncommon, its occurrence is favoured by the languid heart. Still more frequently the patient expires, worn out by repeated attacks of bronchitis, blocking and disabling the limited portions of active lung still left to carry on the functions necessary to life.

Apnœa.—Death from this cause often closes the scene. We can see that the progressive increase of venosity of the blood must find a limit, and in time asphyxiate the patient, but there is a less-recognised cause of apnœa. Towards the close of existence, fibrinous clots form in the large vessels at the base of the heart, and greatly impede the currents through the aorta and pulmonary artery.

The most typical example of this that has occurred to me was in a lady who died in the last month of pregnancy. Though ten years have passed, I still retain a vivid recollection of her distressed appearance, her cyanotic face, the purple lips, and chilly hands. This obstruction in the large vessels explains the curious phenomenon of a fairly strong heart-action, accompanying a pulse feeble and thready in the extreme.

But existence *may* be suddenly terminated by over-exertion, where a previously degenerate heart has been thinned and dilated to an unusual degree. A graphic sketch of such a catastrophe is given by Dr. Wynter, in his essay on "The Effects of Railway Travelling upon Health." "A friend tells us that he was greatly surprised some time since to find a gentleman sitting in a chair, with a hand-kerchief over his face in the open space where they take tickets at the London Bridge Station, on inquiry of one of the porters, he was told that he had just dropped down dead in the room, after running to save the train. It is not often we see such an awful example of the effects of forced bustle thus dramatically placed before our eyes, but be sure that scores of persons drop down dead in the counting-house, or sleep the last sleep in their beds, from this very cause."

Embolism may be the immediate means of bringing about a fatal issue, the mode of death varying with the locality of the spot.

LOBAR EMPHYSEMA—The time will probably come when we shall recognise many more distinct varieties of emphysema. We know now that clinically we must look upon acute lobar emphysema as a separate species, not merely an exaggerated form of the ordinary lobular kind. Its undoubted heredity,* its sudden yet insidious onslaught, its rapid increase without cough or over-exertion, its emphatic tendency under certain circumstances, to lead quickly to a fatal termination, all point to a disease having certain prolegomena of which we know but little ; and to a specific characteristic history, about which we are equally in the dark. Is it arrested lung-innervation ?

Acute lobar emphysema would be a very grave disease, from the fact alone of its giving rise to so few symptoms, till extensive ravages have taken place. We are rarely consulted in the earlier stages, and when our advice is sought, we know so little of the exciting causes, so little of

* Ordinary emphysema is hereditary in 60.4 p.c. (FULLER), lobar emphysema much more so, but we have no data.

the actual pathology, and so little of the influence of remedial agents that, were it not for symptomological therapeutics, our hands would be tied indeed!

In lobar emphysema there are four distinct pathological stages :—

1. Distension of air-sac.
2. Atrophy.
3. Perforation.
4. Parietal absorption.

Dr. Granville Bantock has shown that the greater number of unilocular ovarian cysts are primarily multilocular, but as the *loculi* become distended with fluid, their growth not being proportionate, the septa are stretched, thinned, perforation takes place, and absorption then ensues, leaving no trace of the septum beyond a fibrous ridge on the inner surface of the cyst; this serves very well to show what takes place in the lung. Owing probably to the presence of some dyscrasia, especially gout, and syphilis, the sacs lose their elasticity, they will not tolerate even ordinary respiration-pressure, they dilate in all directions, and sometimes so rapidly as to put an end to life even before the existence of disease is suspected.

Clinically, then, the salient features of this form of disorder, are :—

1. Heredity.
2. Swift and latent course.
3. Obnoxiousness to treatment.
4. Steady tendency to death.

Unlike most other diseases, especially of the chest, the younger the patient—the graver the prognosis.

Treatment.—We shall now consider the treatment of emphysema and its complications. And here, gentlemen, a very important practical point presents itself. I look with confidence that much light may be thrown upon it by your experience and judgment. A typical patient, such as I have pourtrayed, comes to us with the four pathological conditions :—ruptured air-cells ; dilated heart ; engorged liver ; general anasarca. How shall we commence the work of restoration ? Shall we " cover his symptoms " and content ourselves with administering a single dose of the appropriate remedy in the 30th or the 200th attenuation, watching the results, should any ensue, from the serene heights of a calm and lofty philosophy ? I fear that, spite of the solemn Shibboleth of Hahnemannianism still ringing in my ears, *I* must plead guilty to attacking one member of this pathological quartette, at a time. Of the four, I make it a practice to select the most urgent first. Thus, a short time since, a gardener came to me with vesicular emphysema; enlarged liver; slight anasarca and cardiac vertigo. There were present also palpitation, flushing, and morning "biliousness." The giddiness prevented the performance of his duties, stooping, ladder mounting, &c.

I gave *lachesis* 6, for one month. Under its use the vertigo and palpitation passed away. He then had *digitalis* 1, t. d. s. and *ferrum reductum* 1x after dinner daily. Under this treatment he is steadily improving.

In this case I addressed myself first to the cardiac symptoms, because they prevented the poor fellow from earning his living!

But on this point I should especially wish to have the benefit of your practice and experience.

HEAD.—For the flushed face and turgescence of the cervical vessels :—With dyspepsia, *carbo veg.* With constipation, *opium.* With tinnitus, *arnica.* With head and eye symptoms, *bell.* With throbbing headache, *glon.* With spinal symptoms, *agar.* With palpitation, *amyl.* With palpitation and flatulence, *laches.* With vertigo, *dig.*, *nux.*, *sulph.*, *con.*, *agar.*, *solanum.*

THROAT, LARYNX AND LUNG.—Relaxed uvula, *nux. v.*, with the local use of some mild astringent gargle, as Condy's Fluid, at bedtime.

Follicular pharyngitis, the *iodides of mercury and of potassium.* I have seen much benefit accrue from occasionally brushing the follicles with *carbolate of glycerine.*

Very hot drinks, smoking, talking in a carriage, bawling, and the use of coal-gas should be forbidden.

Cough—Loose mucous c. (glairy sputa), *scilla.* With laryngeal tickling, *lach.* With cardiac symptoms, *lach.*, *lycopus*, *sang.*

Nocturnal Cough—With relaxed uvula, *vide supra.* With dreaming *hyosc.* From cold skin, *rumex.** With localised pricking, *ac. nit.*

---

* Warm coverlet, even temperature, moist atmosphere; in these cases the "Bronchial Kettle," which may be used for disseminating a medicated vapour, is admirable. Rapid cold sponging of chest at bedtime, followed by friction with hot towel, is most valuable.

In the tedious course of bad nights, we shall certainly require to call up corps after corps from our reserve. We may then think of the different members of the solanaceæ, the *monobromide of camphor, sticta., succ.-con., verat, viride., cann., humulin, lactucin, lactic acid, valerian.* And as *derniers ressorts* the *bromide of potassium, chloral, chlorodyne, and morphia.*

ASTHMA.—Spasm of hypertrophied, bronchial muscles, *nux v., cupr.*

DYSPNŒA.—With mucous accumulation, *samb., seneg.* (Senile) *tart. emet., kali carb.* With nausea, *ipec., lobel.* With cyanosis, *ac. hydrocyan.* With œdema pulmonum, *ars.* With basic congestion,* *tart. emet., hep.*

FATTY DEGENERATION OF HEART AND LUNG.—*Phos., chalybeates, cod-oil.* Fish and milk diet. Bread made from entire wheat flour.

HÆMOPTYSIS.—From capillary rupture, *arn., millef.* From violence of cough, *ipec.* From pharyngeal varicosis, *hamam.* From cardiac complications, *acon. sec., ferrum acet.*

BRONCHIECTASIS.—*Kali carb., kali bich., phos., stann.* If fœtid, purul. exp. inhale *ac. carbol.,* or *kreos.*

BRONCHITIS.—With mucous rhonchus (coarse), *samb., spong.* (fine), *ipec.* With tenacious exp. or yellow tongue, *kali bich.*

Chronic bronchitis, *copaib., cubeb., tereb., sulph., seneg., silic.*

Senile bronchitis, *kali carb.*

Bronchorrhœa, *puls., scilla.*

Thoracic pains, *acon., bry., kali carb.*

Renal complications, *ars., merc. corr.*

DYSCRASIÆ.—Struma, the so-called " antipsorics," combined with the use of milk and cod-oil.

Gout, *ac. nit., colch., kali hyd.*

Syphilis, *merc., corr., kali hyd.*

HEART.—Palpitation.—With stabbing pain, *spig.* With flushing, *laches.* With dyspepsia, *lycopod.* With constipation, *nux vom.*

Dilatation, *dig. ferr.*

Fatty degeneration, *phos., ferr.*

Cardiac vomiting, *dig., ac. hydrocyan.*

Anasarca, v. dilatation supra, *ars., apoc.* Tea and tobacco may have to be interdicted.

---

* Prolonged inspirations and facial decubitus tend to shorten these tedious cases.

Heart affection, with engorged liver, *dig., nux., chin., sulph., lycopus, cornus, æsculus, hydrast.*

LIVER, *pod., acon., merc., iodine, lept., bry., hep.*

Liver.—It is certainly of vital importance that we should distinguish between primary affections of the liver, and those secondary to emphysema.

However much we may feel inclined to deride the niceties of diagnosis, every man's treatment will depend upon a hypothetical picture of his patient's case existing in his own mind—either consciously or unconsciously.

If we overlook the pre-existent and causative lung-condition, we shall taboo the very elements of nutrition most urgently demanded to prevent the steadily increasing degeneration of heart and lung-tissues.

Thus we shall feed the cause whilst trying to cure the results !

Of course the rule of probabilities will be in favour of " a cardiac liver," as, unless during such a season as the summer of last year, primary hepatic affection is far from common in this country.

GENERAL MEASURES.—I attach the very greatest importance to the *general* treatment of emphysematous patients.

Of course the first thing to do is immediately to interdict all avoidable violent exertion. Then we should aim at removing symptoms such as cough and constipation that lead to straining. Next, remembering to how great an extent the functions of the lung may be carried on vicariously by the skin, we must, by means of friction, hot-air baths, and hydropathic packings, keep that important emunctory in thoroughly good working order. If the belly be pendulous, a good broad abdominal belt, by keeping up the viscera, helps to return the diaphragm to its normal position.

If asthma or dyspepsia be markedly present, we must attend to the state of the stomach in the usual ways.

Knowing what large lungs are seen in the herbivores, whilst pure carnivores, such as some of the reptilia, may be nearly independent of pulmonary appendages, we should on theoretic grounds, order concentrated forms of animal food.

Wine is so apt to aggravate the hepatic complication, that I usually withhold it up to the last stage. The free use of skim-milk well supplants the employment of alcoholic beverages,

CLIMATE.—Where it can be selected, is a question of the last importance. For uncomplicated emphysema, a sedative, yet moderately dry, air is undoubtedly the best. An important point to be borne in mind is not to select a hilly district, lest dyspnœa debar the patient from needed exercise. These indications are to be found in such localities as Leamington, St. Leonard's-on-Sea, Clifton, Weston-super-mare, Ryde, Grange, and those parts of Surrey which are sheltered by the North Downs. Farther from home are Rhodes, the Nile, and Teneriffe. If there be complications, of course they may demand an amount of special consideration that will eclipse the primary morbid element.

CASES.

CASE I.—*Lobar emphysema—arterio-capillary Fibrosis.*

J. G., æt. forty-six, is a tailor by trade, a volunteer band-master by preference, something like another J. G. immortalised by the poet Cowper. He has been under various physicians of various creeds, and is now accounted somewhat of a *bête noir :* he certainly has received more advice than assistance from the excellent members of our cloth, with whom he has come in contact !

I found the patient sitting bolstered up in an arm-chair, with legs dependent. This is his easiest posture, and in it he spends most of his existence. He is of medium height, face pale and pock-marked. He has played a great deal upon large wind instruments. Has felt for some years a progressive difficulty in breathing, with gradually increasing pain over the anterior wall of the chest; the latter symptom is worse during inspiration. Since the dyspnœa, the legs have been observed to swell, they pit deeply under pressure.

Physical Examination.—I find a peculiar sceleroma of the pectorales, and of the serrati muscles. There is considerable general anasarca. There is general lobar emphysema, I can detect no cardiac lesion other than the inevitable tricuspid regurgitant and right dilatation of emphysematous subjects. The urine is deficient in colouring matter, loaded with albumen, but never at any time were casts discernible. Remedies did little for this unhappy sufferer, who died in a few months of anæmic exhaustion. Unfortunately a *post-mortem* examination was not permitted.

This is an example of the idea now gaining ground through the researches of Gull and Sutton that at least one form of "Bright's Disease," associated with "the contracting kidney," is only a local expression of a general condition called by them "Arterio-capillary Fibrosis." Could we have examined this poor fellow's muscles of extraordinary respiration, we should doubtless have found contracting fibrin freely deposited in the intersarcolemmatous spaces.

This condition may be analogous to Vogel's infantile scleroma of the sterno-mastoids.

CASE II.—*Vesicular Emphysema, enlarged liver.* R. C., aged thirty, like the preceding patient, is a tailor, like him he is a rifleman, and like him also he is addicted to the blowing of wind instruments. He is of medium height, clear skin, and bright colour.

There are plentiful strumous scars in neck and in left leg. He is troubled with a very irregular heart-action, and is sometimes faint or giddy. He feels nervous and irritable. He stimulates a flagging appetite with beer. He considers his general health good because he is never confined to bed.

Physical Examination.—The lungs are sound, with the exception of vesicular emphysema of apices and fringes, to sufficient extent to render inspiration and expiration equal in duration. There is no organic affection of the heart. The liver-line is six inches too low, this is partly procidentia, caused by the pulmonary emphysema. I diagnose this to be a strumous liver, dating from childhood. It was too large to be the result of reflux of blood from a dilated right heart, besides there were neither ascites nor general anasarca present.

Treatment.—Under long courses of *digitalis,* of *podophyllum,* and of *bryonia*—with *ferrum redactum,* as a standing dish—his dyspeptic depression disappeared, his heart grew steady, and his liver slowly returned to its normal size. He now enjoys capital health.

I need scarcely say that I interdicted bassoons, beer, and battalion drill!

CASE III.—*Vesicular Emphysema.* W. R., æt. forty four, schoolmaster. Had "inflammation of the lungs" at the age of twenty-six. From twenty to thirty he was an ardent cricketer and rifleman. As a volunteer he held the rank of colour-sergeant. He found that his wind was tested to the utmost by doubling up hill under the weight of accoutrements, &c. At the age of thirty-eight he became prone to headache, from which, however, he is now free. He is a short, sallow, spare man, with restless black eyes, and a bright, intelligent expression. The bowels tend to be confined, but there are no anal symptoms. He feels lassitude in the early morning. The skin is greasy and torpid, the mucous membranes sluggish, for he has marked follicular pharyngitis. He has the characteristic barrel-thorax; inspiration occupies one second, whilst expiration extends over twice that period of time, so greatly is the relation between those processes disturbed.

Treatment.—I ordered total abstinence from athletics. Thanks to frictions, baths, *kali bich.*, *ars.*, and *sulphur*, this patient is now in the enjoyment of fair average health.

You observe, gentlemen, that I cite the three preceding cases, to show the ill effects of spasmodic fits of intermittent extreme exertion. Volunteers drill, on an average, once a week. During the intervals between exercise these men, owing to the nature of their avocations, led sedentary lives. Had they, like soldiers of the line, been drilled twice a day, it is probable that they would have resisted, with a far greater measure of success, the ravages of their insidious enemy.

CASE IV.—*Lobar emphysema, with croupous pneumonia.* M. H., æt. nine months. This little girl was quite well until the spring, when her nurse took her into the garden, and sat in the bright sun, with a cold easterly wind blowing, and the child has had difficulty in breathing ever since.

In 1873 I was summoned to Blackheath to see this case. I found a pale, fragile child lying in its nurse's arms, the eyes were preternaturally bright, pupils dilated. Rapid wheezing respiration, temperature high, pulse quick and weak, skin hot and dry. Frequent rattling cough and occasional vomiting. All the organs were healthy, except the lungs, which were hyper-resonant over their entire area, with the exception of the left base, which was normal on firm percussion. Light, percussion, however, elicited the same tympanitic notes as elsewhere, and on carefully listening with the stethescope fine pneumonic crepitation could be heard at the base. Evidently we had to deal with catarrhal inflammation of the deeper strata of the lower lobe, masked by emphysema of the more superficial portion. The barrel-shape of thorax was well marked in this case. There was a peculiar arrest of development observable on the whole of the left side of this child's body, the left side of the head was perceptibly smaller than the right. Possibly the emphysema was congenital on the left side; the right side giving way in the spring, served to attract the attention of the parents. I gave *tartar emetic* 3x, and applied poultices. Next day there was a marked improvement; when the effect of the *antimony* was expended I ordered *ipec.* 6. The case advanced favourably, and in a week nothing was left of the inflammation but a few points of *crepitus redux.*

This patient afterwards had *sulph.*, *hep.*, *samb.*, *scill.*, *seneg.*, *spong.*, *ars.*, and *puls.*, according to symptoms. *Samb.* φ afforded the most marked relief.

The PRESIDENT : Gentlemen, I am sure we are much obliged to Dr. Edward Blake for reading to us a paper of such elaborate proportions and also for the excellent drawings with which he has illustrated it. Dr. Blake has drawn our attention in the circular which he has very kindly sent round, to two or three points. Now, for my own part, I think that if we do succeed by any medicine in covering the totality of the symptoms present, we shall in all human probability, alleviate the condition of the lungs. (Hear, hear.) At the same time, we must all admit that pulmonary emphysema is not a disease which we undertake to treat with any very great confidence. The utmost we can do, as a rule, is to modify the consequences of irremediable mischief. I have no doubt we shall derive very great advantage from considering this paper. (Applause.)

Dr. ROTH (London)—I have looked over the treatment of Dr. Blake, and I find he has omitted certain auxiliaries which are very useful in emphysematous complaints. In children I have frequently considered their spinal curvatures, and sometimes I have found that which Dr. Blake did not mention —cold extremities. To mention a few of the means which we apply independently of friction and medicine, in order to relieve the heart and the breathing action, while the child or person is in a quiet sitting position, move the feet. In fact the breathing is done for the patient, and as in emphysematous cases with the patient the expiration is the great thing, and he is instructed how to use his expiratory powers. Independently of this they are often unable to bring up a large quantity of mucous. It is often possible to produce a reflex action so as to bring it up. Many of those manipulations and artificial respiratory movements were used 2,000 years ago by the Chinese. I have a number of drawings here in which the patients are represented as going through their processes as if preparing for a religious ceremony, but nothing is done for them but breathing.

After some further observations from Dr. DYCE BROWN and one or two other members the discussion was brought to a close,

The business of the Congress was resumed at two o'clock, the chair being taken by the PRESIDENT (Dr. POPE), who said: Before I call on Dr. Moore to move the resolution of which he has given notice in reference to the London School of Homœopathy, I may mention that I have received a telegram from Dr. Murray Moore, who is now residing at Taunton, and who has for several years lived in the State of California, where he was a member of the Homœopathic Medical Society of that State, and by that society was appointed as a delegate to attend this Congress with a message. That message he has telegraphed to me, as he is unable to be present with us. He says, "The California State Homœopathic Medical Society sends greeting and best wishes to the Congress." It is very pleasant always to feel that we are remembered by our brethren abroad, and I am quite sure we shall all appreciate this kind message from the medical men in the State of California (applause). I will now ask Dr. Moore to bring forward the resolution of which he has given notice ; but previous to doing so I will state that Dr. Bayes has received thirty-two letters from gentlemen who are unable to be present with us to-day, but who are interested in this question. Though I have no doubt he will refer to these letters, I may as well tell you who they are from, and that all, with two exceptions, are opposed to Dr. Moore's proposal, the two referred to being doubtful.

Dr. Neville Wood, Dr. Yeldham, Dr. E. C. Holland, Dr. Leadam, Dr. Hayle (Rochdale), Dr. Bradshaw, Dr. Wilson, Dr. Berridge, Dr. Roche, Dr. Miles, Dr. D. C. Laurie, Dr. Von Tunzelman, Dr. F. Flint, Dr. J. Murray Moore, Dr. Tuckey, Dr. Robinson, Dr. Süss Hahnemann, Mr. Millin, Mr. Thorold Wood, Dr. Tuthill Massey, Dr. S. Morrison, Dr. Ayerst, Mr. Prowse, Dr. Galgey, Mr. Mansell, Dr. James Jones, Dr. Cooper, Dr. McConnell Reed, Mr. Denham, Dr. Matheson, Dr. Shuldham. Having made that announcement I will ask Dr. Moore to bring forward his motion.

DR. MOORE, Liverpool: It has fallen to my lot to take up this vexed question of the change of the title of the new School of Homœopathy, and I am well aware of the difficulties connected with the subject, and of the strong current of feeling that exists against the said change ; and this I must say in introducing the matter, that I believe both sides and parties are equally devoted and earnest friends of homœopathy, and that their differences are of a purely intellectual, scientific, and social character. Albeit unhappy personalities have from time to time cropped up in the discussion of the subject, I trust that the Congress will enter into this discussion without any personalities whatever, and allusions to the past, avoiding all extraneous matter, considering only the abstract merits of the change proposed ; and to whatever decision we may arrive, that the minority will, as in all other rational and self-governing bodies, submit to the expressed will of the majority.

I may state at the outset that the action of the Congress can only be declaratory and recommendatory, as it rests with the donors and subscribers to the school to legislate or otherwise on " the change of title."

This subject has now for about six months been agitating our body, and though all agitations and divisions in large bodies of men are generally over-ruled for ultimate good, in a small body like ours division means disaster. The present effect of this agitation is far from a happy one, hence my desire, and that of many others, to have a final settlement of the question. The late Duke of Wellington remarked that his chief reason for passing the Roman Catholic Relief Bill was "to avoid a civil war." His memorable words were, "That of all wars," and he had seen much of war, "civil war was the worst;" and of all controversies the worst is that which goes on in a small body, banded and held together by their attachment to a great truth, and whose attitude heretofore has ever been that of conflict with the error, prejudice, opposition, and injustice of our great enemy without.

The non-sectarian title of the school, which I propose, is doubtless part of a much wider subject, namely, the future position and prospects of homœopathy in this country, and the title of the school, therefore, cannot be considered apart from this without leaving out the most material elements to guide us in our decision.

Is homœopathy ever likely to be recognised or legalised here as in America, with its separate colleges (in six or seven States of the Union), all with power of granting degrees ? Or is it most probable that it will be amalgamated with general medicine, taught in our schools, with or without the name, as a part of general medicine ? Let us pause for a moment to consider these questions ; and here we are furnished at once with an answer from what has already taken place.

Homœopathy is taught already in some of our schools under the cover of legitimate medicine—imperfectly taught, dishonestly and dishonourably taught, without a word of acknowledgment or approbation of the source from which it has been derived, or with derision of that source if mentioned at all.

Then as to establishment and legal recognition of homœopathy in America, let us note that the circumstances of an old and monarchical country are so different from those of a new republic, that no comparison can be made ; yet it is very remarkable that the most recent and most successful establishment of homœopathy in America (four years ago)—most successful both in a scientific and popular sense—was the union of the Boston School of Homœopathy with the new University of Boston. Note what has taken place there in reference to the title of the school; it is now called " School of Medicine," the incongruity of styling it " School of Homœopathy " being felt in an institution where an all-embracing title should be employed. In the report of this school we are told that " Its curriculum is of the broadest character, and includes all the collateral branches of modern medical science."

This—the Boston University School of Medicine—is the type not only for our school, but for its title, and let us follow this practical example of the great country, and though we may not, like them, be taken up by any of the universities, we shall, ere l ong, receive the recognition of those who have the power of granting degrees, the more speedily, if our hospital be raised to the required standard.

One subject closely connected with the future of homœopathy must be touched upon, namely, the present attitude of the medical profession towards us. Our President's address having touched upon the recent attitude of the profession, I pass over that subject briefly.

Now there are strong symptoms of awakening justice towards us amongst our brethren of the so-called orthodox school; these symptoms were first manifested at Birmingham two and-a-half years ago; still more recently in London, Manchester, and Bradford. At the latter place conspicuously and nobly so by one in authority and position. Now what five or six men have expressed, five or six hundred are ready to express if they had the moral courage to do so, or if it were made easy for them to do so. I deny that two or three waspish remarks by editors are to be taken as expressing the genuine feeling of the profession towards us; they express, if you will, the feeling of the tyrannous section of the profession—that part which is ever clamorous respecting its so-called dignity, and which cares far more for what is thought respectable than for what is true and good, more for its own interests than for the interests of mankind; but we believe that this class is on the decrease, and it has been brought about partly by the advocacy of the laity, who have always been witnesses to our unjust treatment, and partly by the consistent perseverance in a conscientious attachment to what we believed to be the truth in medicine.

Apropos of this professional movement in our favour, I deeply regret that no flag of truce has yet been held out to us in Liverpool, and that the medical institution of this great town contains as its second law a statute for excluding homœopaths from its membership, and all its advantages; I hope that some of its brave members will initiate, and speedily carry out, the repeal of this obnoxious law.

But to return. Our good friend Dr. Bayes has recently dwelt much on the position of the school as an extra-academical school, and has justified its existence on that ground. Here let me say that however this discussion may terminate, the homœopathic body owes a deep debt of gratitude to Dr. Bayes for his most laborious and successful efforts in obtaining the means of establishing such an efficient school.

Now there are two serious arguments against the school existing " as an extra-academical school," and they are these :—

1st.—The difficulty of obtaining students ; and

2nd.—The isolation involved.

1st.—The students' difficulty.—At present there are so many lectures to attend, required by the hall and college and universities, that the student has no time for extra studies ; nor has he money generally to spare ; for I need not tell you that medical students usually come from the upper middle class of society, or are the sons of professional men, whose pecuniary means are limited, their parents often with difficulty giving them the mere supplies absolutely necessary for the positive and peremptory requirements of the college and hall or university, as the case may be ; so that students' attendance will, I fear, be very small, and the audience therefore be composed of amateurs, who will attend irregularly and capriciously ; only a few enthusiastic students may be looked for—perhaps very few.

2nd.—The argument of isolation.—By establishing it as an extra-academical school we are just pushing ourselves into that very isolation and sectarian position of which we have complained as being obliged to assume heretofore, in consequence of our persecution by the orthodox school ; and now we take up, spontaneously, a very marked dissenting position, which, though it might have advantages for a time in teaching pure homœopathy in contradistinction to Ringerism, would eventually stamp it as a sectarian school, and exclude it for ever from legal recognition. Having now noticed the objections to the title " school of homœopathy," I pass on to the positive arguments for a non-sectarian school title.

1st.—By giving the school such a title we place it in a position to receive and apply any newly acquired truth or remedial process whatever that may be discovered hereafter, or that now exists, in addition to maintaining and upholding the great law of similars, bequeathed to us by our illustrious master.

2nd.—We place it on a scientific level with all other schools of medicine.

It is not scientific to call a school homœopathic, allopathic, or antipathic; these terms are only expressive of one feature of medical truth, but " school of medicine " is broad and large, and comprehensive of all medicinal measures and appliances.

Dr. Cockburn in his recent pamphlet has worked out the scientific argument fully, and shown in analagous cases, as divinity, that we do not establish chairs of Calvinism or Arminianism, though we teach all these, and far more than these in the chair of divinity.

3rd.—By adopting a non-sectarian title we place the school within the pale of possible legal recognition by the licensing bodies. The lectures will count as ordinary medical lectures at other schools, whereas, if a sectarian title be continued, the school can never be recognised, but is doomed to perpetual isolation. If asked, How do you know that it can never be recognised with its present title ? I reply that our friends who originated this movement have ascertained most positively that it cannot be recognised if called " School of Homœopathy " or any other *pathy*, and therefore if we continue the name as it is, we shall lose in the future the high position we claim of perfect equality with our brethren of the old school, and, what is of far greater importance, the opportunity of saturating the whole medical world with that truth which we believe God has entrusted to us for the benefit and blessing of our noble profession, and through it of the whole brotherhood of man.

Finally : If you believe that homœopathy is the " Be-all " and " End-all " of medicine, of course " School of Homœopathy " is the title to adopt, and there is an end of all further agitation of discussion ; on the contrary we believe that larger views are held of the future of medicine by the majority of our body ; and if we take the right course now, we shall succeed in elevating and establishing homœopathy in this country in the only way it can be established,—by bringing the hospital up to the required standard, and by opening the school on a broad basis as already indicated.

The cries which have been raised against such as have advocated this view—of being "renegades"—of "striking the flag"— of " eating the leek "—of having "lost faith." in homœopathy, are not applicable to men who have advocated the great homœopathic law in its darkest days, and when they stood alone in this country, and who now naturally desire that the wars of David may be followed by the peaceful reign of Solomon.

I can only speak for myself without compromising anybody else when I say that to whatever decision you may come this day on this subject, whether for or against my views, and the views of those who advocate the broad basis for our school, I shall stand by the school, as the channel of teaching that great truth to the practice of which I have devoted nearly thirty years of my life, and to which I purpose adhering through the remainder of my days on earth, because I believe it to be the true law of healing.

Dr. Moore added : I have now the pleasure of moving the following resolutions, first, " That this Congress regrets that the executive of the London School of Homœopathy has adopted a special instead of a general title." (Dr. Moore also read a second resolution to the effect that the school should be called the Bloomsbury School of Medicine.)

Dr. Hayward (Liverpool): I have very great pleasure in seconding both those resolutions, but I would very much prefer that Dr. Moore had placed only one before us at once, because it is necessary we should be as definite as possible in this matter.

Dr. Moore: Then, I will be happy to do that. I move, " That this Congress regrets that the executive of the London School of Homœopathy has adopted a special instead of a general title."

Dr. Hayward : I have very great pleasure in seconding that resolution. I think it is a matter of very great importance; and that now is the time for us to take a stand definitely and pointedly, and by adopting the special title of " The Homœo-pathic School," we preclude ourselves from the opportunity of teaching besides homœopathy. It is therefore, in my opinion, a very short-sighted policy indeed to adopt a special name. It is very important to select a general title, in accordance with which we can introduce into the school all professional knowledge, whether homœopathic or allopathic, medical and surgical, and we shall not be excluded from applying any. Of course, if we adopt the term " homœopathic " we shall be expected to stick to it. Now, are we prepared for that ? I don't think any gen-tleman in this room would like to say that our school must be restricted narrowly to the teaching of homœopathy. (Cries of " Yes, yes.") If, gentlemen, we teach nothing but homœopathy we shall teach a very narrow, and I was going to say very sectarian aspect of the profession. As medical men we ought to teach the whole of that medical knowledge which qualifies medical men, and if we adopt a special name—as it would seem by some to confine ourselves to strict homœopathy—we exclude the right to teach what is more general. I maintain that by doing that we really put a veto on the lectures already given, because I maintain that in the lectures given by Dr. Hughes and Dr. Dyce Brown we have taught more than homœo-pathy. If we have taught more than homœopathy, we intend to teach more than homœopathy ; therefore if we adopt a title which precludes us from teaching more than homœopathy, what an anomalous position we place ourselves in ! I think that now is the time to adopt a title by which we can teach anything we like. By the movement throughout the profession at the present time we have, I believe, got an opportunity which will never again present itself in the present generation. I am not an old

man, but I feel that if we do not take the present opportunity
we shall never see such another. I think the feeling of everyone
in this room is that we ought to take advantage of the opportunity
we now possess. I have great pleasure in seconding the resolution that the title of the school ought to be general and not
special. (Applause.)

Dr. NANKIVELL (Bournemouth) said : I have been asked to
propose an amendment on that resolution which I think will
meet with acceptance from the majority of the members of this
Congress. That resolution is a very short one, and perhaps
before I speak to it I had better read it to you. It is, " That
the name of the school remain for the present The London
School of Homœopathy." (Loud applause.) I remember at the
last Congress at Bristol this matter was considered, and it was
passed by an almost unanimous majority that a School of
Homœopathy should be established in London. I think that all
we have to consider to-day is, not whether the institution shall
continue, but whether it shall be called by that name. This
matter was first brought to my knowledge by a circular which I
received from my friend Dr. Black, and afterwards I received a
second note from him, asking whether or not I acceded to the
proposition signed by himself, Drs. Drysdale, Dudgeon, and
Ker ; I replied that I had no objection whatever to the School of
Homœopathy having a wider name than School of Homœopathy,
but that I thought that if we changed the name we were bound
to change the scope of the school ; that if we called it a school
of medicine, we were bound to make it a school of medicine, and
teach anatomy, physiology, and everything else to students who
liked to attend it. From Dr. Moore's paper and motion there
appears not the slightest desire on the part of any of these gentlemen to increase the funds or the scope of this school. The
mere question is shall it be called a school of medicine. I think
it is very much better to call things by their right names. What
is taught is therapeutics. Therefore, it is not in a true or
technical sense a school of medicine at all. (A voice : " A medical
school.") No, it is only a homœopathic school. Another point
is we have got funds together—Dr. Bayes has got funds—for a
school where homœopathy should be taught. Therefore, it is a
very serious matter in the first year of its existence to change
its name. I am the very last person in the world to stick to a
name, if by changing it we could gain anything without sacrificing principle, but at present we cannot cast it overboard without
sacrificing principle. If the other medical men in the schools
and through the medical papers come to us and say, " We will
recognise your school as a school of therapeutics if you change
the name ' Homœopathic,' " it would be another matter. But
they will do no such thing. They will only come round as

the position of things gradually alters. The *Lancet* offers no right hand of fellowship, and if at present you effect this change, you will be in the wrong position all the time. If we give up the title "Homœopathic" as applied to the school, do so as to the *Journal*. (A voice : There is no connection whatever.) If we can get appointed a lecturer on Materia Medica in another school who is not ashamed of homœopathy, or of Hahnemann, let us call the school by another name; but until that is a practicable and feasible thing, I believe we are only following the interests of science by calling the institution by the name it has, a School of Homœopathy. (Applause.)

DR. DYCE BROWN (London) : I have great pleasure in second-ing the amendment moved by Dr. Nankivell. My view in favour of keeping the name as it is, rests upon one point alone. The allopathic section of the profession refuses to teach homœopathy at all. We come in and say, "We will supply the existing want." That bits of homœopathy are taught in other schools is a strong reason for our present name. We do not start a medical school, but a school to teach that which other schools do not. We shall not teach bits of homœopathic practice ; but show the principle on which such treatment is based, and we will teach the students to apply the principle to medicines and diseases in general. Therefore, it is necessary for us to say precisely what we mean to teach. Now, what we mean to teach is homœopathy. Dr. Hayward says we ought not to teach that alone, but all therapeutics.

Dr. HAYWARD (interrupting) : May I be allowed to rise to correction. I never said such a thing. I never said we should teach allopathy as well as homœopathy. I merely said we might teach anything we liked.

Dr. BROWN : I beg Dr. Hayward's pardon. Of course we take the right of doing so ; but believing as we do that homœo-pathy is the best system of medicine, and knowing that allopaths do not believe in their methods, we don't want or profess to teach anything but homœopathy, except when we come to a case where we should say to the students, "This is beyond the pale of homœopathic law." But except in these cases we want to teach the students what we do, and not that which we do not believe in. There is one other point. Dr. Moore said our classes are small. I think that for the first year they were remarkably good. Students did not all come regularly, but there were half-a-dozen regular attenders out of a dozen enrolled. Now, as it was a summer session, which is not favourable, I think half-a-dozen regular attenders out of a dozen is remarkably good. We have only to continue, and the more distinctly it is known that we mean to teach homœopathy the more will students come and hear what we have got to say. (Applause.)

Dr. WYLD (London): I don't so much wish to make a speech as to ask a question of Dr. Brown, because I think the answer may to some extent influence the meeting in deciding upon a name. If I am not much misinformed, the facts are of this nature. There were fourteen or fifteen students at the school, but I understand that only four or five or six paid fees; the others were free admissions. That is a very small number of students to be attracted after the expenditure of £100, and the distribution of 20,000 handbills. I understand there were five or six, or there may be seven students who paid the entrance-fees, and that these lectures began with twelve, fourteen, or fifteen students, that sometimes there was an attendance of five or six, or sometimes fewer, but I have been informed that latterly the attendance dropped down to two, and that on one occasion there was only one student present. What I would submit is—Does not that amount to a proof that the name has been a failure? With 20,000 circulars and £100 expenditure, is not that a failure?

Dr. BROWN: I don't think it was ever reduced to a smaller audience than four. I don't remember it.

Dr. HUGHES; I must inform Dr. Wyld that I was the unhappy person whose audience was reduced to that number.

Dr. CAMERON (London): I have but one or two words to say in reference to the name of the school. In Dr. Dyce Brown's lectures, reported in the last number of the *Homœopathic Review.* he has certainly gone beyond homœopathy in telling those who treated a certain complaint of the throat that if that complaint is very difficult to treat they are not to go into the homœopathic treatment of the disease, but they are to swab the throat with nitrate of silver lotion. If that is not allopathic treatment, I don't know what is.

Dr. GIBBS BLAKE: I quite follow Dr. Nankivell's arguments, especially where he says that the school should be called by a proper name. If a student goes to Great Ormond Street to learn the practice of his art, he ought to be taught there, not only the cases where the therapeutic principle is of value, but, I take it, that he ought to be taught the exceptions to that principle, and, therefore, that a professor at Great Ormond Street should go into the subject fully, and should teach a student, who attends there for his knowledge of his profession, the whole of therapeutics, which Dr. Brown thinks it right for him to follow. (Applause.) Therefore, I submit that a thing should be called by its proper name, and the proper name of this school is not a "School of Homœopathy," but it is a "School of Therapeutics." A school of therapeutics includes the teaching of Materia Medica. It seems to me that that meets the difficulty. It certainly is not, and never will be, a school of medicine in the strict sense of the term. The schools of medicine in London are so numerous that it seems absurd to suppose we should ever get the chairs filled up by the means suggested; but our school is, and should be, a school of therapeutics. This becomes a second amendment on the resolution before the meeting. I submit whether it is not the best solution of the difficulty.

Dr. HALE seconded Dr. Blake's amendment, regarding it as the best solution of the difficulty.

Dr. DRYSDALE (Liverpool): I rise to support the resolution proposed by Dr. Moore; and, in the first place, I must protest against being confounded with those, if such there be, who seem to think that it depends upon us whether we give up the title homœopathic as a body. It does not depend upon us. As long as we believe that the homœopathic is the law of the action of specific medicines, so long must we, in common honesty, openly confess that we do. While our professional brethren separate themselves from us on that account, and falsely brand us as sectarian, we must be content to bear the accusation. Until the majority of medical men return to the behaviour of men of science and gentlemen, and allow homœopathy to be discussed like any other theory in medical literature and societies, there must exist a separate literature and societies, to which no more appropriate name than homœopathic can be given. Here it indicates not a creed, but merely the cardinal point on which free discussion is required; it is otherwise with a school where the name must imply a defined creed. Meantime, I protest against the accusation of desiring a neutral name for the school from any desire to shirk the opprobrium of bearing the name of homœopathist. I may remind you that I was one of the founders of the *British Journal of Homœopathy*, a journal addressed to purely professional readers, at a time when there were not a dozen qualified homœopathic practitioners in Britain—(applause)—and I still approve of its name. (Renewed applause.) In describing the lectures in our school as extra-academical, Dr. Bayes is, I think, mistaken in the meaning of that term. In Edinburgh it was applied to all lectures delivered without the walls of the University, and which did not qualify for the privilege of its degree. But these lectures were sufficient to qualify for the rights and privileges of other professional licensing bodies. Now this is denied to the lectures of our school, and, therefore the word Dr. Bayes ought to have used is extra-professional, and not extra-academical. This is an imputation and a grievance which I call upon you to protest against by voting for Dr. Moore's motion. Our remedy is pointed out by the course followed in the case of the University of Boston, in America. A few days ago I met Dr. Helmuth, who related the history of that institution. It was founded by a rich citizen, and for some time contained only the faculties of arts and theology; in process of time it was thought desirable that the faculty of medicine should be added. Among those interested, such as favoured the homœopathic theory were in the majority, and it was proposed that they might fill up the chairs, but it must be called the faculty of medicine simply, not homœopathic medicine. Immediately parties were formed, and it was said, " If you go in there and teach medicine, you are a traitor to your camp. You must not go in there ·unless the university admits the faculty as that of homœopathic medicine." Fortunately a more rational view prevailed, and all the chairs belonging to the medical faculty are now filled by homœopathists, although they are named just as in the ordinary schools. The chair of Materia Medica for example is called simply the chair of Materia Medica, but the teaching is on the homœopathic principle. That is the position we wish here. There is no chance of a charter being granted in England, but all the licensing bodies are in the same position to us as the Boston University. The University of London, for example, is not an allopathic university; therefore, we have the same right to teach there that anybody else has, and if we abdicate that right, we are unworthy of our principles : Shall we sink into a corner and say we are afraid to teach medicine? We are not afraid. We must claim our right to teach Materia Medica in the way we think proper to *bonâ fide* students, as a part of the curriculum which qualifies for the license to practice, and not be content with extra-professional lectures to dilletanti. The only practicable way to do this, we have been informed by a member of the senate of the university, is to adopt a neutra ·title, such, for example, as the " Bloomsbury Medical School;" any other at once compels a definition of homœopathy, and that has never been given to the satisfaction of any considerable number of our body. The name of "London School of Homœopathy" for example, is repudiated as a misnomer of the teaching in our school by Dr. Fenton Cameron, who objects to the treatment of sore throat therein recommended, viz., aconite and belladonna, followed in obstinate cases by swabbing with a strong solution of lunar caustic, as not homœopathy. The objection is just from his point of view, and none who think with him can consistently and conscientiously allow the present establishment to bear the name of School of Homœopathy, although they could not have the same logical objection to such teaching in the " Bloomsbury Medical School." A creed and a strict definition are thus essential to please homœopathists if you will call it a School of Homœopathy, while so much of creed as is expressed in this title is an absolutely fatal barrier to our sharing in the recognised medical schools of our country, just as it was to obtaining the Boston University for our cause. With a neutral name, such as the

Bloomsbury Medical School, the very same lectures as now, in the very same words, by the very same lecturers may be given; and we should still have a starting point for agitation to overcome the partisan resistance to our claim of recognition, whereas by the present title those very lectures are condemned to perpetual extra-professional isolation. Why then should this title be insisted on from the false and unfounded fear that changing it, in compliance with the wise, just and far-seeing rules of the London University, might appear a loss of faith in our distinctive principle in the eyes of ignorant laymen, or for any other subsidiary motives? Let us, therefore, beware how we trifle with this chance of asserting our claim to teach openly and honestly, and with equal privilege of recognition, those homœopathic principles of therapeutics which are now taught secretly and dishonestly in many allopathic schools.

Dr. Dudgeon (London): I do not think the proposal of Dr. Hale would meet the objections of those who think with me, that we should take our stand upon our rights, and our rights are to enjoy all the privileges presented to us by the University of London. Now, the University of London would no more recognise a School of Therapeutics on the principles of homœopathy than it would recognise a School of Allopathy, or a School of Homœopathy. We may justly consider that we have arrived at a time when we can claim to be the representatives of the true scientific medicine, and if we put ourselves into a sectarian position, in reference to our school, we thereby put ourselves into a position of obscurity and deprive ourselves of all the advantages of our University, which belongs as much to us as any other members of the medical profession. (Applause.) Then, let us consider why should we not call ourselves a school of medicine or a medical school? When Hahnemann, in his brilliant days, which were so graphically described by Dr. Hughes (that is to say in the vigour of his age), published his *Organon*, he did not call it the *Organon of Homœopathy*. He called it first the *Organon of Rational Medicine*, and in the first edition he everywhere speaks of the physician, who practises according to his method, as the "rational physician." (Applause.) And he calls his system throughout the system of rational medicine. (Applause.) Now then, are we to go back to ante-Hahnemannic days, are we afraid to take the position that Hahnemann asserted for himself? In the later editions of his *Organon* he drops the word homœopathist, and he speaks everywhere of the physician who practises his method as the true physician, and of the system of medicine as true. Shall we then go back and deprive ourselves of any chance of recognition by the University of London? No! I say let us, like Hahnemann, assert our claim to be the representatives of true medicine. True medicine must be practised according to the principles of homœopathy, and if we teach true medicine we shall teach homœopathy. (Applause.) And in those rare cases where homœopathy is inapplicable we may resort to the other method which our brilliant lecturers in the School of Homœopathy recommend. (Applause.) We have been told that Dr. Dyce Brown teaches to supplement homœopathic practice by allopathic measures, and Dr. Hughes in his very interesting lectures on Materia Medica points out the allopathic use of drugs. When many years ago I was engaged along with Lord Ebury and Mr. Cowper-Temple, concocting that clause of the Medical Act which is the charter of our rights, do you think that that question was not discussed among us? Of course it was, and I heard from Lord Ebury, and from Mr. Cowper-Temple as representing the House of Commons, that any mention of the word "homœopathy" would not have been allowed. We went upon general principles. We said " any theory of medicine," and we did not mention homœopathy particularly. Shall we go back from those days? Shall we abandon the charter we then obtained? No; don't let us go back; let us go forward. Our position is that of the representatives of true medicine. Have we not had experience of schools of homœopathy in this country? There was a school of homœopathy established in Hanover Square. Immense · sums were expended on the establishment of that school. It was ushered into the world with a great flourish of trumpets, as great as anything witnessed in these days. What has become of that school? We know it has been consigned to the limbo of oblivion. There was another school connected with the Bloomsbury Hospital, and I occupied the position of one of the lecturers in that school. Probably the talent brought into that school was not equal to the talent brought into the present School of Homœopathy, but we had had some experience, and the talent brought into that school was probably about the average talent we could muster in those days. What has become of that school? We all know what has become of it. It is dead. (Laughter.) With these examples of schools of homœopathy, which flourished for a time and then passed away, although they have done some good work, shall we now repeat the same experiment which has failed? No; I say let us take our stand as citizens, as men who will insist upon enjoying the privileges our country offers. Let us not exclude ourselves from the privilege we have a right to. Let us be bold for once and say "We are the representatives of true medicine." If you object that our school does not teach anatomy and botany, you object to what is beside the question. If we have a school of therapeutics we have a school which is a school of medicine. It is not a school of medicine *plus* the other sciences; it is a school of medicine, or, as Dr. Drysdale suggests, you may call it a medical school. Our decision to-day, although it may not be binding upon the directors of the London School of Homœopathy, if it is in favour of the catholic term "Medical School," will have an enormous effect upon the future of homœopathy. (Applause.)

Dr. HUGHES (London): I think, Sir, it is time we descended from the high and lofty considerations to which my friend, Dr. Dudgeon, has raised us, to the more practical question of whether we will change the name "School of Homœopathy," under which the institution has been working for the last six months in London. This school has been established, and a large amount of work has been done for it. Its establishment has been made known to our colleagues in all parts of the world, and has been hailed with gratification everywhere. We are asked now to alter the name under which it has been known during this time. We are not now discussing the preliminary question as to what name should be given to our infant just born, but whether the name should be altered—whether there are sufficiently weighty considerations to induce us to do that. We are asked to do it at a time when, what I must call, a certain unfortunate letter, animated by the best intentions but not couched in the most judicious language, has appeared—a letter which has already caused much anxiety on the part of our body. I venture to say that if at this time we were to alter the name to anything which would drop the term "homœopathy," we should give discouragement to all our friends, and encouragement to all our enemies. (Applause.) We should appear to be giving countenance to the idea amongst our friends or our foes that we were false to our principles. Our colleagues abroad could not but consider us pusillanimous, if not disloyal. I believe that this is the view in which our action would be considered. (Cries of "No, No.") I submit that that is the view in which our action would be considered. But then comes the further question (I would not rest wholly upon this view) which is of no little importance—the further question, should we call it the London School of Homœopathy? or should we call it by any other name, "The London Medical School," or "The School of Therapeutics?" I think not, and for this reason. We have hitherto been driven to establish homœopathic journals, hospitals and societies, because we have been forbidden our rights to be represented in the old journals, hospitals and societies. We have called our journals *The British Journal of Homœopathy* and *The Monthly Homœopathic Review*; and now we call our school The London School of Homœopathy. Because we are not allowed to teach homœopathy in the halls, we are driven to teach it in The London School of Homœopathy; and the *onus probandi* lies on the other side if a change of policy is made. Now, the object of the School of Homœopathy is, as Dr. Bayes has well said, extra-academical. Although in the Edinburgh sense of the term it may not apply to our position, in the large general sense it does. Our object is not to get medical students to come and learn the Materia Medica with us, instead of in the schools with which they are affiliated. I believe it would be injurious to get them to do so. I believe it would be injurious to our cause to do so. Our object is to provide for men whose studies are nearly if not quite complete, homœopathic teaching; our object is to provide some means for their learning their work before they go forth to the practice of their profession. Therefore we do not wish that students should come to study the Materia Medica with us in the first instance. We hope by our name to get many more students of the kind we want than we should do by the proposed plan. It is argued that we should give up the distinctive name of the school, because we do not absolutely limit ourselves to teaching pure homœopathy there. But let me ask whether the officers of any homœopathic institution bind themselves entirely to homœopathic practice; do the officers of any homœo-pathic institution bind themselves not to give any kind of medicine but such as is homœopathic? (Applause.) I think not. By adopting the term homœopathy, they mean that homœopathy is to be the leading practice pursued; but if they find patients who cannot be benefited by anything else, they give them allopathy. I believe that our great object is to teach homœopathy in the school. When I say that I shall "neglect no known actions and uses of drugs," I do not mean that I shall advise my students to follow them. My great object is to teach them the homœopathic action of drugs. Dr. Brown's great object is to tell them how to treat cases homœopathically. If he comes to a case that he cannot treat homœopathically he tells them so. Therefere, I maintain that the name of the school is justly applied. Consequently, the *onus probandi* being on the other side, why we should change our practice of calling our journals and societies by the name " homœopathic," I call upon gentle-men, seeing the serious consequences which might follow from the proposed change of front in the face of the enemy, I do call upon them, in the name of common sense and manly practice, to term our school what it is, and what we, as long as we con-tinue to officer it, intend it to be. (Applause.)

Dr. WOLSTON (Croydon): Mr. Chairman, I hope we are all equally interested in the progress of homœopathy, and in its progress and teaching; we are all equally interested that, for the time, the Homœopathic School of Medicine shall continue and be a prosperous and successful institution. My own idea is that calling it by the name London Homœopathic School is to blot it out. (Hear, hear.) In the interests of the School of Homœopathy, and for no other purpose, we have to consider whether it is desirable that the school shall have the title given to it "homœopathic;" I never went in for the name from the beginning as many others did: I myself proposed a name which I hoped might be a sort of compromise: I prefer the name suggested by Dr. Gibbs Blake, of the "School of Therapeutics:" What I object to is "The Homœopathic School of Medicine:" The only question with me is, according to an American expression, "Will the thing run?" I understand the object of our school is not to teach men who are already medical men; our object is to obtain students who are not qualified, and more than that, that we are to have the lectures recognised by such a body as the London University: My own feeling is this, and I have had some little experience, I affirm that it is the name which is the bugbear, and if we could get for the school a name which represented that which was taught there, students would be attracted to the school, and the university would recognise these lectures. We have to decide the question whether by adhering to the present name we do or do not further the interests of the school itself: My own opinion is, that to call it the School of Homœopathy is to put the school very soon out of the light altogether. (Hear, hear.) I believe there are many subscriptions that would flow into the school from persons of a more generally liberal disposition than if the institution were denominated the School of Homœopathy. A rose is a rose, whatever you call it; but I want the school to be progressive, and for my own part I think the retention of the name "homœopathy" in connection with it would prevent many persons from coming to it. I don't want to surrender the name as applied to our journals or societies; I simply change the name of the school. As to the advantage or loss to the school by being called therapeutic, my own conviction is that I should serve the interests of our opponents against the school if I designated it the School of Homœopathy; on the other hand I think I should be serving the best interests of the school by eliminating the word "homœopathic;" call it therapeutic if you like, but leave out "homœopathic." (Applause.)

Dr. Hewan: I vote most heartily for the amendment that it should be called the London School of Therapeutics. I think it is a great pity that the matter has been allowed to remain over so long. We have heard of the importance of recognition by the examining boards. We want to get the lectures recognised by the London University. Well, then, in order to do that you would require in the lectures to teach the whole of therapeutics, and if you could get a medical school established, by all means go in for that. If you could get a medical school established, with instruction in therapeutics, I would most strongly support it. We are not going, however, to establish a number of lectures. What we desire is, to teach therapeutics and the law of similars. I shall vote most readily that instead of its being called a Homœo-pathic School it be designated a School of Therapeutics. (Applause.)

Dr. BAYES (London) : I will be as short as possible, and in-deed I don't think I need be very long. I must say that before this meeting I was very much opposed to this agitation being continued, and many of our friends were very anxious that the name of the school having been given to the institution, we should have rest for two years, just to work the practical part of the whole matter. But, seeing that my opponents—as I may call them in a friendly way—had such a strong wish to bring the subject before the Congress, I think we have to thank them very much for keeping thoroughly to the point—not digressing in any way—and I will try to do the same. Now, my friend Dr. Moore, expressed a wish that whichever way the majority might go in this matter, the minority would yield to that decision. (Hear, hear.) But we are a standing illustration of the rights of mino-rities. We homœopathists have not gone with the majority, and I don't think Dr. Moore was quite correct in saying that whichever way the majority went the minority ought to go with it. The school has been founded, the funds have been given, lecturers have been appointed, and many of our opponents have told me that if they had had the appointment of lecturers them-selves they could not have selected better men. (Applause.) Under these circumstances I think we cannot do better than leave matters as they are. We had no expectation that our lectures would be recognised. We wish to teach what at present is not taught in the schools, and if that is well taught we have no doubt but that in a short time, by its own virtue—its own weight, it must be brought into the allopathic school. But, first, we must have no fear that what we teach is thoroughly good. First of all as to what is taught, I think its character commends itself very much to us. We teach homœopathy, and we call the institution a School of Homœopathy. The next point is, suppose that by sinking the title we could gain a few more students, I think this a chimera, a fool's paradise into which some have got. With regard to the suggestion that to call the school one of Homœopathy when other things are taught there, is dishonest, I admit that, at first sight, in a school of homœopathy, it appears reasonable that nothing else but homœopathy should be taught ; but I contend that we have as much right to apply that title as Mr. Brassey has to call his yacht a steam yacht. Mr. Brassey went round the world in his yacht, though of the 52,000 miles he only steamed some 20,000 miles, yet nobody says he is not perfectly right in calling the vessel a steam yacht. Then, another question, which Dr. Drysdale has reminded me of, is recognition. In the first place, we don't want our lectures to be recognised. (Applause and cries of "Oh, oh.") I have had several letters from students, in which they say that if our lectures were recognised lectures, they would not come, because they say this, that unless you have a complete medical school they would not, if the lectures were recognised, come from their complete medical schools. They would be marked men. I have spoken to a good many, and they all say the same thing —that they would not attend our lectures in place of those at the old hospitals. They are willing enough to be taught, after they have obtained their degree, and some are brave enough to come before they have obtained their degree. I must also explain, in reference to Dr. Wyld's statement about the school, that we have not circulated 20,000 handbills, or any handbills at all.

Dr. WYLD : I beg to state that the statement was made in your house, and you did not contradict it.

Dr. BAYES : I may not have contradicted it, but it is, nevertheless, not the fact. It is something like the reports the public are receiving from the East of the number of killed. What we have done is to send out circulars to all in the London Medical Directory every year, which is about 3,600. As to Dr. Gibbs Blake's suggestion that the institution should be named the School of Therapeutics, that name is indefinite. Neither has the name proposed by our excellent friend, Dr. Moore, either appropriateness or definiteness, and as we have a name which is appropriate, definite and honest, I think we had better keep it. (Applause.)

Dr. DRURY (London) : I regret exceedingly that the discussion has taken place with reference to the school, because myself and some others very strongly dislike the way in which the institution was started. (A voice : The question. The question is the name of the school.) In regard to the name I am unwilling to give up the name "Homœopathy." I would be no party to the striking of the flag. I should greatly wish to see this vexed question settled by a compromise. Now, we have a name in connection with the London Homœopathic Hospital : I don't think any of us wish to say we are not homœopaths : I don't wish to say so, and I suggest that the institution be called the London Homœopathic Hospital and Medical School : I much prefer the word "medical" to the word "therapeutics." Therefore, if the word "homœopathy" in connection with the school were dropped, lectures might be announced on the homœopathic Materia Medica, or on homœopathy as applied in medicine. I am quite sure of this, that a homœopathic school will never be recognised, and I don't think it is desirable that any sectarian school should be recognised.

Dr. BLACK (London) : If I had remained silent it might be supposed that I agreed with Dr. Bayes and other members. My idea was that this was a great propaganda agent. If this School of Homœopathy is only to teach the few who have applied in past years, my idea is that we have spent a great deal of time unnecessarily : I believe the success of the school depends upon our getting for it a general name. I see nothing in the state of homœopathy and in the state of the period to favour the impression that men will come to examine more now than they have done in the last ten years. On the contrary, the men who come to homœopathy are those who seize the advantages of the system, and who will not expose themselves to the disadvantages which those who openly profess the system endure.

Dr. MOORE then replied on the discussion. He said : Though there has been a great deal said, there has been a very little said to the purpose. The point as to recognition has been set aside. I was quite surprised to hear several speakers, including Dr. Dyce Brown, who must take as deep an interest as any one of us in the matter, pass over that important part of the subject, because, it is, to my mind, certain you will never have a number of students unless homœopathy is part and parcel of their curriculum. We abandon the term " homœopathy," not to meet the wishes of our opponents, though we know it is an offensive term to them, but the subject of a homœopathic school narrows itself into this—if you continue your present name you will never be recognised, and the longer it remains the more it will be talked of, and the greater will be the opposition to it when it changes its name ; and change its name it must do. We must call it by a medical or some other name, and the sooner it is done the better. As to the importance of recognition, I think this is just the time for that. The medical mind is waking up towards us— waking up to a sense of the injustice it has dealt out to us, and we should put ourselves in a position to be recognised. I think we shall lose a very great opportunity if we allow this one to pass. (Applause.)

Dr. HITCHMAN said that before this question was put, there was one important point he wished to notice, viz., What is our position with regard to the public ? How are the public to distinguish in times of sickness if there should be no distinctive name for homœopathic practitioners ? After making a few remarks on this topic,

The PRESIDENT said : This discussion has now extended over a couple of hours, and as my views on the matter are already sufficiently well known, it is unnecessary for me to say anything excepting this, that I have listened very attentively to what has been said this afternoon in favour of changing the name, and I must say that I have heard nothing calculated to alter my views. With regard to the question of the School of Medicine, I certainly think that if the teaching in Great Ormond Street were like the

'aculty of the Boston University, that of a complete school of
medicine, it would be inappropriate to call the institution a
School of Homœopathy, but, inasmuch as that term, as understood by the profession and the public, comprises not only
therapeutics, "the supreme end"—as Sir Thomas Watson
called it—of our existence as professional men, but the foundation upon which the practice of medicine rests, and as we do not
profess to, and as we have not the opportunities for teaching the
whole of medical science as taught at the present day, I think it
would be incorrect to call the school a School of Medicine.
We call it a School of Homœopathy because it is a School of
Homœopathy. To that it has been objected that Dr. Dyce Brown,
and others, direct attention to remedies other than those which
are homœopathic, but if you teach homœopathy you must also
point out those cases in which homœopathy cannot be applied.
We all concede that homœopathy has its limits, and you must
teach those limits. Then Dr. Cockburn, in his pamphlet, "No
Sectarianism in Medicine," has said, "We don't establish
chairs of Arminianism and Calvinism, but we establish chairs of
theology." That is true, but, though the word "Arminianism"
is not used, you establish chairs in colleges having sectarian ·
titles. You have the Independent College, the Baptist College,
and others. Then, again, Dr. Dudgeon referred to the comparative failure of the Hanover Street School of Medicine, and of
that in Bloomsbury Square, of which he was a distinguished
ornament, and where he produced a well-known and valuable
series of lectures on homœopathy. Those schools flourished at
a time when the feeling with regard to homœopathy was very
different from what it is at ·the present day. The bitterness
against it has been very much mellowed. Therefore I do not
see why the failures of these schools should influence us at the
present time; neither do I see that their failure was in any way
due to their being known as homœopathic. These are the points
I wish to draw attention to, and I hope this meeting will sanction
the action of the governors and subscribers to the London
School of Homœopathy in having given it that name. Dr. Gibbs
Blake wishes to withdraw his amendment.

After some discussion on points of order, the PRESIDENT put the
amendment moved by Dr. Nankivell. On the return being made
it was found that 45 had voted in favour of the amendment, and
14 against it.

Dr. MOORE then withdrew the second resolution to the effect
that the Congress recommend that the title should be the
Bloomsbury School of Medicine. Dr. DRURY had an amendment
to the effect that the Institution be known as the London
Homœopathic Hospital and Medical School. Notwithstanding the
determination the Congress had expressed to retain the existing

name for the School, Dr. Drury requested that his amendment—
now become by the withdrawal of Dr. Moore's second motion, a
substantive motion—be put. It was so, and lost by a large
majority.

Mr. Procter : Before you go to the next business, will you
allow me one word. This matter has been settled for some time
to come, and as there has been a proper discussion of it, I hope
that as loyal subjects, the minority will consent to be guided by
the majority. It is to be hoped that the minority will fall in
with the prevalent tone of mind and give their hearty assistance
to the School. (Hear, hear, and applause.)

Dr. Hughes then read the following report of the committee
appointed at the last Congress, to make arrangements for holding
a " World's Convention " in London, in 1881.

Your Committee beg to report that they have had several
meetings, and after much consideration, and in conference with
the lamented President of the last Convention, Dr. Carroll
Dunham, have agreed upon the following recommendations, which
they present for the acceptance of the present Congress:—

" Scheme for the World's Homœopathic Convention, 1881.

" 1.   That the Convention shall assemble in London at such
time and during such number of days as may hereafter be
determined.

" 2.   That this meeting take the place of the annual British
Homœopathic Congress, and that its officers be elected at the
Congress of the preceding year; the Convention itself being at
liberty to elect honorary Vice-Presidents from those foreign
guests and others whom it desires to honour.

" 3.   That the expenses of the meeting be met by a subscription from the homœopathic practitioners of Great Britain ; the
approximate amount to be expected from each to be named as
the time draws near.

" 4.   That the expenses of printing the Transactions be
defrayed by a subscription from all who desire to possess a copy
of the volume.

" 5.   That the Convention shall be open to all medical men
qualified to practise in their own country.

" 6.   That all who attend shall present to the Secretary their
names and addresses, and a statement of their qualifications ;
and, if unknown to the officers of the Convention, shall be introduced by someone known to them, or shall bring letters credential
from some homœopathic society, or other recognised representa-
tive of the system.

" (a)   That members of the Convention as above characterised,
shall be at liberty to introduce visitors to the meetings at their
discretion,

"7. That the Committee be authorised to enter into communication with physicians at home and abroad to obtain—

"(a) A report from each country supplementary to those presented at the Convention of 1876, recounting everything of interest in connection with homœopathy which has occurred within its sphere since the last reports were drawn up.

"(b) Essays upon the various branches of homœopathic theory and practice, for discussion at the meetings, and publication in the Transactions ; the physicians to be applied to for the latter purpose being those named in the accompanying schedule.

"8. That all essays must be sent in by January 1st, 1881, and shall then be submitted to a committee of censors for approval as suitable for their purpose.

"9. That the approved essays shall be printed beforehand, and distributed to the members of the Convention, instead of being read at the meetings.

"10. That for discussion the essays shall be presented singly or in groups, according to their subject-matter, a brief analysis of each being given from the chair.

"11. That a member of the Convention (or two, where two classes of opinion exist on the subject, as in the question of the dose) be appointed some time before the meeting to open the debate, fifteen minutes being allowed for such purpose, and that then the essay, or group of essays, be at once opened for discussion, ten minutes being the time allotted to each speaker.

"12. That the order of the essays be determined by the importance and interest of their subject-matter, so that, should the time of the meeting expire before all are discussed, less loss will have been sustained.

"13. That the Chairman shall have liberty, if he sees that an essay is being debated at such length as to threaten to exclude later subjects of importance, to close its discussion.

"14. That the authors of the essays debated, if present, shall have the right of saying the last word before the subject is dismissed.

"15. That, as at the first Convention, the subjects of the essays and discussions shall be—

"(a.) The Institutes of Homœopathy.
"(b.) Materia Medica.
"(c.) Practical Medicine.
"(d.) Surgical Therapeutics, including diseases of the eye and ear.
"(e.) Gynæcology."

The adoption of the report, moved by Dr. HUGHES and seconded by Dr. BAYES, was then carried unanimously. The Committee was also re-appointed.

The following report of the Hahnemann Publishing Society was read, and its adoption moved, by Dr. HAYWARD.

" The annual meeting of this Society was held at Liverpool, September 12th, 1877, Dr. Drysdale in the chair, in the absence of the President, Dr. R. Hughes.

" Present : Drs. Drysdale, Black, Dudgeon, Hayward, Bayes, Bryce, Blackley, J. G. Blackley, Mahoney, J. G. Blake, E. T. Blake, Skinner, A. C. Clifton, G. Clifton, Moore, Hawkes, and Harris.

" After reading the notice calling the meeting, and the minutes in the previous annual meeting, the hon. secretary read the report of the operations for the year ending August 31st, 1877, of which it was stated that fifteen new members had joined during the year, of which six were American and one Australian ; that no member had resigned, but two—Dr. W. Hering and Dr. Slack—had died; and that the total number of members now was 106. That the sum received in subscriptions was £28 19s. 0d., for books sold £1 5s. 0d., and for bank interest £1 10s. 0d., making a total of receipts of £31 14s. 0d. That there had been paid for postage and carriage of letters and books, &c., £1 17s. 11d. ; for two parts of the Repertory, 8s. ; and to Mr. Turner for Repertories supplied to members, £15 8s. 4d. ; making a total of payments of £18 8s. 3d. ; and leaving a balance on the year in favour of the society of £13 5s. 9d. ; which, with £65 8s. 6d. balance remaining last year, makes a total of £78 14s. 3d. as the present funds of the Society. Fourteen copies of Part I. of the Materia Medica, fourteen copies of Part II., and sixteen of Part III. had been disposed of during the year ; eight copies of the Encyclopædia and eleven and a half sets of the Repertory ; showing an increased appreciation of the publications of the society. Sixty copies of the Encyclopædia remaining in the hands of Dr. Dudgeon, unknown to the secretary, had been sent in ; so that there are sixty-six copies on hand. A large number of the circulars referred to in the last annual report had been posted to North America and South America, and some to Australia, New Zealand, Germany, France, Belgium, and India ; and it has been published in nearly all the North American homœopathic periodicals.

" Dr. Dudgeon has finished the supplement to chapters Disposition, Mind, and Head of the Repertory, and it is now in the hands of the printer. Dr. Clauber, of Mentone, has promised to arrange the symptoms of a medicine for the Materia Medica ; Dr. Burnett is assisting Dr. Drysdale in the General chapter of the Repertory ; and Dr. E. T. Blake assisting Dr. Black in the Therapeutic part. The other workers are continuing their labours: Dr. Galloway having nearly finished the arrangements of the symptoms of Natrum Muriaticum ; and Dr. Hayward having made progress with that of Crotalus ; and Drs.

Simpson and A. C. Clifton with the chapters of the Repertory they have undertaken. Drs. Drysdale and J. G. Blake are engaged on Rheumatic Fever, Dr. Drysdale on Gout, and Drs. Black and E. T. Blake on Inflammation and Dropsy for the Therapeutic part.

"After some discussion it was agreed that the Society should accede to the president's proposal to bring out a new translation of Hahnemann's *Materia Medica Pura*, including his Introductions and Notes.

"In view of Mr. Turner's giving up business it was agreed to make him an offer for the purchase of the remaining copies of the Repertory, the price not to exceed £10—Dr. E. T. Blake undertaking the negotiation.

"The various officers and committees were re-appointed, Dr. E. T. Blake being added to the Therapeutic Committee; and it was agreed to hold the next annual meeting at the time and place of the meeting of the next Congress, or of the annual assembly of the British Homœopathic Society."

In seconding it Dr. HUGHES said that he desired to enlist the sympathies of the Congress in behalf of the translation of the volumes on chronic diseases, in conjunction with another, who, although not so good a German scholar, has a better knowledge of the Materia Medica generally. I shall be glad if any gentleman willing to engage in this work will communicate with Dr. Hayward.

The resolution was carried unanimously.

The place of meeting next year was, on the motion of Dr. BLACK, seconded by Dr. GIBBS BLAKE, fixed in favour of Leicester. The meeting was arranged to take place on the fourth Thursday in September.

Dr. GIBBS BLAKE was then elected President, and Dr. ARTHUR CLIFTON, Northampton, Vice-President.

Dr. HUXLEY was elected General, and Dr. GEORGE CLIFTON Local Secretary.

Dr. EDWARD MADDEN was elected Treasurer.

Owing to the lateness of the hour it was impossible to hear the paper of which Dr. SKINNER had given notice, and the proceedings were closed.

Milton Keynes UK
Ingram Content Group UK Ltd.
UKHW040929180224
437992UK00003B/112